Praise for Sara Richardson

"Sara Richardson writes unputdownable, unforgettable stories from the heart."

—Jill Shalvis, *New York Times* bestselling author

"With wit and warmth, Sara Richardson creates heartfelt stories you can't put down."

—Lori Foster, *New York Times* bestselling author

"Sara [Richardson] brings real feelings to every scene she writes."

—Carolyn Brown, *New York Times* bestselling author

HOME FOR THE HOLIDAYS

"Fill your favorite mug with hot chocolate and whipped cream as you savor this wonderful holiday story of family reunited and dreams finally fulfilled. I loved it!"

—Sherryl Woods, #1 *New York Times* bestselling author

"You'll want to stay home for the holidays with this satisfying Christmas read."

—Sheila Roberts, *USA Today* bestselling author

FIRST KISS WITH A COWBOY

"The pace is fast, the setting's charming, and the love scenes are delicious. Fans of cowboy romance are sure to be captivated."

—Publishers Weekly (Starred Review)

HOMETOWN COWBOY

"Filled with humor, heart, and love, this page-turner is one wild ride."

—Jennifer Ryan, *New York Times* bestselling author

NO BETTER MAN

"Charming, witty, and fun. There's no better read. I enjoyed every word!"

—Debbie Macomber, #1 *New York Times* bestselling author

Home for the Holidays

ALSO BY SARA RICHARDSON

HEART OF THE ROCKIES SERIES

No Better Man
Something Like Love
One Christmas Wish (novella)
More Than a Feeling
Rocking Mountain Wedding (novella)

ROCKY MOUNTAIN RIDERS SERIES

Hometown Cowboy
Comeback Cowboy
Renegade Cowboy
Rocky Mountain Cowboy (novella)
True-Blue Cowboy
Rocky Mountain Cowboy Christmas (novella)
Colorado Cowboy
A Cowboy for Christmas

SILVERADO LAKE SERIES

First Kiss with a Cowboy

Home for the Holidays

SARA RICHARDSON

FOREVER

New York   Boston

Copyright © 2020 by Sara Richardson
Reading group guide copyright © 2020 by Sara Richardson and Hachette Book Group, Inc.

Cover design and illustration by Daniela Medina
Cover photography © Shutterstock
Cover copyright © 2020 by Hachette Book Group, Inc.

Forever
Hachette Book Group
1290 Avenue of the Americas, New York, NY 10104
read-forever.com
twitter.com/readforeverpub

First edition: September 2020

Forever is an imprint of Grand Central Publishing. The Forever name and logo are trademarks of Hachette Book Group, Inc.

The publisher is not responsible for websites (or their content) that are not owned by the publisher.

Library of Congress Cataloging-in-Publication Data

Names: Richardson, Sara (Romance fiction writer), author.
Title: Home for the holidays / Sara Richardson.
Description: First edition. | New York : Forever, 2020.
Identifiers: LCCN 2020014839 | ISBN 9781538718216 (trade paperback) | ISBN 9781538718223 (ebook)
Classification: LCC PS3618.I3452 H66 2020 | DDC 813/.6—dc23
LC record available at https://lccn.loc.gov/2020014839

ISBNs: 978-1-5387-1821-6 (trade paperback), 978-1-5387-1822-3 (ebook)

Printed in the United States of America

LSC-C

10 9 8 7 6 5 4 3 2

For my beloved aunties.

Chapter One

Dearest Dahlia, Magnolia, and Rose,

I know we haven't spoken in many years, but I'm sending you these packages in hopes that we might finally reconnect after all this time. When your mother decided to stop visiting me, I suppose she was doing what she thought best. Maybe she thought things would be easier for all of us. It hasn't been for me. I can hardly believe it's been eighteen years since we last played in that old camping trailer you took over here at the inn. It still sits near the pond, full of your old dress-up clothes and jewelry and the many stuffed animals we invited to our parties. Oh, what fun we always had when you would come visit. Do you remember? The fancy afternoon teas and the cookie baking, and the magical Christmas extravaganza we would host at the inn every year? Those memories are some of the very best moments of my life, and I hope you think of them fondly, too.

As another Christmas draws near, I have been thinking more about you, about the love and the laughter you brought into this old place. I know you've all grown into beautiful young women, but not much has changed at the Juniper Inn. All of the cozy cottages remain tucked among the pines, which are already covered with a healthy dusting of snow. The mountain peaks still stand guard to the west, looking almost like an ice castle hovering on the horizon. You three always swore the inn was really part of a fairy world, even though no one else could see the magic as clearly as you girls could. I always saw it though. I still see the magic. Even as it's aged, there's always been something enchanting about this place. Do you remember how we would sing and dance around the Christmas tree? How we would bundle up in soft woolly layers and gather outside on Christmas Eve for s'mores at the campfire? I wanted to remind you of those simple, cozy days, so I'm sending you each a piece of Christmas from the Juniper Inn.

Dahlia, for you I chose the snowflake music box that always sat on the mantel. You used to wind it up over and over again, singing along to "Let It Snow!" at the top of your little lungs. When it broke the year you turned seven, you spent hours working to fix it—making it sing sweetly again. Even back then there was no problem you couldn't solve.

Magnolia, for you I chose my Christmas tree rolling pin. What fun we had baking all those cookies for the hordes that would come to the Christmas extravaganza! You had such a gift for baking with love, and I'm thrilled to see you've followed one of your greatest passions.

Rose…sweet little Rosie…for you I chose the angel that sat atop the Christmas tree. You used to call her the princess angel, and spent hours admiring every detail of her dress and the flowered halo circling her blond curls. You always had such a sense of style, my dear. It's no wonder you've gotten to where you are today, starting your own design firm. I'm sure your upcoming wedding to Gregory Cunningham will be the most beautiful event Savannah has ever seen. (I know how to use the Internet!)

Time passes so incredibly quickly. I remember the days you were all born. You have grown into beautiful young women, and I am nearly bursting with pride over each of you and your wonderful accomplishments. Though I haven't been part of your lives for a very long time, I still love you as though you are my own daughters and I hope these keepsakes will spark memories of our Christmases together, just as they did mine.

I must admit I'm not only writing to reminisce. I am also hoping that you will come to see me, to spend Christmas with me at the place we all loved so. I know you are all busy—Dahlia with your children, Magnolia with your bakery, and Rose with your upcoming wedding, but I would love to see you again, my dears. I would love to share the magic of Christmas with you one last time. Please come. It would mean so very much to me.

Love always,
Aunt Sassy

Chapter Two

Dahlia

One last Christmas? Oh, God.

Dahlia leaned into the counter where the open package sat, the music box playing an out-of-tune rendition of "Let It Snow!" Aunt Sassy only had one more Christmas? She was *dying*? It seemed impossible. She couldn't quite imagine the vibrant red-headed beauty as a sick old woman. Dahlia set down the letter and lifted the dainty music box so she could admire it closely. The sparkly silver snowflakes now turned slower than they once had, and the song skipped. Parts of the glitter had chipped away from the snowy base, but somehow the music box's flaws seemed appropriate. Relatable, even. The years had chipped away some of her sparkle, too.

Especially this last year.

Dahlia turned the box over to examine the underside. When Rose had accidentally knocked the music box off the mantel the Christmas she'd turned three Dahlia was sure her heart had shattered, too. The dancing snowflakes were one of the most beautiful things she'd ever held in her hands—something she looked forward to seeing each year. Her aunt had assured her they could find a new music box, but Dahlia spent the entire day gluing pieces back together and tinkering with the wires, determined to save the trinket. That's what she did—she fixed things. That's what she had always done.

Even as her marriage had fallen apart over the last several years, she'd fixed everything around it, desperately trying to hold her little family together right up until her husband walked out the door and into another woman's arms. And she'd spent every day since his abandonment trying to make it okay. Okay for her kids, okay for her. Okay in the eyes of everyone else. *It's for the best, really*, she'd told all the other PTA moms. *We're better friends than we are husband and wife. We're going to be great co-parents.*

It was strange the lies you told when you were going through a crisis, when you didn't know what to say so you said what you knew people wanted you to say, what they wanted to hear. *I'm doing great. The kids are fine. No, we don't need anything.* As if it were all simply a speed bump on their straight-and-narrow road through life. No one had wanted to hear the truth—not even her own mother. No one wanted to hear that instead of hitting a speed bump, the divorce had been more like careening off a cliff— sending her spiraling downward, the car around her in flames. She'd always excelled at putting out fires, but the divorce had left her feeling like she was trying to spit on an inferno.

The front door banged open, bringing with it a whoosh of frigid air that seemed to make the music box drone even slower. Minneapolis had experienced a bitter start to winter—which seemed appropriate this year, too.

"Mom! Mom!"

Dahlia set down the music box before it toppled out of her hands, and turned to greet Maya and Ollie, who were supposed to be with their father this weekend since she'd had them most of Thanksgiving week.

"Hello, my loves." She gave them each a squeeze, not even needing to ask what they were doing home. She's seen the email about the Christmas bake sale from the school and had already anticipated they would show up since their father couldn't bake his way out of a paper bag.

"What's this?" Ollie snatched up the snowflake music box in his grubby hands. In kindergarten, he still hadn't grasped the concept of regular handwashing, and always came home with paint and dirt from the playground sealed into the creases of his skin.

Dahlia gently took the music box away before he dropped it. "It's a gift from my aunt," she said, setting it on the higher shelf where she kept her cookbooks. Maybe it was silly to try to protect those snowflakes when they were already old and decrepit but holding a memory from her past had given her back a small piece of herself, and she couldn't bear to risk seeing it broken again.

"My aunt Sassy sent it to me for Christmas." Along with a request. And somehow Dahlia wasn't surprised. She'd lived enough to know that sometimes fate stepped in. This year, more than any other year, she needed to go back to the Juniper Inn for Christmas. She needed to see her sisters who lived so far away, and she needed to be there for her aunt.

"Aunt Sassy?" Maya rose to her tiptoes as though trying to get a better look at the music box. "Is she your sister like Aunt Rose and Aunt Mags are?"

"No." Holding back a sigh, Dahlia lifted the music box off the shelf, wound the knob, and set it in front of the kids so they could get a better look. They were dying to examine it, to touch it—she could tell from their eager little expressions, and she remembered how the music box had once entranced her. "Aunt Sassy is Grammy's sister." Though she doubted her mother would claim her. Dahlia had no idea what had happened between the two of them eighteen years ago. Her mother had refused to tell her, so Sassy had remained almost an enigma from Dahlia's past.

"I didn't know Grammy had a sister." Ollie had quickly lost interest in the singing snowflakes, opting instead to rifle through the pantry until he found a bag of gummy snacks.

Dahlia tsked at him, carefully took the package away, and handed him a clementine from the bowl on the counter instead. He peered up at her from underneath his long lashes, his dark eyes so full of light as he offered her the sheepish grin that brought hope blooming in her heart all over again. For all the struggles they'd endured over the past year, her children were pure tangible joy. "Grammy does have a sister," she told him. "But they don't talk."

"How come?" the boy asked, ripping off pieces of the orange peel and letting them fall on the floor. Yes, her children were pure tangible joy and they were also a whole heck of a lot of work. "Grammy and her sister had some problems years ago." Dahlia handed him the broom along with a look that told him he'd best clean up his mess.

"You always tell us to work out our problems." Maya was still gazing at the music box. "Dad's in the car, by the way. He's on the phone," her daughter informed her as though she couldn't resist the temptation to remind Dahlia of the one problem she hadn't been able to solve. The poor girl. Even at eight years old she was so like Dahlia—always taking more on her shoulders than she should. Always aware and informing and orchestrating. Dahlia would have to remember to bring that up with their therapist next time. She didn't want Maya to become a mini her.

The front door opened again, the sound automatically putting steel into her spine. She always braced herself when Jeff walked into a room—not out of fear, but out of a need to prove to him she was fine, that he hadn't broken her with his betrayal.

"Hey there." Her ex-husband walked into the kitchen from the hall, a sheepish grin etched into his handsome features. As had become her custom, Dahlia greeted him with a bright, capable smile.

"Hey." She quickly busied herself with unpacking the kids' lunch boxes from their backpacks. Being busy took the edge off just about anything, she'd learned. That was how she'd ended up on the PTA and the healthy school lunch committee and the school accountability team. That was how she'd been named Volunteer of the Year at the kids' school. As long as she kept busy, she could keep moving forward and eventually she wouldn't feel so much like she was spinning her emotional wheels.

"Soooo, I was hoping these two rug rats could stay with you this weekend." Jeff leaned into the counter across from her, his smile as boyish as their son's. That smile had done wonders for her once, but now it brought a cold hollowness that reached into the deepest part of her stomach.

"We have to bring three dozen cookies to the bake sale on Monday," Maya explained, always the informant. "And I told Dad we were absolutely not going to buy them at the store. They *have* to be homemade or I'll be the laughingstock of the entire third grade."

Even with each painful pound of her heart, she kept her smile intact. *Doesn't Jade bake?* She fought the temptation to voice the question. It would only be to make a point. Jade didn't bake. Jade was a personal trainer. She'd been Jeff's personal trainer when they'd met. The woman had helped him lose over forty pounds, and then had also made sure he lost his 130-pound wife.

And yet…Jade wasn't nearly as useful as Dahlia, which was why Jeff always showed up or called when he needed something. In some ways, Dahlia felt like she was still his wife—managing the kids' schedules, taking care of them when they were sick. He'd even asked for her help in organizing the three-week European vacation he and Jade had planned with the kids over Christmas, since this was his year to have them. *You know the kids the best,* he'd told her. *I need you to help me figure out where to stay with them, what they'd like to see.*

So, she'd helped him. She'd made hotel reservations for him. She'd put together a list of the best restaurants that could accommodate Ollie's dairy allergy. Because she wanted her kids to be okay. Because it was something for her to do—a way to keep busy, a way to be useful. It was a way for her to be part of a once-in-a-lifetime trip they were taking without her…

"I wanna make those frosting cookies!" Ollie was still slurping his way through the clementine. "The ones with lotsa sprinkles."

Grasping for the joy, Dahlia went to the sink and wet a paper towel before handing it to him. "I think that can be arranged."

"Do we still have the snowflake sprinkles?" Her daughter had wound the music box again and was humming along.

"I believe we do." Dahlia went to the pantry and pulled out the Tupperware container of sprinkles she'd stocked up on for an occasion exactly like this one. "I'll tell you what. Why don't you two go change out of your uniforms and we'll get this cookie-baking party started."

"Yes!" Ollie pumped his fist in the air, sending the rest of his orange flying. Giggling, he scurried over, snatched it off the floor, and popped it into his mouth before Dahlia could stop him. "Ten-second rule!"

Dahlia decided not to remind him that it only took one second for germs to cling to a juicy orange.

Maya followed him out of the kitchen telling him how gross it was to eat off the floor.

"You'll get Ebola," her daughter said in her know-it-all tone.

Jeff chuckled as the two of them argued their way up the steps, but Dahlia finally let her smile slide. How long could she keep this up? Playing the role of Jeff's personal assistant while he loved another woman?

"Thanks, Dal. I really appreciate this." He started to turn, but she slammed her palms into the counter. "Wait."

She couldn't let him walk away without saying something. Maybe because Christmas was getting closer and he was taking her babies away from her for three weeks. Maybe because he used her every chance he got, and she let him. Maybe because she was tired of putting out fires, so she'd finally let one consume her.

"Yeah?" He turned back to her with a glance at his watch.

Dahlia simply studied him for a minute. While the years had taken a toll on her, he'd hardly changed at all. They'd met their junior year in college. In the business school. He was good-looking with that thick black hair, perceptive dark eyes, and a slight dimple in his right cheek, but it was his charisma that had drawn her in. She hadn't planned on seriously dating anyone, and she hadn't planned on getting married right after they graduated, but Jeff had swept her up with his energy and optimism and enthusiasm. That's what he did. He made people get carried away. But he didn't sweep her up in his charm now. She didn't love him anymore. Maybe she'd never really loved him as much as she'd loved the idea of him, the idea of who they could be together. But she'd still given up everything for him, for their family. And she couldn't keep doing that for the rest of her life. Not when they were no longer a family.

"The kids can stay here. And I'll bake cookies with them." She steered her gaze to the snowflake music box, which had gone silent. "But you'll have to pick them up on Sunday."

"Ohhhh…" He drew out the word with concern. "I'm afraid Jade and I have plans Sunday. It would work better for us to pick them up Monday night since we're heading to the airport early Tuesday morning."

Why wasn't she surprised? This whole cookie-baking situation was really just a way for him to find free childcare. "Well that won't work for me." Her heart thumped harder, pushing heat through her veins. "You come pick them up on Sunday. Because I'm leaving town." She wasn't going to do it anymore. She wasn't going to let him take advantage of her love for her children like this. He'd wanted this divorce and now he had to learn to do things for the kids on his own.

"Leaving?" His smile tightened into confusion. Ah, yes. Because what life did she have outside of her kids? None. But that had to change.

"Where are you going?" he demanded.

"I'm going to spend Christmas with my aunt Sassy in Colorado. Not that it's any of your business. In case you've forgotten, we're not married anymore." And it was past time to stop acting like they were.

Chapter Three

Rose

Rose's nerves kicked in the second Gregory pulled up in front of the high-end bridal boutique with its intimidating stone façade and sleek glass windows. "Keep driving," she told him, only half joking. "We could drive all the way to Tybee Island and spend the afternoon in bed."

Her loving fiancé glanced at his watch. "Wish I could, but I have a meeting on the other side of town in twenty minutes."

When they'd first started dating, he would've gladly canceled a meeting to steal some time away with her. In those days, they were constantly sneaking out to his parents' beach house on Tybee Island, but these days...well, between all of his meetings and the constant wedding plans, she couldn't remember the last time they'd been spontaneous.

"It'll be fine." Gregory leaned over and brushed a quick kiss across her cheek. "Go pick out your dress. I can't wait to see it."

"I'm just not sure I want to go with anything fancy." She eyed the storefront that *Wedding Bliss* had labeled the only place to purchase a dress in all of Savannah. "I was hoping I could make my own dress." She'd even sketched out a few different designs and had gone to look at potential fabrics. But when she'd shown them to Gregory's mother, the woman had simply laughed and told her she couldn't possibly make one that would fit such a grand occasion.

"You don't have time to make the dress," Gregory said, sounding an awful lot like his mother. He sat up straighter, staring at something down the block. "Oh, good. Sydney is here." Relief loosened his frown into a relieved smile. "You two have fun. I'll see you later tonight."

"Right. See you tonight." At nine o'clock when he finally got home from work. Rose pushed out of the car and had barely gotten the door shut before Gregory peeled away from the curb.

"Sheesh. Did he rob a bank or something?" Syd asked, watching the Mercedes take a hard right.

"He has a meeting." A meeting that was more important than spending the afternoon in bed with her apparently, but she didn't want to talk about that. Instead she faced the massive glass door in front of them. "We'd better get in there." They were only five minutes early, which, in Evaline Cunningham's world, meant they were ten minutes late.

Sure enough, the second Rose and Syd walked in, both Evaline and Rose's own mother Lillian ambushed them. "Good, you're finally here. We found you the perfect dress."

A horrified gasp hurtled up from the very center of Rose's chest, but she caught it in her throat and gave her mother and Evaline a practiced smile. "I'm not sure it's the right style." That was Southern speak for *There is no way in hell you will ever see me wearing that.* Especially at her wedding.

She eyed the atrocity dangling from the padded hanger that Evaline held in front of her face. It looked like an owl had gotten tangled up in a roll of tulle. And the gems and sequins—good golly, Miss Molly. She'd have to hand out sunglasses to the guests.

Leave it to Gregory's mother to pick the most ostentatious dress in the entire store. As the matriarch of a family that had virtually become royalty in Savannah, Evaline didn't bother with subtleties. Normally the woman didn't bother spending time with common folk either, but she hadn't had much of a choice when it came to Rose.

Eight months ago, Rose had been minding her own business—going about her very ordinary, but happy, life, and—BAM. She'd fallen in love. She'd been cleaning the fourth floor of the Cunningham Enterprises high-rise downtown. Vacuuming, actually. Which happened to be one of her least favorite activities, but she'd taken the custodian job to increase her savings so she could keep her fledgling interior design business afloat. That evening, she'd put in some earbuds, and danced her way around a conference room with one of those industrial vacuum cleaners that had a long hose. After one too many twirls, she'd gotten a bit tangled and had nearly toppled over when, suddenly, strong hands had taken hold of her shoulders to steady her.

She'd turned around and there stood Gregory Cunningham in all of his tall, dark, and handsome glory. His tie had been loosened, and the top four buttons of his starched white shirt were undone, only adding to his charm. *You're a good dancer*, he'd said. *And you're handsome and kind*, she'd immediately thought. Because she was most definitely not a good dancer, as evidenced by the fact that her legs were still tangled in the vacuum hose.

Gregory had twirled her the opposite direction to free her and then he'd taken her out for a drink. The drink had turned into dinner and then dinner had turned into breakfast and before she knew it, she and Gregory were spending romantic weekends at his family's beach house on Tybee Island. Within six months, they were engaged because Gregory said, and she quoted, *It's taken me my whole life to find you and I don't want to wait anymore.* So, they were getting married in only five months. Much to his mother's staunch disapproval.

But the wedding would change Evaline's mind. Rose would show her she could fit in with their friends and their family. She just wouldn't do it wearing that hideous dress.

Chin raised, Rose looked into her future mother-in-law's cutting blue eyes. "I think I should keep looking." She had already decided there would be no feathers at her wedding. No gems either. It was going to be at Red Gate Farms, for the love of God. She needed something nostalgic and romantic. "Brown feathers simply aren't right for a late spring wedding." Or any wedding where the bride didn't want to be mistaken for an owl.

Rose's mother and Evaline shared *the look*. They stood shoulder to shoulder in a desperate unified force as though they'd already decided this was the dress before Rose had even arrived.

Rose tried to smooth over Evaline's scowl with a bright smile. "It is a very…*interesting* dress. I guess I've always had my heart set on something else, that's all." The statement resonated with a subtle vibration in her heart, strumming unknown chords. It was that feeling again—the one that nudged at her hopes. The wonder of something else. Something more, something different, something…deeper. She loved Gregory—he was her fairy tale come true. The man she'd dreamed about since she was a little girl—but trying to earn his family's approval had started to make her feel like someone she wasn't sure she wanted to become.

"Rosie?" Her mother fluttered a hand in front of her face. "Are you absolutely positive you don't like the dress, darling?" She glanced at Gregory's mother with a placating smile. "Because I think it's absolutely lovely. Evaline has such exquisite taste, you know. And I think it would be very flattering on you with that empire waist."

Ah, yes. Her mother had always made a point of helping Rose find a way to dress around her curvy hips. Lillian also never disagreed with Evaline, no matter what. Her mother had spent far too long trying to climb the social ladder to ruin it all with one wrong word to Evaline Cunningham.

"It would be perfect if you were doing a *Game of Thrones* theme for the wedding," Syd commented as she gave the dress a good long look. "It screams tragic medieval princess."

The voice of reason. Thank God she'd brought Syd along. With an ally she might actually manage to walk out of here with something she adored rather than something her mother-in-law deemed perfect. As her college roommate, Syd had proven time and again she could keep her wits about her in the most stressful of situations—like that time Rose had accidentally started a small fire in their dorm room with a candle and a dozen cute firefighters had shown up to put out the blaze.

"*Game of Thrones?*" Evaline stalked back to a rack and slammed the hanger onto the bar. "I think it's elegant. Unique."

"But we don't want a barn owl landing on her head in the middle of the ceremony thinking he's found his true love, now do we? Think of the scandal that would cause." Syd batted her mascara-free eyelashes innocently at Gregory's mother. She didn't care what the matriarch thought of her. Didn't care what anyone thought of her, actually.

Rose couldn't remember the last time she'd left the house without mascara. Or lipstick. She couldn't remember the last time she'd worn her hair back in a ponytail. After all, you never knew when someone from the local media would want to snap a picture, her mother liked to remind her. She glanced at Syd, who'd opted to dress in black yoga capris and a rainbow tank top that said "Good Vibes" for this little outing.

Oh, what she wouldn't give to spend a day in yoga pants…

"I think we should all trust Rose's judgment," Syd said helpfully. "After all, she *is* an interior decorator. She has a great sense of style."

Uh-oh. Warning bells started to clamor in her chest, bringing an ache just beneath Rose's breastbone. Sydney wasn't going to bring up Rose's idea. Surely not now. Not here…

"In fact," her friend went on, encouraging Rose with an excited lift of her eyebrows, "Rose was just telling me the other night how much she'd love to redecorate your family's beach house."

Evaline's gaze shifted to Rose, casting her in an awkward spotlight.

She was going to kill Syd for this. Yes, she'd said she wanted to redecorate Evaline's beach house, but she never would've brought it up to the woman herself! Everyone seemed to be waiting for her response. "Um, right. Yes. Sure," she stammered, searching for words. "Because you said you were interested in having it redecorated at some point and I have ideas." Okay, she had more than ideas. She had completed a whole design scheme, but she hadn't had the guts to show it to Evaline yet.

"You would be a great client for Glamour Girl Design," Syd prompted when Evaline said nothing.

"A client?" Gregory's mother belted out a rare laugh that

caught Rose so off guard she nearly toppled over onto the marble floor. "Surely you're not still talking about continuing your little hobby." Evaline shared a long look with Rose's mother.

"I'm not talking about it." Rose found it difficult to meet the woman's eyes. "I *am* going to keep my business." The business she'd been working on for well over three years—ever since she'd graduated with her design degree. Glamour Girl Designs may not have taken off yet, but all she needed was one big client…

"When do you plan to do that?" Evaline marched over and gazed down at her. "There are going to be certain expectations of you in this family. Committees you'll need to participate in, charity events you'll need to attend. When are you going to have time to run your own little design *business?*"

Gregory kept asking her the same question, so she told Evaline the same thing she always told her fiancé. "I'll find the time. It can be flexible. I can take on only a few clients as my schedule allows." She tried her best to hold up her shoulders in the midst of the woman's stare down.

"But it won't be necessary." Evaline shook her head. "We already have interior decorators for all of our properties. You'll need to focus on the things that are important to this family."

And obviously Rose wasn't important. Her goals didn't matter.

"Evaline is right, Rose," her mother chimed in. "You're going to have such a visible position now. So many responsibilities. It's not a good time to get distracted with a hobby."

"It's not a *hobby*. It's a career." And it was what she'd been doing her whole life—taking average or mundane spaces and giving them vibrancy, personality, beauty…

"You can give our designers your recommendations," Evaline

said as though that was settled. "I'm sure they'll take your thoughts into consideration."

The dismissive tone drew Rose to her feet. It was one she'd heard too often as the youngest of three sisters. No one ever took her seriously. Her hands balled into fists, but she couldn't argue with Evaline. Not in front of everyone else.

"Why don't we all take five?" Rose asked instead. "I need to freshen up." Southern speak for *I can't stand the sight of you right now so I'm escaping to the restroom.*

"That's a fabulous idea." A saleswoman who had been watching from a distance hurried over to Rose's mother and Evaline and prodded them toward a spread of small tables near the back of the store. "We have a refreshment area over here. There's peach iced tea and a platter of fresh fruit and some of the most darling pastries you'll ever see."

"Pastries?" Syd suddenly perked up, but Rose linked their arms together and dragged her in the opposite direction.

"We're going to visit the powder room. Be right back."

"But I don't have to pee." Her friend tried to resist. "And look! They have green macarons back there."

"You can have one later," Rose muttered all but shoving Syd through the bathroom door. The restrooms were every bit as opulent as the boutique itself—everything seemed to have been plated in gold, shimmering under the light of more chandeliers. The calming scent of lavender drifted in the air.

"Whew." Rose finally managed to inhale a full breath. She walked to a mirror and checked her lipstick. Amazingly still intact, but that shiny spot on her forehead...wow. She dug around in her purse for her compact. "Things were getting tense in there, huh?"

"Ohhhh." Syd hopped up to seat herself on the marble vanity. "I see. This is where I give you a pep talk, right? That's why we had to sneak away to the bathroom?"

Rose concentrated on powdering the oil field on her forehead. "A pep talk for what?"

"You know. About how everything'll be okay. Things may seem bad now, Rosie," her friend recited dutifully. "But I'm sure it'll all work out. You'll find someone else."

That stood her up straight. "What'd you mean things seem bad?" And…"Find someone *else*?" She'd only brought Syd in here so they could complain about her mother-in-law for a few minutes, not so they could pick out a whole new future for her.

"Well, this is the third shopping trip we've been on and you can't find a dress." Her friend gave a shrug. "Isn't that a sign or something? Like the universe telling you not to marry Gregory?"

Rose dropped the compact back into her purse. "It's not a sign." It couldn't be a sign. She and Gregory were compatible in nearly every area. They'd done all of those personality tests. Relationship therapy, too—which he'd pushed back on since they got along fine most of the time, but she'd wanted to make sure. That their relationship was right. That they could communicate. In the end, the therapist said they had the best communication skills she had ever seen in an engaged couple.

See? Rose didn't need anyone else to give her a pep talk. She could do it by herself. She hoisted herself up on the flawless counter next to Syd. There was something about sitting there with her legs dangling that made her feel like a little girl again. If Evaline walked in right now, she'd have a conniption. For some reason that made her smile.

"The perfect dress is out there," Rose insisted. "I'll find it. The wedding is still months away." That would be plenty of time to still have alterations done. "I don't want to find a dress too early. What if I lose weight?" Or dear God, gain it?

Syd gave her the assessing look of a best friend. She had these round, gorgeously dark eyes that could be as cunning as Maleficent's. "Are you sure this is what you want? One. Hundred. Percent. Sure?"

A wild thumping started in Rose's heart and she had to look away. "That's not fair. You're asking me this at a very inconvenient time." At a time when her future mother-in-law had just completely discounted her hopes and dreams. Having a few doubts right about now made sense.

"In my opinion this is the absolute best time to ask." Her friend turned to face her, giving her no escape. "Can you do this? Can you be who that woman wants you to be? Can you be who Gregory wants you to be and still be happy for the rest of your life?"

The words twisted the knife on the stab of doubt she'd been trying so hard to ignore over the last month. If it were only she and Gregory they were talking about, she had no doubt they could be happy. But with his family, it would likely never be just she and Gregory.

Syd leveled her with an honest stare. "I'm asking because I can't imagine spending one day with that woman, let alone the rest of my life."

"I won't be spending the rest of my life with *her*." Even as she said it, Rose knew it wasn't true. Gregory might complain about his mother behind her back, but he tended to do everything he could to keep her happy. Their family had to live up to certain expectations, his mother always said. And Evaline had been trying to convince Rose and Gregory to move into the guest quarters on their estate after they got married. "Maybe we'll move away."

"And leave the family business?" Syd looked skeptical. "Isn't Gregory next in line to take his father's throne?" Her friend pronounced the words with a British accent.

She rolled her eyes at the theatrics. "He is supposed to take over as CEO eventually, yes." Ever since Gregory had graduated from business school, his father had been grooming him to take over the family's fast-food conglomerate as well as run their growing portfolio of professional sports teams. "But his father won't retire anytime soon, trust me. So maybe we'll live somewhere else for a few years." Wouldn't that be a dream? Just she and Gregory off on their own. She could start her design business anywhere, and, surely he could easily find a job being a Cunningham and all…

"Would Gregory ever go somewhere else?" Leave it to Syd to always ask the hard questions. "Would he walk away from his family?"

No. The answer came right from Rose's gut. Not for her. Not for anyone.

"You need to make sure, Rose," Syd said quietly. "It's not too late for you to call off the wedding. I'm not saying you *should*. But you need to make sure this is what you want for your life."

"It is." Or it was. Oh, mercy, she didn't know. Why did it all have to be so confusing? Why couldn't she just be with the man she loved? "It's too late to reconsider anything. Everything's already planned. The invitations have gone out…"

"It's not too late until you say 'I do,'" her friend insisted. "Maybe you should take some time to think things through. Give yourself some space. Hey!" Her eyes lit. "You could go to your aunt's place. It's perfect! She wanted you to come out anyway."

Syd had been over helping her look up ideas for the brides-maids' dresses when Rose had received her aunt's package. Her friend had been intrigued that Rose had an aunt she knew noth-ing about. But maybe Syd was right. Rose thought about Sassy's note, about the angel sitting on her counter at home. *You always had such a sense of style...It's no wonder you've gotten to where you are today, starting your own design firm...* How would she ever start her own design firm without the support of her husband? Of her family? "Evaline has us all booked over the holidays." She'd lost track of the parties and the galas and the charity events she and Gregory were supposed to make appearances at.

Syd hopped off the bathroom counter and stood facing her. "Didn't you say your aunt is dying? Sounds like the perfect excuse to disappear for a while."

"I'd love to be there for her." She had no idea why her mother and Sassy had a falling out all those years ago, but her aunt had never had children of her own and she obviously needed help. She'd tried to talk to her sisters about the letter, but they were all so busy, they'd been playing phone tag. "I don't know if there's any way I can make it happen though. Not with all of these events I'm supposed to attend with Gregory." Evaline would have a conniption if she left town.

"At some point you need to start standing up for yourself," Syd insisted. "If you want to go visit your aunt go. You're not married yet. Gregory could survive one Christmas without you."

"I guess." Any anyway, how could she say no to her aunt? Surely Gregory would understand. "It sounds like my sister is going. My aunt specifically asked all three of us." According to Dahlia's last message, she had decided to visit Sassy. Maybe the Juniper Inn would provide Rose with the perfect escape.

She hadn't been there in years, but she still remembered her aunt's beautiful boutique resort in Colorado. She remembered stumbling out of the cramped car with her sisters and feeling like she'd stepped into the pages of a storybook, someplace magical and removed from the rest of the world. The resort had eight gingerbread house–like cabins nestled in the trees, and a perfectly lovely pond for ice-skating. Oh, it had been so long, but she could still almost smell those pine trees. The inn had been a place she'd wandered and laughed and dreamed with her sisters. Her heart swelled just thinking about it. "I think a trip to Colorado is exactly what I need right now."

"Atta girl." Syd gave her a supportive pat. "I'd go with you but—"

The door flew open and Lillian charged into the bathroom. "Rose Marie, just what do you think you're doing?" She didn't wait for an answer. "Evaline has a busy schedule, and you're chitchatting in here. Don't you know how this looks?"

"Like she had to go to the bathroom?" Syd asked.

Lillian fixed her scorching gaze on Rose's best friend. "Will you give us a moment, please, sugar?" she asked in full Southern decorum.

"If I must." Her friend started to back toward the door. Once she was behind Lillian, she mouthed *Stay strong* and flexed her biceps.

Right. Stay strong. Unfortunately, that was much harder to do without reinforcements.

Once the door had opened and closed, Rose's mother closed her eyes in a dramatic pause. Rose knew from past experience this was her mother's way of collecting herself, so she leaned against the sparkling marble countertop to wait.

"Evaline thinks you're having doubts." Lillian finally opened her eyes, staring at Rose as though trying to analyze her. "But I told her that's not true. You're not having doubts. What is there to doubt?" She walked over and smoothed her hand over Rose's hair. "Gregory is the best thing that has ever happened to you. He's smart and he's handsome and he will be able to provide for you for the rest of your life."

All true. And yet…he hadn't wanted to sneak out to Tybee Island with her earlier…

"That man is more than your father and I could have ever dreamed for you…" Sighing loudly, Lillian snatched a tissue from the golden box on the counter and dabbed at her eyes. Her mother always cried when she talked about their father. "If your daddy was still here, he'd be ecstatic about this wedding."

"I know." But he wasn't here. He'd passed away four years ago after having a stroke. And Rose had hardly left her mother's side since. Being a businessman much like Gregory, her father probably would've loved her fiancé. They would've played golf together. They would've talked business and profit margins and stock options. "I'm not having doubts." For some reason, she always lied when her mother started to cry. She said whatever she had to in order to make things better. "It's all a little overwhelming, that's all." The wedding, sure, but also what would come after.

"I know it might feel overwhelming." Lillian reached into her purse and pulled out a compact, proceeding to powder Rose's forehead for her. "But, sweet pea, hiding in the bathroom isn't going to help. Especially when Evaline is out there waiting. You're only overwhelmed because we still have so much to do. You haven't found a dress and we're running out of time before the holidays. Once we check things off the list, you'll feel better."

Yes, but would she be able to check Evaline's controlling nature off the list? That's what had started to grate on her more than the wedding details.

"Speaking of the holidays," her mom went on, handing her a lipstick. "Evaline wanted you to decide on the cake before Christmas. That way the order won't get lost in the rush they're bound to have in the next few weeks. Should I make an appointment with the baker we liked for next week? Evaline will have to approve it—"

"No." The word came out harsher than she meant it to, but it was almost a relief. Rose shoved the lipstick back into her hands. "Next week won't work. I won't be here next week. I have to go out of town for a while."

"Out of town?" Her mother lowered her voice as though afraid Evaline was listening outside the door. Which she probably was. "Whatever for?"

At first Syd's idea to get away had sounded crazy, like wishful thinking, but now getting away felt like it was the only thing that could save her. "Sassy got in touch with me. And Mags and Dahlia." She watched her mom's face carefully. She had the loveliest skin tone—olive and smooth—but those familiar worry lines had appeared around her eyes.

"Sassy contacted you?" Rose couldn't tell if the wobble in her mother's tone was anger or fear. "What does she want?"

Originally Rose had wondered whether she should tell Lillian about the letter. She hadn't wanted to get her all worked up. But there was no going back now. "She wants us to come see her. Honestly, it sounds like she might not be doing so well. She asked us to spend Christmas with her, and—"

"That's impossible." Her mother turned away, but not in time to hide her obvious shock. "You absolutely cannot go."

"Why not?" Rose stepped around to face her. "What happened between you two? Why did we stop going out to see her?"

"That is none of your business." Her mother pressed her fingers to her forehead as though she had a headache coming on. "You can't leave right now. Not when the Cunningham family needs you here. I forbid it. You can't ruin this chance, Rose."

Defiance rushed through her. She never told Lillian no. She always did what her mother asked. Maybe because Rose was all her mother had. Dahlia lived in Minnesota and Mags hardly ever visited from Florida. They hadn't been here when their father had died. They'd come for the funeral, but Rose was the one who'd sat up all night with her mother while she'd sobbed. Rose was the one who'd begged her to get out of bed those horrific weeks after they'd lost him and her sisters had gone back to their lives.

But she had to do this. She had to be there for her aunt. She had to get away and clear her head. "I'm sorry, but I'm going," she told her mother. "Sassy needs us, and I need to go."

She had to make sure the life she was walking toward was the one she truly wanted.

Chapter Four

Magnolia

The flowers showed up right on schedule. Ten o'clock on the nose, well after the morning rush. Magnolia Buchanan-Diaz saw the delivery girl coming from all the way down the block. A bouquet of lush red roses and crisp white magnolias and full-bodied yellow dahlias plumed from a blown-glass vase the same variegated turquoise and blue color as the sea across the road from where her mobile bakery sat.

The arrangement earned a gasp from her assistant Coral, who had been wiping up the espresso machine until the flowers came into view. "Oh, my gawd. Eric sent you flowers again, didn't he?" She tossed the rag onto the counter, a literal throwing in of the towel. "He did. He's always sending you flowers. Such a romantic! And I can't even find a guy who'll call the next morning." That might be true, but since Coral was in her early twenties, she still had plenty of time to find the right man.

It was, however, too late for Magnolia. Eric had called twelve times that morning, leaving message after message apologizing and begging her to come home so they could talk, but Mags couldn't bring herself to respond. Now, she simply watched the

Home for the Holidays

flowers bob closer and closer until the delivery girl stood right in front of the bakery's open window. They were beautiful flowers, so colorful and vibrant, but she couldn't enjoy them anymore. Eric always went to great lengths to choose the arrangement, selecting roses, magnolias, and dahlias to remind her of the sisters she rarely got to see anymore. The first time he'd sent flowers after they'd argued about the cost of the fertility treatments they were doing, it had sent Magnolia running back into his arms, but after too many apology bouquets now the sight of one made her want to turn and run away. Away from him. Away from them…

"Delivery for Magnolia Buchanan-Diaz," the delivery girl said baring a peppy I'm-here-to-make-your-day smile. She was probably used to gasps of surprise and exclamations of joy when she presented her offerings, but Magnolia couldn't muster the energy for any of that nonsense. She'd slept in her car last night and had been walking around all morning in a numb, sleep-deprived fog.

"Where do I sign?" Magnolia asked, not bothering to look at the card. She already knew what it said. *I'm sorry. Please come home so we can talk.* She couldn't go home. Not after last night. Not after this argument. This one had changed something. It had forced a part of her to completely shut down. Usually she came away from one of their quarrels feeling angry or sad, but now she felt nothing. Empty. Hollow. Detached.

The delivery girl frowned slightly, confusion pulling at her young features. But she handed over an iPad. "You can sign right there."

With her hand trembling, Magnolia scribbled something illegible across the line and handed it back to her. "Thanks." She felt bad for her flat reaction, so she quickly bagged up the last of the white chocolate raspberry muffins. Better that than her finishing them off later. "Take these for the road," she said, handing them over across the counter. "On the house."

That seemed to erase all traces of disappointment in the young woman's expression. "Really? Thanks! I've heard people say your stuff is the best, but I've never had the chance to try anything."

"Well, in that case…" Magnolia eyed the baskets, which had nearly been picked empty over the course of the morning. "You really have to try the lemon scone." She bagged one up. "And these petite birthday cake donuts."

"Wow!" The girl shoved the iPad into a satchel that was draped across her body and gathered up the bags. "You're the best. Thanks so much! I'll totally tell everyone to come here!" Digging her hand into one of the sacks, she turned around and started munching on the scone as she walked away. "This is amazing!" she called over her shoulder. "Best scone I've ever eaten!"

"Have a nice day." Magnolia sent her off with a wave, but the compliments lingered, filling the cold hollowness still left over from her fight with Eric. That's how she knew this was what she was meant to do—to feed people sweets and treats, to fill them with a happiness that fueled her own. That's why she'd taken out the loan from her parents to start her own bakery.

Oh, Lordy. Her parents. What would her mother say if she knew the truth about her marriage? Actually, Mags already knew the answer. Her mother came from a long line of carefully groomed wives. *It's your job to make your husband happy*, Lillian liked to say. Well, Magnolia had made Eric happy once upon a time. She'd thought they had the perfect marriage. There'd been passion and spontaneity. When she would come home from working at the bakery on Eric's days off, he'd surprise her with elaborate dates he'd secretly planned—scavenger hunts around the city and picnics on their favorite stretch of beach. She would try to outdo his surprises—cooking him dinner wearing only an apron and buying tickets to hockey games where they both screamed themselves hoarse rooting for the underdog. But that was before the lost pregnancies, the failed fertility treatments, the attempts at trying to be okay with it all.

"My God, these flowers are beautiful." Coral pressed her entire face into the bouquet and inhaled deeply. "I swear your husband always has great taste, but he really outdid himself this time, didn't he?"

"You could say that." Mags lifted the hefty arrangement and carted it to the back counter where it would be out of way for the after-dinner dessert rush. She'd already made a full arsenal of cupcakes, which was what she was best known for—chocolate mint, salted caramel, s'mores, and another round of pumpkin spice, even though fall had somehow moved to the rearview mirror. Yesterday she'd sold out of those babies in less than an hour, so she'd made a double batch today. It took her mind off things—the baking, the mixing, the measuring. It was so easy to follow recipes, so formulaic. There were no decisions to be made, no questioning what was right. She could just move about freely, doing what she loved, caught up in something that promised to rescue her from her crushed hopes. If only it could rescue her marriage, too.

"Call me crazy, but you don't seem exactly thrilled about the flowers." Coral poured herself another mug of black coffee and leaned into the counter next to Mags, peering up at her with a pair of questioning green eyes. "What's up? You're not yourself today. You seem…" She paused as though she wanted to choose her words carefully. "Subdued."

It happened to be the perfect description of how she felt. Subdued. Smothered under a blanket of her own disappointment. Lately it had started to suffocate her. After their most recent failed in vitro attempt, desperation had kicked in. Last night she'd made Eric a nice dinner—fresh grilled scallops and a creamy Parmesan risotto. He'd already been in a bad mood because the water heater went out again, so she'd wanted to cheer him up, to lure him out of the grumpiness so they could talk about trying for another baby.

He'd picked at the food and hardly responded when she'd brought up going back to the doctor. Four failed in vitro attempts didn't mean they would never get pregnant, she'd reminded him. *We can try again…*

"Seriously. You okay, girl?" Coral asked glancing at her with concern. "You don't look so good."

Magnolia stared back at her friend, but she hardly saw her. No one knew about the infertility, about what it had done to her marriage. She stared at the flowers until they blurred into a shapeless splotch of colors. "I think I have to leave him." The words had to come out. Too much pressure had built in her heart and she couldn't hold it all back any longer.

"What?" Coral jolted upright, her coffee sloshing out of the mug. "Gawd, Mags, *what?*"

"I have to leave. Maybe not forever, but for now." She'd known it before this moment. Maybe she'd known it for a while, but she'd so hoped she'd end up pregnant after that last treatment. And a baby would fix what had broken in her marriage. She wouldn't have to obsess anymore, over hormones and the right timing and what to eat and what to avoid and what to force Eric to avoid. If she'd only gotten pregnant those tired sad circles under her eyes would finally be hidden beneath the healthy glow of pregnancy. If only she'd gotten pregnant this time, she and Eric wouldn't be crumbling under the stress of the financial sacrifices they'd made so they could simply hold a baby in their arms.

Her mind wandered backward again, pulling her into the thoughts she hated most. Maybe she and Eric never should've gotten married. It had all happened so fast. She'd met him during a vacation to Islamorada, Florida, four years ago. The hotel she and her friends were staying at had a small fire, and he'd been one of the first firemen on the scene. As they evacuated, she'd struggled with smoke inhalation, and he'd taken care of her. Well, he'd done more than that—he'd captivated her. Eric had been strong and charming, spontaneous and a bit wild. Passionate. Best of all, he'd been free of the expectations she'd lived under most of her life.

Oh, how she'd wanted a taste of that freedom. A life that felt like it truly belonged to her, a life that was deep and adventurous and maybe even flawed but also real. Instead of playing a rehearsed role in her mother's perfect family, Eric had given her the chance to simply be Mags. To explore, to wander, to dance on the beach under the stars, to go skinny-dipping in the ocean. Theirs had been one of those whirlwind romances—the one she'd always dreamed of having.

What had happened to those two spontaneous, carefree, loving people? She didn't know. She only knew she didn't want to be this person. The one who obsessed over hormones and diets and treatments and anything that might give her hope of finally getting pregnant. She didn't want to be the woman who fought with her husband because he didn't want to keep trying for a baby they might never have. She didn't want to be the woman who spent the night sleeping in her car.

"Okay. Okay." Coral steadied her hands out in front of her.

"Obviously you and Eric had a fight or something. That's totally normal in a marriage. My parents fought all the time." She gave Mags's upper arm a gentle squeeze. "But honey, that doesn't mean you have to leave him. You'll work it out."

"We've tried." They'd been trying for two years. Ever since she'd had her first miscarriage. They'd done the counseling, the relationship retreats, the podcasts. And things always got better for a while. But it had become a cycle they couldn't seem to break no matter how hard they tried. They were both so intense, so passionate. They were too much alike. Or…they had been so much alike. They'd both wanted a family. They'd talked about trying for a baby right after their wedding, and spent hours daydreaming about how many children they would have. Eric used to say he hoped she'd have twins. Or triplets even.

But last night…

Mags stared hard at the counter, her lungs contracting so hard her ribs began to ache. "It wasn't just a fight this time." It was a turning point, a shift in the foundation of their entire relationship. "Eric told me he doesn't want a baby. That he's not willing to try anymore." He'd said exactly what he knew would wreck her. *I'm done*, he'd said. *I can't do this anymore. We can't afford to do this anymore. Our savings are gone, Mags. And you've become a completely different person.* She had; she knew she'd become a different person. With each disappointment they'd endured she recognized herself less and less. Having a baby had become an act of desperation, of obsession. But she couldn't give up now. She had to try again. "We've had to do all these fertility treatments and they keep failing," Mags whispered. "It's been so hard."

"Why have you never said anything?" Coral asked quietly. "I didn't know. I had no idea."

No one knew. Not even her own sisters. It was so grueling the things they'd gone through. The testing and the procedures. And the results—that was always the most frustrating moment of them all. The *I'm sorry, not this time, you can try again.* It didn't matter how much money they paid or which doctor they worked with or how much her heart pleaded with God, their answer was always the same. No.

"I know it must be hard to talk about," Coral prompted.

"I don't even know what to say anymore." She'd always been independent, the peacemaker in her family. She worked hard. She loved hard. So how come she didn't deserve a baby? How come she couldn't have the one thing she wanted most in life, the one thing she felt would complete her?

"I understand." Coral covered Mags's hand with hers. "I can't imagine how painful this all must be. Have you gotten any outside support? From family? It's too much to carry on your own."

"I haven't talked about it with anyone." Not even the people she loved most besides Eric. But she'd been thinking about her sisters ever since she'd received Sassy's package. Holding that rolling pin her aunt had chosen for her had given her the first flicker of hope she'd felt in so long. Dally and Rose had texted her just this morning that they were both going, and they'd begged her to come, too. "I think I'm going to take some time off," Mags told Coral. "To go stay with my aunt in Colorado. Just until after the holidays. Can you run things while I'm away?" They were only open three days a week in the winter as it was. This would be the absolute best time for her to get away.

"I can handle things." Coral stood and started to tidy up the counter like she wanted to prove herself. "You go, Mags. Take all the time you need."

"Thank you." Tears sprang to her eyes. Maybe the Juniper Inn would help her find the healing she so desperately needed.

Chapter Five

Dahlia

Dahlia drank in the dazzling white-capped peaks lining either side of the two-lane highway. God, she'd forgotten how much she loved the mountains.

Even in early December the snow had already piled up in the Colorado Rockies, but it was crystalline and powdery instead of grimy like the snow back in Minnesota. So pristine and lovely. It looked exactly like one of those postcards her aunt used to send before the big falling-out in their family—like the inside of a snow globe. The sight gave her the first flicker of Christmas spirit she'd felt since Jeff had told her he wanted to take the kids to Europe.

Truthfully, she'd been dreading Christmas and everything that came with it this year, knowing she would be separated from Maya and Ollie for the first time in their lives. But the view out the windshield loosened the sadness that had settled in Dahlia's chest when she'd kissed Ollie and Maya goodbye. Her sweet son had taken her cheeks in his chubby hands, tugging her face close to his. *I asked Santa to bring you the specialist surprise since we'll be so far away on Christmas,* he'd whispered. *I can't wait, Mama. I'll bet it's gonna be so amazing, whatever it is. You're gonna love it.*

She'd held him tight, silently gagging on the tears she'd refused to let fall. Now they filled her eyes once again, blurring the ice-glazed road in front of her. She'd better slow—

A form materialized out of nowhere. A man in the middle of the road! She hit the brakes and cranked the wheel, sending the car spinning off the asphalt down a small embankment. White whirled around her—sun and then shade, trees and then sky. The car came to an abrupt stop in a puff of snow, facing the highway.

Adrenaline pounded through Dahlia's chest, hammering against her heart. What. The. Heck? The man—who she'd thought might've been an apparition—materialized again, sauntering casually toward her car like he had all day to get there. He might've been whistling for all she knew.

Fury stormed through her as she ripped off her seatbelt and threw open the door, barely remembering to cut the engine before she flew out of the rental car.

"What are you thinking?" she demanded, taking a step toward him. Immediately, her leg sunk into the snow all the way up to her mid-thigh. Letting out a grunt of frustration, she planted her hands onto the snowbank to free herself, but both arms sunk in all the way to her chest. Goldarn it! How was she supposed to give him a proper talking to when she was stuck like this?

A shadow eased over her and Dahlia craned her head to look up. It was a shame she'd given up on swearing when the children were born.

"Need some help?" The man wore something between a smirk and a smile. He was clad in flannel, from the trapper's hat on his head to the heavy coat that made it difficult to tell just how big he really was. Could that all be muscle under there? Or more layers?

She hissed in a breath, unable to contemplate anything other than the freezing sting in her hands.

Seeming to take her silence as a cry for help, the man leaned down and plucked her from the snowbank, hoisting her up into his arms and delivering her to the road with two giant steps. Definitely all muscle.

"There." He set her down. "You okay?" He seemed to look her over. "I mean you look good. Really good." Suddenly he seemed to blush—or was it the cold air freezing him too? And then he cleared his throat. "But it's best to make sure."

Ugh! Was he seriously trying to hit on her right now? The fear and the cold all seemed to converge on her at once. "Of course I'm not okay!" she blurted. "I could've hit you! I could've hit a tree!" She could've died and then what would happen to Ollie and Maya? They'd be stuck with their father!

"But you didn't. You're fine. Your car is fine. Mostly." The man's nonchalance ground down against her nerves. He'd almost been hit by a car and was acting like nothing had happened.

Breathe, she commanded herself. But her ribs seemed to have tightened, and oxygen was harder to come by at this altitude. "I can't believe this."

"Hey, nothing to worry about," the man said in a reassuring tone. "Spinouts happen all the time up here. No big deal."

Dahlia's jaw hinged open. He took her irritation with him as embarrassment? "Spinouts don't happen to me." She was from Minnesota for the love of God. She knew how to drive in the snow. Now that the adrenaline had started to subside, she studied the man's face. He looked about her age, maybe. It was always hard to tell with men. There was something boyish and playful about his hazel eyes, but the Paul Bunyan jawline and stubble gave him a more rugged appearance. Still, his good-natured smile kept her from checking her pocket for her pepper spray.

"You weren't going fast enough to get too far off the road," the man told her, one corner of his mouth hiked into a sly grin. "You could've hit a moose though." He gestured to their left.

A massive bull moose stood about twenty feet up the road staring them both down.

"Oh God." Dahlia immediately stepped back and sank into the snow again.

"Easy." Paul Bunyan clasped her hands in his and pulled her out. "Don't panic and make any sudden movements. He's assessing the situation, making sure we're not a threat."

Oh, was that all? "He's huge." The whisper scorched her throat. How had she missed that? The moose was massive and imposing and quite possibly angry. *Oh, dear God, don't force my kids to grow up with their father.*

"I was trying to flag you down, so you'd stop in time," Paul Bunyan commented softly, keeping his eyes on the animal. "But you must've not've seen me until the last minute."

"Um, no." She didn't mention that she hadn't seen him because she'd been crying. Her eyes heated again. This trip had been a huge mistake. She shouldn't be here. This was crazy. What if something happened to her? Who would make the kids their lunches and get them to their music lessons on time? Who would read them stories before bed and make sure they actually bathed once in a while?

"What should we do?" she hissed. The moose still stood frozen, every bulging muscle seemingly tensed. Weren't moose dangerous? She'd always heard you were supposed to stay away from them. "He looks mad." Panic rose into her throat.

"He's not gonna hurt us," Paul Bunyan insisted.

As if wanting to refute that statement the moose clomped a few steps closer, tossing his head this way and that. It was a wonder he could even keep that head lifted with all the weight in his rack.

Dahlia's lungs pressed out a whimper. "Call 911."

The man next to her laughed. He laughed!

"By the time Timmy got here, the moose would be long gone," he assured her. Easing closer, he linked her arm through his. "We're gonna slowly back up. Keep your head down and whatever you do, don't look him in the eyes."

Don't look him in the eyes? Why? Would he attack? A tremble recoiled through Dahlia's upper body as she pressed her chin to her chest. Somehow, she managed to stumble backward alongside the man, even with her knees weakening.

"There he goes." Paul Bunyan stopped, and Dahlia forced up her head. Sure enough, the moose was sauntering to the other side of the road where he disappeared into a thicket of trees.

Letting out the breath she hadn't realized she'd been holding, Dahlia propped her hands on her knees to hold herself up. "I can't believe…what in the…that was a *moose.*" Walking down the middle of the road. He could've flattened her…

"I see him all the time. I call him Brutus." Paul Bunyan turned to face her, shielding his eyes from the late-afternoon sun. "You're not from around here, huh?"

"I'm from Minneapolis." They had moose in Minnesota, but she couldn't remember the last time she'd ventured into the North Woods. And she'd never seen one that close up before.

"So, what brings you to Juniper Springs?" Paul Bunyan started walking in the direction of her car while Dahlia gimped along behind. Her knees apparently couldn't believe the danger had passed.

"My aunt." She tried to sound as breezy as he did. "She's dying and she asked my sisters and me to come spend one last Christmas with her." This trip might not be all that uplifting, but it was important. That's why she had to come here—even if it meant braving icy roads and grumpy bull moose.

"Three nieces…" The man paused from seeming to assess the damage to her car and gazed back at her. "Are you talking about Sassy?"

"Yes." Dahlia quickly closed the distance between them, anxious for any update on her ailing aunt. She'd tried calling Sassy multiple times since receiving the package in the mail, but the woman never answered her phone. Sassy had simply texted Dahlia saying she couldn't wait to see her. "You know Aunt Sassy?"

"Everyone knows Sassy." Paul Bunyan dug a set of keys out of his pocket and pointed them toward a black truck parked on the other side of the road. "Looks like the car is okay, but we're going to have to dig you out." Then he added, "Sassy is not dying, by the way."

"Yes, she is." Dahlia followed him to the truck where he pulled out a shovel. "She sent us each a package with our favorite Christmas decoration from when we were young, and specifically asked us to spend one last Christmas with her." That's what Dahlia had been preparing for all week—nursing her aunt through some terrible illness, making herself useful.

The news didn't seem to ruffle Mr. Bunyan any. He simply crossed the road back to her car, toting the shovel along with him. "I'm Sassy's doctor," he said, shoveling the snow away from the wheels. "Pretty sure I'd know if she was dying."

"*You're* a doctor?" Normally she didn't resort to categorizing people, but she would've pegged Paul Bunyan as a lumberjack or a forest ranger. Definitely not a doctor.

Her surprise reinstated his grin. "That's right. *I'm* a doctor." He stuck out his hand. "Ike Songer and you are?"

"Dahlia." She straightened her shoulders. Just last week she'd done a presentation for the entire PTA at the school, and there hadn't been one internal flutter, but now butterflies were beating their wings against her ribs.

"Nice to meet you, Dahlia." A grin lit his eyes. "I should've known you were related to Sassy. You have her eyes."

Well, he would know being her aunt's doctor and all. She did her best to ignore his captivating grin. She recognized a charmer when she saw one. Heck, she'd been married to one. "There must be some mistake." Dahlia steered the conversation back to her aunt. "Sassy *is* dying. Maybe she hasn't told you. Maybe she doesn't want anyone around here to know." That was the only explanation.

"I'm telling you, she's not dying." Dr. Ike stomped through the deep snow to the back tires of her rental and started to shovel. "She was in the office not three weeks ago for a full-on physical. Your aunt is as healthy as that bull moose."

"That's impossible. Why would she ask us to come out here for one last Christmas then?"

The man shook his head in amusement. "Knowing Sassy, she has her reasons." He slipped off the thick flannel coat he wore and wrapped it around Dahlia's shoulders as though he could tell she was chilled. "Let me tow your car out of the snowbank and you can ask her yourself."

Chapter Six

Magnolia

By now she should have learned chocolate couldn't fix everything, but that sure didn't stop her from trying.

Dusting brownie crumbs off her hands, Magnolia scrambled out of the rocking chair she and Eric had bought for the baby almost two years ago when they'd first started trying to get pregnant. She'd thought it would be so easy, that she'd go off the pill and within a couple of months she'd be glowing and rounder. She stood in the center of the baby's room now staring at the furniture she'd found on clearance at Target. It had all seemed so serendipitous when she'd bought the crib and changing table and matching plush chair. Eric hadn't been exactly thrilled with the purchase, but like she told him—it had been an incredible bargain and they would need it eventually.

Now, though, looking around the room, she wasn't so sure.

She should've been more careful about getting her hopes up, like Eric had said, and yet over the months she'd added things to the room—the *Goodnight Moon* book and the cute bookshelves shaped like trees. The gender-neutral koala wall hangings she hadn't been able to walk past at a baby boutique. The sign with cursive lettering that read, "We love you to the moon and back." And the little Christmas stocking she'd bought last year, because after all the trials and tribulations of trying to conceive, she'd been sure their little miracle would be on the way by then.

They'd done everything right—they'd followed all the procedures and schedules and recommendations and old wives' tales. She'd prayed and begged and pleaded and read every blog she could find. She'd followed special diets and had always made sure to get the recommended amount of exercise. She'd reduced her stress through meditation and gentle yoga. And yet this room was still empty. Somehow the decor and the books and the subtle yellow paint she'd slathered on the walls made it feel even emptier.

Magnolia walked to the changing table where the Christmas stocking hid in the top drawer. Eric didn't know it was there. She'd stopped showing him the things she bought for the baby. She wanted to stop hearing his gentle cautioning. *Maybe we should wait. This is only making it harder…*

Tears stung the rims of her eyes as she opened the drawer and pulled out the stocking that still had a blank space where she had planned to stitch a name. The gnawing emptiness inside her seemed to open up again, spreading all through her. The stocking was soft and velvety—so delicate with white faux fur trim around the top—just like Santa's hat. She'd dreamed of hanging it up on their fireplace mantel, of filling it with little surprises. Christmas was supposed to have become even more meaningful, more significant because they would have a baby to share it with.

Not letting the tears fall, Magnolia shoved the stocking back into the drawer. This year, Christmas had lost its meaning. She and Eric were skirting around each other, and for the first time in their marriage they were spending the holidays apart. She was leaving for Colorado that very afternoon, and she didn't know when or if she was coming back.

A sense of defeat crowded out the desperation she'd felt for so long. Once so full of love and hope, her heart seemed to have shriveled. Tears threatening to fall again, Magnolia pulled the koala pictures off the wall and shoved them into the closet. Next went the "We love you to the moon and back" sign. Eric had been right. This was only making it harder. The room, the reminders. She needed to get away. She needed to figure out how to weave her broken heart back together.

And she desperately needed another brownie. Slipping out of the room, she closed the door firmly and then stumbled into the kitchen to where she'd left the pan of brownies on the stove to cool. Crap. Had she really eaten four already? A familiar self-loathing closed its fist around her heart.

Four? Seriously? Why couldn't she ever stop at one? Before she'd moved away from home for college, her mother had always told her exactly how much she could eat, and now she couldn't seem to make responsible choices without hearing her mother's voice whisper *You don't need more* in her ear. These days she always felt like she needed more. Even with the weight she'd put on—even with being four sizes larger than she'd been three years ago—she still needed more.

Screw it. Mags shoved half of another brownie into her mouth. Chocolate might not fix anything, but it took the edge off her emotions for a few seconds. And anyway, that would be the last one she'd ever eat. She swore. She'd never take another bite of chewy chocolaty goodness as long as she live—

A key turned in the lock across the room. Eric opened the door and cautiously stepped inside as though he knew she wouldn't want to see him.

Mags stayed where she was, almost afraid to look into his eyes and see the disappointment, the distance between them. It seemed to have grown so vast since their last argument. "What're you doing here?" He was supposed to be on his twenty-four-hour shift. That's the only reason she'd come home tonight. She'd stayed with Coral for the last few nights, but she couldn't stay there forever.

"I got someone to cover the rest of my shift." Eric walked over to where she stood. He was still dressed in his starched navy-blue firemen's uniform, and his dark hair was mussed as though he'd recently had his helmet on. That look used to seduce her. Not quite three weeks ago—two weeks after the in vitro had failed and before the big fight—that uniform had seduced her to fall into bed with him. It had been so long since they'd made love without the schedule, without the rules, without the knowledge that it could make or break their chance to have a baby. It had simply been the two of them again—showing love, taking love, comforting each other in the most intimate way possible. And then, only days later, he'd told her he was giving up on their dream.

"I had to come home and see you." His arms reached out halfway and stopped as though he was afraid to touch her. "This is making me crazy, Mags. I don't want to fight with you." His dark irresistible eyes and long lashes made him look so sincere. Those eyes and his handsome face had always drawn her in. It was the captivating contrast between his squared broad jaw and the two small dimples that appeared when he smiled. So rugged, but tender, too. Except, he didn't smile at her much anymore. Not since before all the fertility treatments.

Avoiding his gaze, Mags dragged herself to the stove and helped herself to another brownie from the pan. She'd do double duty on the cardio tomorrow.

"Please say something." Eric hovered nearby but didn't crowd her.

"I don't know what to say." She carted the remaining brownies over to the trashcan and dumped them. She'd never had much willpower. For chocolate or for men in uniform.

"We were happy." Behind her, Eric's voice teetered on the verge of desperation. "We were happy before all this started. We don't need kids, Mags. We don't need a baby to be happy."

And that was the difference between them. "I do." Mags took the empty brownie pan to the sink and started to wash it. "It's what I've dreamed about my whole life. Being a mother." And now that she knew how he really felt, things would never be the same. He didn't want a child and she did. What middle ground could they possibly find to stand on? "I'm tired." Bone-weary tired. "I'm tired of fighting. Of trying so hard. I can't do it anymore." There was that sense of defeat again, washing over her, dragging her back into the riptide.

"We won't fight anymore," he promised. "We'll go see that counselor you liked. Or maybe we should take a vacation together. You've always talked about going up to Martha's Vineyard—"

"I don't want to go on vacation." Mags shut off the water and spun to face him. Nausea churned through her. "I'm going to stay with my aunt Sassy for a while. Rose and Dahlia and I are going to spend the holidays with her." Maybe she should've told him before she'd bought the one-way ticket to Denver.

Eric's shoulders caved. "You haven't seen your aunt in years. Why now? Are you going to spend time with her or are you leaving me?" His voice cracked on the last word but he cleared his throat and continued, "Which one is it?"

"I don't know," she admitted. "I need some time. Some space. This isn't all your fault, Eric. Our problems are my fault, too. But I'm not sure we can fix them."

"We can. I know we can." He approached her slowly, as though he didn't want to scare her away. "I love you, Mags. But I can't keep doing these treatments and watching your heart break every time. We can't *afford* to keep trying. I'll make you happy without a baby. Like we were before…"

"Too much has changed." A familiar pain wrung out her heart. It was so much easier to push him away when she was mad at him. "I'm sorry."

"Don't give up on us." Her husband carefully reached his hands to her face, holding it gently while he looked deeply into her eyes. "You go to your aunt and sisters. Do whatever you have to do. Take time. But please, Mags…don't give up."

Chapter Seven

Rose

In the eighteen years Rose had been away from Juniper Springs, not one thing seemed to have changed.

She pulled into a slanted parking spot and cut the engine, leaning back with a nostalgic sigh at the familiar sights along Main Street. The square brick storefronts had all been elaborately decorated with garlands and lights and wreaths fashioned from the juniper pine branches. Snow encrusted the windows and the ledges, making the whole scene very Norman Rockwell. A few people hurried down the sidewalk all bundled in their stocking hats and scarves and puffy jackets, greeting each other as they passed.

It was strange that coming back here gave her a sense of coming home—she could feel it, something settling deep inside her. Growing up, their family had moved more than a dozen times. As soon as her father got a raise at work, their mother insisted they move to a bigger, better house. But no matter where they went, Rose never felt as though any of those places were home. Not in the truest sense of the word.

Moving around so much had scattered her memories. Did her

first kiss happen at the house on the south side, or the one in Midtown? Did she fall down the stairs and break her arm at the house in Rincon or the one in Richmond Hill? She couldn't quite remember, but she remembered every one of her visits to Juniper Springs with Technicolor clarity.

Rose climbed out of the car so she could smell it—that fresh, crisp mountain air, the hints of pine, the swirling scent of hot chocolate and coffee wafting from Grumpy's Place, the coffee shop down the street.

Wow. It was exactly like stepping into a memory. Suddenly she was transported back in time, to the day when she'd been eight or nine years old and Sassy had brought her into town just the two of them the day before Christmas. Rose had bounced along beside her aunt, oohing and aahing over every window display in those storefronts. They'd taken a detour through the park across the street. Rose turned to face it now. The gazebo still stood there, snowflake Christmas lights dangling from the rafters, and every tree in the park had been wrapped in lights. She could still picture the sparkling colors that had made the park seem so magical back then. She'd have to come back at night to see the light display in all its glory.

Pulling her scarf up tighter around her ears, Rose headed across the street to get a better look at the park. She'd only stopped in town to see if she could still get a cup of Grumpy's coffee, but now that she was here, she couldn't resist a walk down memory lane.

The crown jewel of all the Christmas decorations had always been located front and center in the park. Each year, one of the local businesses sponsored the giant Christmas tree that stood next to the gazebo. The Yuletide Committee hiked out to some remote area of the nearby forest and selected the perfect spruce or evergreen. Then the sponsoring business always took great care to decorate the tree with beautiful ornaments and festive lights...

Oh! There it was. As always, it was impressive, at least twenty feet tall and covered from top to bottom in silvery tinsel. She smiled. This town really hadn't changed.

Rose took it slow on the sidewalks. The snow had been cleared, but patches of ice still shone in the sun and her cute Uggs didn't give her much traction. Gregory had bought them as a gift for her before she left for Colorado. To keep her feet warm, he'd said. The reflection almost startled her. That was the first time she'd thought of her fiancé since she'd left Savannah. It had been a crazy trip with the flight delays and overbooked connections. Evaline had offered their family's private jet, but Rose only suspected that was so she could control when Rose departed and when she returned, and Rose didn't want to plan her return. Not yet. Not until they knew what they were dealing with in regard to Sassy's health.

She paused in front of the massive fir tree. It was stately and perfectly shaped, but now that she drew closer, the trimmings on the tree...yikes.

Glancing around, Rose frowned. There seemed to be no thought put into how the ornaments had been placed on the branches. Instead of spacing them out and varying the color patterns, the red, green, and silver baubles had all been clumped together.

Walk away. This is not your problem. And it wasn't her place to fix it, either. But, holy moly would it look so much better if those ornaments were spread out in a thoughtful color arrangement. Rose glanced over her shoulder and smiled at a young mother and her daughter walking by. She studied the ropes cordoning off the tree. A sign stood nearby: "This year's Christmas tree donated by Fixers Hardware Store."

Oh, no wonder! With the holiday rush, those hardware store workers were likely much too busy to take the time to arrange the ornaments carefully. They'd probably just piled all those ornaments on the branches without another thought.

She *was* thinking though. A tree this regal should be dressed exquisitely. It should be balanced and coordinated. It should look like someone had put thought into Juniper Springs' hallmark Christmas display.

She couldn't walk away, or she'd keep thinking about it all night. That's what she did. She overanalyzed everything when it came to design. She obsessed over it and couldn't rest until she did something to fix it. If she could at least get the bottom of the tree straightened out right now, she could find a ladder at Sassy's house and come back tomorrow to rearrange the top. Shooting another quick glance down the sidewalk, Rose stepped over the rope barrier and approached the tree. The ornaments appeared expensive—real glass balls with varying intricate designs, so at least the tree had that going for it. With a little rearranging it would actually be beautiful.

Standing back, Rose started to formulate a plan to highlight the tree's natural shape and stature. Carefully, she started to pluck some of the red ornaments off the branches, setting them in the snow next to her. Next went the green. She carefully tucked a few into her coat pockets to keep them from getting lost. Obviously, she'd have to go shopping later to find more ornaments. The tree should be filled with them. Oh! Maybe she could even find some locally made ornaments. She'd be happy to donate some new ones to the collection to give the tree more personality.

Happiness bubbled up inside of her at the prospect of a project. Anything to take her mind off what she was about to hear once she arrived at the Juniper Inn. The thought of losing Sassy stole the breath from her lungs.

"What're you doing?"

Rose spun, knocking a branch in the process. A tangle of gold ornaments fell to the ground and scattered, getting lost in the deep snow.

A man stomped over the rope barrier. She couldn't see much of him with the green stocking hat pulled down over his forehead and the flannel scarf wrapped around his neck and mouth, but his eyes were dark and glowering.

"Great," the man mumbled. "Now we're gonna have to wait till spring to find those." He shot her a glare that immediately knocked her off-balance. Those eyes of his were so sharp they could cut right through a person.

"I asked you what you're doing." His glare shifted to her bulging pockets. "You want ornaments to take home there's a secondhand store a few blocks away that sells them for cheap."

Despite the bitter chill in the air, heat flashed across Rose's cheeks. "I'm not *taking* the ornaments." Seriously. What kind of person would steal ornaments off the town tree? "I was fixing the tree." She tried to glare back at him, but glaring had never been her strong suit. This man had obviously practiced a lot.

"You're *fixing* it?" He repeated as though she'd just told him she was burning it down.

"Yes." Rose raised her shoulders and stepped closer to the man to show him he couldn't intimidate her. "It's a mess. I'm sure the hardware store meant well, but there is absolutely no order to the placement of these ornaments. I mean, look." She gestured to the silver balls she hadn't gotten to yet. "They're all grouped together. It's like someone just threw them up there."

The man's deep-set eyes narrowed. They were an interesting shape, those eyes. Slightly upturned in the corners, large and perceptive somehow. "Who the hell are you?" he asked in a growl.

Oh, right. Well she supposed he did have some reason to be suspicious. Everyone in Juniper Springs probably knew everyone else, and no one in town had seen her in almost two decades.

"I'm Rose." She attempted to melt the ice in his stare with her brightest smile. "Rose Buchanan."

The man simply blinked at her as though waiting for her to elaborate.

"I'm Sassy's niece," she went on, doing her best to keep up the wattage in her smile. "She's asked my sisters and I to spend Christmas with her this year like we did when we were younger." See? She actually did belong here. "I'm also a designer," she added, and then immediately shut her mouth. Why did she always feel the need to justify herself?

"So, you think being a designer qualifies you to mess with the Christmas tree?" His condescending tone seemed to chill the air even more. "We don't need help from someone like you."

Someone like her? Suddenly Rose felt trapped in her coat. Embarrassment and anger swirled together in her stomach. He didn't even know her! "I'm only trying to help."

"We don't want your help." The man swiped a few of the red ornaments off the snow and hung them back on the tree exactly the way they had been before—all clumped together. "The tree is fine," he snapped digging through the snow until he found one of the gold balls. He bumped past her and hung it back on the tree as though making a point. "If you'll kindly empty your pockets, you can be on your way and I'll put everything back where it goes."

Rose simply stood and gaped at him. She certainly hadn't anticipated running into the Grinch in Juniper Springs of all places. But she wasn't going to let him ruin her Christmas cheer. "Maybe I should talk to the person who sponsored the tree." Surely some rational person with the holiday spirit would welcome her help redecorating the tree.

"I'm the one who's sponsoring the tree this year." He didn't turn around to look at her. Somehow, he'd located all the ornaments— holding the lot of them in his large gloved hands. "And if we'd wanted anyone to fix the tree, we wouldn't have put up this fence around it." Impatience flared in his eyes. "You can go on now. Or I'll have to call the sheriff out and tell him you're trespassing."

"Trespassing?" In a public place? "Like I said, I didn't mean to cause problems." She *hadn't* caused any problems. "I accidentally dropped a few ornaments, but that doesn't mean I deserve to be treated like some criminal." Rose whirled indignantly and went to step over the rope, but the toe of her boot caught and tripped her. Instead of stalking away, she fell flat on her face in the snow.

Chapter Eight

Magnolia

This couldn't be right.

Mags checked the GPS again. Surely, she'd made a wrong turn somewhere. She squinted out the windshield ahead of her. How could this be the Juniper Inn? You used to be able to see the pond and a few of the cabins from the road. There was evidence that a driveway had once been there, and tire tracks had packed down the snow, but where were the beautiful cabins? Where was the large hand-carved sign that used to welcome visitors to the property? Where was the main house where her aunt lived? She couldn't see anything past the overgrowth of the forest. The pines and evergreens and aspens had inundated the place, hemming in the driveway.

Mags eased a foot onto the rental car's gas pedal and urged the SUV forward, staying in those tire tracks. Thank God she'd rented the four-wheel drive vehicle, or she'd never make it through. Shadows slid over the car as she navigated the path she assumed the driveway would follow. Even at three o'clock in the afternoon, the sun already hovered low, spilling through the trees like liquid gold. The lane was so narrow that branches scratched along either side of the rental, so it was a good thing she'd gotten the extra insurance, too.

Riding the brakes around another curve, Mags checked the GPS again. It had to be right, but—

She eased the car to a stop. The trees had started to thin enough that she could see a few buildings in the distance. But they weren't the same charming cottages that had once dotted the lake. They were old and run-down, the siding rotted and peeling, their front porches collapsed in. Worse yet, there were no Christmas decorations. Not one wreath or string of lights visible anywhere.

Sassy used to go all out in decorating for Christmas—she'd had every cottage outlined with colorful lights. Each front door would have a wreath made of fresh evergreen branches. Red velvet bows used to dress up the porches, but now there was...nothing. Nothing except for tumbledown buildings and snow and trees that had grown in too thick.

The sight sunk Mags's heart. Aunt Sassy really must not be doing well. Why had she waited so long to reach out? Guilt edged in. Her aunt probably thought she and her sisters didn't care about her. And who else did Sassy have?

Mags cringed remembering how she'd called her mother to talk about Sassy's letter. Lillian had dismissed the whole thing and quickly changed the subject. She'd refused to even acknowledge the possibility that her sister's health was declining. Instead, she'd asked if Mags had gotten her measurements done for her bridesmaid dress yet. That was what her mother truly cared about right now. Rose's upcoming wedding. Though they hadn't talked in a month, Lillian hadn't even asked Mags how she'd been. Her mother had never really known what to do with Mags. Dahlia had been her overachiever, getting straight As and securing every academic honor. Rose had always been the one who lived to make Lillian happy, but Mags had been closer to her father, bonding over the baseball games they used to attend together, and since his death, it was like she and her mother had no connection at all anymore.

It had always been easy to connect with Sassy though. In her memories, their aunt only had positive things to say to them. She'd told them she loved them. She'd told them how brilliant and beautiful they were. Mags couldn't wait to see her.

Last week, when she'd tried to call her aunt to tell her she was coming, she'd only been able to leave a message. Sassy had replied with a text asking her to send her travel information and had said she couldn't wait to see her. But she'd reveled nothing about her condition.

Whatever it was, she and Rose and Dally would get Sassy though it. Mags steered the car up the small hill and felt her heart sink even further the second the main lodge came into view. The house had once been so pristine and well cared for, but now the massive stained logs were peeling and faded. One of the large picture windows that overlooked the property had cracked, and a few broken bird feeders were scattered across the wide front porch. The house almost looked as sad as she felt.

Only one other car sat in front of the garage—a rental from the looks of it. Dahlia had texted that she'd already arrived at the inn but had offered no other details—no warning about what they were walking into.

Mags parked the rental behind Dahlia's car and climbed out straight into a drift of snow, her whole body shuddering. There was a reason she'd moved to Florida. She absolutely detested the cold. Zipping up the ski jacket she'd borrowed from Coral before she'd left Florida, Magnolia tromped through the snow in her borrowed Sorels, trying to follow the tracks Dahlia must've made when she'd gone into the house earlier. By the time Mags reached the front door she was huffing and puffing from the altitude and from the frigid air—which really did take your breath away. She stomped snow off her boots and knocked on the door, her knuckles already halfway to freezing. This was colder than cold. Mind-numbing. She simply wasn't going to be able to leave the house once she got in there.

The door swung open quickly—thank God—and Dahlia appeared. "So, Aunt Sassy isn't dying," her sister announced before Mags could even greet her.

"What'd you mean she's not dying?" Mags scooted inside the door past Dahlia before her toes froze off.

"I mean Aunt Sassy is as healthy as a bull moose, according to her doctor, who I happened to meet on the road when I almost *hit* a moose, and he told me Sassy was in for a checkup a few weeks ago and there's absolutely nothing wrong with her."

Relief loosened the tightness in her rib cage. "Thank God." Mags took in her sister's indignant expression. Out of the three of them, Dahlia looked the most like their father, with a slender nose and cheekbones made softer by the roundness of her face. Mags had always been envious of Dally's olive skin and strawberry-blond hair, not that she'd ever admit it to anyone. "Isn't it a good thing that Sassy's not dying?" Mags leaned over to untie the laces of her boots so she didn't tromp snow all over the house. Although it might not've mattered much if she did. Judging from the dust on the floor in the entryway and the clutter stacked in the corners, the place hadn't been cleaned in a while.

"Of course it's a good thing she's not dying." Dahlia's voice softened. The relief was evident on her face, too. "But why would she basically say she was then? In our letters. I mean, you read it the same way I did. So did Rose."

Mags stood and shook the boots off her feet. "To be fair, she never actually said she was dying."

"She *insinuated* it." Her sister had always been a literalist. "She must've known how it sounded." Dahlia led her through a sitting room with a misshapen old couch and two overstuffed chairs facing a river-rock fireplace before bringing Mags into the kitchen. It was cheery and warm—with yellow walls and blue accents, but this room hadn't been cleaned in a long while either.

"And, when I arrived to ask her about it, she wasn't here." Dahlia promptly went to the antique stove and grabbed a teakettle, that had just begun to whistle. "She left us a note saying she had a last-minute errand to run and she'll be back with dinner, so I guess we'll have to wait and ask her what's going on then."

"I guess so." Mags glanced around the kitchen wistfully.

There had been so much laughter in this kitchen while Sassy had shared her secret cookie recipes, teaching the girls to sift flour and measure out the right amount of baking powder for the high altitude, and how to cream the butter and sugar. Mags had fallen in love with baking in this kitchen. Sure, the house was a little older, a bit run-down, but this was where she'd uncovered one of her deepest passions.

"Here's some peppermint tea." Dahlia carried over two mugs. The same Santa face mugs they'd used to drink hot cocoa from. Except now Santa's nose was missing.

"I added some honey and lemon," her sister said, setting the mug in front of her. "It'll warm you up."

Dahlia was always doing things for people—feeding them, cleaning up after them, organizing them, bringing them peppermint tea with a splash of lemon and honey. Her sister liked to be busy.

Not that Mags was going to complain. The mug warmed her hands right away. "Thank you. It's good to see you, Dally." Mags appraised her sister's face. Dahlia's eyes were still bright and animated, but a sadness hid in them, too. Her sister never would admit it, but the last year—the divorce—seemed to have taken a toll on her.

"It's good to see you, too." Dahlia's face relaxed into a smile. "I can't believe we're here. After all these years." The bridge of her nose crinkled slightly, reminding Mags of the face her sister used to make when their mother would make her cat peas. Dally had hated peas with an undying passion.

"It's a mess though, right?" Her sister's voice lowered as though she was afraid someone might overhear. "I mean, it doesn't look like the place has been cleaned in eons." She seemed to inspect the surface of the Formica kitchen table. "And not one upgrade in all those years. Everything's the same, except for older and messier."

Mags had to laugh at that. "Then I guess we'll fit right in." She winked at her sister. "Older and messier is how I feel, too." Now that she was inside, she didn't mind the state of disrepair so much. When they were children, twirling around in this kitchen with their aprons on, spatulas in their hands, everything had seemed so perfect, so easy. But that was the façade of childhood— the trust that everything was just as it should be when all along beneath the surface things had always been messy. Back when she was a kid, Mags hadn't paid attention to the dysfunction, but her mother and Sassy obviously had had plenty of issues. She sipped the tea, letting it warm her. "So, Dally...how are you?" She asked her sister this question on the phone often, and Dahlia always deflected. She wouldn't be able to do that now that they were face-to-face.

"Fine. Great actually." Dally's eyes had always flared slightly wider when she lied. They'd learned it from their mother, the lying. The smoothing over of details. It was why Mags hadn't shared her fertility struggle, what it had done to her marriage. It was why Dally couldn't tell her how broken her heart was, even though Mags could see it in her slightly sunken posture. It was why Rose pretended to be excited about the wedding, even though Mags had noticed her hesitations the last time she'd visited Savannah. They were always supposed to be fine.

She shouldn't blame only her mother. Over the years, Mags had learned that was the expected response from a strong, independent, capable woman. *I'm fine. Great, actually.* Anything less would show weakness, a vulnerability most people feared. Including her.

"How are the kids?" she prompted, mostly because she'd grown tired of the song and dance. She sure as hell wasn't *fine, great actually*, and she would be willing to bet her marble rolling pin that her sister wasn't either. What was wrong with needing each other anyway? What good was having sisters if you couldn't rely on them? "I bet they're missing you like crazy right now." Once again, Mags wondered what kind of jackass took his kids on a vacation with his new girlfriend over Christmas? That was an easy one. Jeff Martindale. She'd never liked her sister's husband. He'd always been slightly obsessed with himself.

Tears welled in Dahlia's eyes. "Yeah. I'm missing them more

than I even thought I would. I can't stop thinking about them even for a second. I hate it. Not knowing what they're doing, how they're feeling." She sighed. "From the little I have heard, it sounds like things aren't exactly smooth sailing on the trip right now."

"Well of course they're not." Mags set down her mug so she could throw up her hands. Some conversations required dramatic gesturing. "What does he expect? They want to be with their mother on Christmas, not at some hotel in France." With some young bombshell who couldn't keep her hands off their dad. How awkward would that be? Mags had seen plenty of pictures of the two of them on social media.

"It's okay—"

The front door banged open and a muttered string of curses drifted down the hall. That sure sounded like Rose...well, minus the curses. Their youngest sister was still entrenched in the whole Southern manners thing. Thank God Mags had escaped.

Mags looked at Dahlia and the two of them stood at exactly the same time, hurrying down the hall to greet their sister.

"Whoa." Mags stopped short of hugging Rose. "What happened to you?" Soggy was one way to describe Rose's current look. She seemed to be wet from head to toe—her beautiful golden hair hanging in strings around her shoulders.

"I fell!" Rose practically wailed, shaking off her coat with force. "Face-first in the snow!"

Mags held back a chuckle. When they were young, Rose had been the most dramatic of the three of them. Over the years she'd mellowed out, but every once in a while Mags still caught a glimpse of Rose's inner diva.

"And then when I was trying to get up, I couldn't get my

footing, and I fell again!" She blew inside with the same swiftness as a cold wind and slammed the door shut behind her. "All in front of the most incorrigible, surliest man I've ever met."

"Well that sounds like a story." Mags moved in to help Rose slip off her dripping-wet suede jacket.

"You're completely soaked!" Dahlia hustled around, coming back with a stack of blankets she proceeded to wrap around Rose's indignant shoulders.

"All I was trying to do is to clean up the Christmas tree in the park. I mean, seriously! It looks like a horde of raccoons decorated the tree, ornaments all over the place, thrown about in no particular order. So, I took a few off to rearrange them, and the man accused me of stealing!"

Mags couldn't tell if the ruddiness on her sister's cheeks had come from anger, cold, or humiliation. Most likely a combination of all three. Rose hated to make a fool out of herself and embarrassed easily.

Together, she and Dahlia escorted Rose into the kitchen and sat her in a chair.

"There." Dally offered their sister her peppermint tea and tucked the blankets in tighter around her shoulders. "I'm sure it was all a misunderstanding."

"I mean, do I look like someone who would steal Christmas ornaments off a public tree?" Rose demanded.

Mags decided not to answer that. At the moment, Rose did happen to have a little crazy in her eyes. "So, you drove into town and got to work right away redecorating the place?" Mags couldn't help but tease her. "Like some kind of Mary Poppins for Christmas trees?"

That at least made Rose smile. "I was reacquainting myself

with the magic of this beautiful little town, and I saw something amiss. I mean, remember how stunning that tree used to look all lit up in the center of the park? Well believe me, this one looked nothing like I remembered."

"Just like everything else around her," Dahlia muttered, dragging another chair to the table. "It seems a lot has changed."

"There's no stopping change." Magnolia said as she took another sip of her tea. "But I'm glad we're all here." They hadn't spent any quality time together since high school. Not for more than a week at a time. And never just the three of them without their parents or spouses or kids.

"Yes, at least we're together." Rose's eyes brightened with tears.

Mags studied her sister, seeing a familiar weariness in her features. "Other than the Christmas tree caper, how have you been?" she asked.

"Oh, I've been great." Rose sat straighter. "The wedding plans are really coming along."

Mags could've mouthed the response along with Rose. Her sister's heart wasn't in the words, though. They rang too hollow.

"By the way, I have it on good authority that Aunt Sassy isn't dying," Dahlia informed Rose. "According to her doctor, she's perfectly healthy."

"What?" The blankets fell away from Rose's shoulders and she finally smiled. "That's the best news I've heard all day. But if she's not sick, what are we doing here?"

Mags wrapped her hands around the warm mug again. "We're reconnecting. Escaping. At least that's what I'm doing." Whatever Sassy's reason for bringing them out here—and Mags was sure she had one—the timing was perfect.

"I'm surprised Eric didn't come." Rose started to comb out

her hair with her fingers. "You two have never spent a holiday apart."

"He couldn't get off work." The words tumbled out, a perfectly reasonable explanation. Except it wasn't true. But how did you just come out and tell your sisters that your marriage was in shambles when you'd been pretending things were *great* for so long? She and Eric hadn't spoken since she'd walked out of the condo with her suitcase, but she couldn't get his sad expression out of her mind. He'd looked like he was in pain. The same pain that seemed to run through her heart like a fault line.

"What about Gregory?" Dally asked Rose. "I'm surprised he let you come. You two seem to keep such a busy schedule and I'm sure it's even busier around the holidays."

Before Rose could answer, the back door blew open, sending in a gust of wind and swirling snowflakes.

"Whew! It's colder than a polar bear's tonsils out there." Sassy seemed to float in on the wind, shutting the door tightly behind her before leaning against it. The woman had bundled herself in a red and black plaid scarf along with a matching flannel beret. Her flaming red hair—always in artful disarray—stuck out beneath the cap. In her hands, she balanced a large box, and it only took seconds for Mags to realize what was in it. The Christmas ornaments she remembered so well.

"My girls." Sassy set down the box on the counter and shook her head slowly back and forth. "You're here. Finally! You're here!"

Mags had forgotten how melodious her aunt's voice had always been.

"We're happy to be here." She stood up, ready to greet her aunt with a hug. Sassy hadn't changed a bit. Her aunt's dazzling smile and her expressive green eyes still exuded warmth, and tenderness. Mags embraced her, detecting the scent of jasmine that always used to make her nose twitch. "We couldn't resist coming to the Juniper Inn for Christmas."

"Especially when we were so worried," Dahlia added, taking her turn for a hug. "The way you wrote that letter, we thought something might be wrong."

"Whatever would be wrong?" Sassy asked, gathering Rose into the hug.

Mags traded looks with her sisters. It seemed not even Dahlia wanted to admit they'd assumed she was dying.

"Well, um…" Rose delicately cleared her throat the way a Southern belle would. "It's just you said you wanted us here for your last Christmas at the Juniper Inn."

"Oh, that." Sassy scooted past them and picked up the box again. "Well, yes. I guess I owe you an explanation, don't I?" She headed for the hallway smiling at them over her shoulder. "Let's move into the living room so we can decorate the tree while we chat. I need to tell you the whole story."

Oh, the tree. Mags fell back into a memory. They'd always had such fun decorating Sassy's tree. It had been so different than the one in their own home—with its matching ornaments and stately ribbons. Sassy had all varieties of decorations for her tree. Little trinkets she'd handmade and ornaments guests at the inn had brought from far-off places. Mags followed her aunt to the living room. She couldn't wait to see them all again.

The evergreen tree in the corner couldn't have stood more than five feet tall. It was bare in certain places and full in others, but somehow it fit the inn perfectly. And it smelled like Christmas with that fresh pine scent.

"I suppose it's always best to start at the beginning." Her aunt set the box in front of the tree and sat down next to it. Mags and Rose and Dally all joined her, and Mags couldn't help but start to pull out some of the ornaments she'd treasured as a child— the pink and brown gingerbread man, the fat, jolly Santa made out of clay. Oh! And there was the miniature nutcracker with the tall red hat.

Sassy reached into the box and hung a stained-glass heart onto a branch. "Many, many years ago—when I was in my early twenties—I was very much in love with a young man. Larry Douglas." She sighed a happy sigh as she said his name.

"You were in love?" It shouldn't have surprised her, but Mags had never thought of Sassy as the type to swoon over a man. In her memories, their aunt had been happy and complete on her own.

"I was," Sassy confirmed. She carefully selected an intricate star made out of silvery paper and placed it on a low branch. "Larry and I were desperately in love. But my parents forbid me to date him. He was black," she explained. "And they said it would be too hard for us to make a life together. Back in those days, people didn't take kindly to a black man marrying a white woman. And—"

"But that's not fair," Rose interrupted. She set down the funny octopus ornament she'd been holding. "You should be free to marry whoever you want—"

Mags nudged her to quiet down so Sassy could continue.

"It wasn't fair," Sassy agreed. "But that's the way it was." Her green eyes took on a wistful tint. "Larry and I didn't care though. We were determined to be together. He was the kindest man I'd ever met up until that point in my life. A hard worker. Honest. We talked about running away together. We wanted to secretly get married and move to New York where people were more open-minded than they were in Savannah." Her aunt peered into the box and carefully lifted out a delicate snowflake. "But in the end he couldn't do it." She stared past Mags at the tree, seemingly caught up in a memory. "He said he would never feel right about sneaking me away from my family. So, he asked my father for my hand in marriage."

Mags found her hand moving over her heart. She could almost feel her aunt's emotions crackling to life in her chest. The love, the hope it had brought her. That was exactly how she'd felt when she'd met Eric—like she would do anything to be with him. "What happened?" She was almost afraid to ask. It couldn't have been a happy ending if Sassy had never married him...

"After he asked my father, my parents decided to send me away." Though emotion seemed to brighten her eyes, Sassy spoke matter-of-factly. "They sent me here. To the Juniper Inn." She added another snowflake to a twisted branch. "My mother's brother owned it back then. He'd had the place built brand-new from the ground up, and they told him I could help him manage it."

"Oh, Sassy," Dahlia crooned from the other side of the box. She'd laid out six ornaments on the floor in front of her, but none of them had made it onto the tree. "That's so sad. How could they do that to you?"

"They did what they thought best," she said simply. "I think they liked Larry, if you want the truth. My parents weren't the sort of people to judge based on someone's skin color, but they were afraid for me. They were afraid for him, too."

A tear rolled down Mags's cheek, and she quickly dabbed her eyes with her sleeve. All this time their aunt had a tragic love story in her past, and they'd had no idea...

"What happened to Larry?" Rose demanded. "After you left? Did you stay in touch with him?"

"For a while." Sassy picked up a beaded candy cane. She seemed determined to get the tree decorated. "But it was too hard. Knowing we would never be together. He wrote me a letter and told me he loved me, but he said he couldn't pursue a relationship anymore knowing my parents were against it."

"But you were a grown woman!" Mags couldn't help the anger that spilled out of her. How unfair. Her grandparents had never been overly warm, friendly people, but to destroy their daughter's chance at true love? That wasn't right.

Sassy chuckled as though the outburst amused her. "Things were different for young women in those days, my dear." This time she hung a crocheted stocking with a few pulled threads on the tree. "We didn't have as many options, as much say as you do these days."

What would that have been like? Mags couldn't imagine. She dug through the box and found one of her absolute favorite ornaments of all time—a beautiful glass butterfly with colorful wings.

"My parents knew how strong my feelings were for Larry." Sassy stood up to hang a pine cone on a higher branch and then sat back down. "They knew if I stayed in Savannah, I wouldn't be able to stay away from him. So, they moved me here."

Unbelievable. Mags didn't say it out loud. Her mother hadn't been thrilled when she'd met Eric. He was only a firefighter, after all. Instead of coming from a high-society Southern family, his parents had emigrated from Puerto Rico just before he was born. But even Lillian hadn't forbidden her from marrying him.

"So you lost touch with the man you loved?" Rose finally added an ornament to the tree—a delicate ballerina that was missing one toe shoe.

"I heard he married someone else a few years later." Sassy's soft smile appeared genuine. "He seemed happy. And I was happy here." She looked around the cozy living room, the smile fading. "I was happy here for a long time. When my aunt and uncle wanted to retire, they offered me the inn, and by then I loved it too much to let it go."

But she'd told them it would be her last Christmas here... "You don't love it anymore?" Mags asked.

Their aunt took her time answering. "I will always love it. But it no longer serves me. I don't have the sense of purpose here I once did." Her eyes misted over. "It used to be a busy place. I got to know many of the families who would come year after year, but as time went on, they stopped coming. They found other places to travel. Nicer, more luxurious places. I tried to keep up with things, but the buildings were aging quickly, and good help was hard to find." She shook her head sadly. "No one has stayed here as a guest in over two years. And... well now it feels like a lonely place to be."

Mags's heart crumpled thinking about her aunt living here all alone. Watching things change. Watching the place age and not being able to do anything about it. "Well, we're here now." Thank goodness they'd come.

"Yes. We are," Dahlia added, placing a rooster ornament on the tree. "And we can help you, Sassy. We can do whatever you need us to do."

Rose gasped, nearly dropping the glass globe she held in her hand. "We can redecorate!"

Their aunt laughed—a delighted joyous sound. "I can't thank

you enough for coming. It's true what I said—this will be my last Christmas at the Juniper." Her gaze fell on the box again. "But I certainly hope it won't be yours." This time she selected a tiny framed picture of the four of them, placing it right on the front of the tree. "That's why I asked you to come. I might be ready to start a new journey, but I can't let this place go completely. Not when it has been so much a part of this family."

Mags froze and stared at their aunt in disbelief. "Are you saying what I think you're saying?"

"You're giving us the inn?" Rose asked breathlessly.

"I specifically asked you to come for Christmas because I need your help to pull off one last Christmas extravaganza at the Juniper Inn." Her expression sobered. "You all know how important our holiday party is to this town and we only have a few weeks to get things in order. We'll have to decorate this whole place and make the desserts." She paused as though she wanted to give them time to digest the information. "And then, if you so choose, I'm offering to give you three ownership over the inn. You would each own a third. That's the deal. You own it together, keep it in the family…or I sell to some developer who'll likely level it to build condos."

"But…" Mags couldn't believe Sassy would ever want to give this place up. It had always seemed so much a part of her. "What are you going to do?"

"I'm not exactly sure yet." Sassy hung a gold bell on the tree. "All I know is it's time for me to move on."

"So…what?" Dahlia's expression bordered on panic. "You want us to stay here and manage the inn?"

Sassy shrugged. "I want you to do whatever you want with it. Make it whatever you want it to be. Redecorate it and open it again, if you want. Or keep it for your families as a place you can get away."

"But we all have lives far away from here." Mags pictured the beach, the beautiful Florida sunshine. As much as she loved the inn, she wasn't sure she could stand the snow half the year.

Sassy seemed to wave their concerns away. "You don't have to decide now. We'll fix this place up, pull off the best Christmas extravaganza this town has ever seen, and then you can let me know your decision on Christmas. But keep an open mind, my dears. It's never too early or late to start over, to choose the life that will bring you the most joy. Anything is possible."

Never too late. Mags held on to those words. Could they be true for her and Eric too?

Chapter Nine

Rose

What in heaven's name was that incessant buzzing? Rose pawed her way out from underneath a pile of soft pillows and the downy quilt that made her want to lounge in this lumpy queen-sized bed forever...or at least for another couple hours.

She couldn't remember that last time she'd slept feeling so cozy and tucked in, but she forced her eyes open and squinted at the nightstand where her phone sat bouncing across the surface.

She reached for it but let her head fall back to the pillows as a weak "Hello?" croaked from her throat.

"Rose?" Gregory's voice projected through the line, much too loudly.

"Yeah?" She held the phone an inch away from her ear.

"What's wrong, babe? Are you sick?"

"No." She cleared the frog from her throat. They'd stayed up well past midnight reminiscing, and discussing Sassy's crazy proposition. "Not sick, just sleeping." She closed her eyes ready to get back to it.

"Sleeping?" Gregory's voice echoed through the speaker. "But it's almost nine o'clock there."

"Really?" Rose pulled the phone away and squinted at the time on the screen. Sure enough. "Huh. I had no idea." Because she'd been *sleeping. Peacefully sleeping, thank you very much.* Granted, Gregory had every right to be surprised. She couldn't remember the last time she's slept past six. Back home, she and Gregory woke up at five o'clock every morning so they could hit the gym together before he had to be at work at seven. Man, she'd forgotten how much she loved sleeping in.

"You must be sick." Gregory now lowered his voice like he didn't want anyone to overhear their conversation. Someone must've walked into his office.

"I'm not sick. In fact, I feel great." A contentedness seemed to weight her body to the bed as she glanced around the room. Nothing had changed since she'd last slept in this same cozy bedroom all those years ago. Back then, she'd had a slight obsession with princesses, and Sassy had been happy to oblige. Her aunt had painted the room a soft baby pink and had made a gauzy tulle canopy for the bed along with matching curtains for the window. Framed fairy-tale pictures hung on the walls, depicting each princess's happily-ever-after—Cinderella, Snow White, Rapunzel, and her personal favorite—Sleeping Beauty. Her aunt used to tell her that if she went to sleep surrounded by happily-ever-afters, she would find hers someday, too.

As she looked around, her heart seemed to settle back into place. She didn't know if it was being back at the inn or being with her sisters or looking forward to the prospect of spending the next few weeks caught up in Juniper Springs' simplicity rather than rushing around from holiday event to holiday event, but a blissfulness lightened her heart.

"You need to get up," Gregory said. "Half your day is wasted. Why don't you go for a run outside?"

Rose propped herself up on her elbows so she could peer out the large picture window on the other side of the room. "It's snowing." She would not be going for a run today. In fact, she didn't have much on the agenda for the day except getting reacquainted with the property and figuring out what they had to do to get the place in shape for the Christmas extravaganza. "Besides, I'm on vacation."

"Vacation?" Gregory paused and said something she couldn't make out. He must've been asking whoever was in his office to give him a minute. "I didn't realize you were going on vacation. I thought you were there to take care of your dying aunt."

"Oh. Right. About that…" Relief washed over her yet again. Gregory knew how worried she'd been when she'd received Sassy's package. "Aunt Sassy isn't dying. She's not even sick, actually. It was all a misunderstanding." Silence lingered on the other end of the line, so Rose continued. "She looks amazing, actually. Almost exactly like I remember her. Isn't that great?"

"Yes, babe. That is truly great news." Finally, his tone had softened. "I'll go ahead and send out the jet so you can come home."

Home? Rose sat all the way up, the old bedsprings groaning beneath her. "No. I can't come home."

"Yes, you can." Gregory's voice always took on a nasally tone when he got annoyed. "Your aunt doesn't need you there and I need you here." He groaned. "You heard my mother go over the list of events we're supposed to appear at over the next two weeks. I can't do this alone."

Exactly. His mother had committed to the events. It was his family. Those were their events, not hers. Not yet. "I promised Sassy I would stay. We're all staying. Dahlia and Magnolia, too. It's already settled." She left no room for him to argue.

There was a long pause before Gregory spoke again. "I don't understand. Why would you stay?" He sounded genuinely confused, but for some reason Rose didn't want to tell him about her aunt offering them the inn at the end of their stay. It wasn't like they'd get to keep it anyway. How could the three of them possibly manage the place from three different states? Mags didn't seem open to moving to the arctic tundra, as she referred to Juniper Springs. And Dahlia kept saying she was too busy to even think about adding something else to her life. Gregory didn't need to know any of that though. Not yet.

"Sassy has asked us to spend the holiday with her. She needs some help fixing this place up, and she's lonely. Spending one Christmas with her isn't too much to ask." She let a chord of annoyance slip into her pitch, too. If he could always be catering to his mother and his family, she could fulfill her aunt's request this one time.

"What am I supposed to tell everyone?" Gregory asked. "It won't look good if you're not by my side. Everyone will expect my fiancée to be there. I can't very well tell them your aunt is dying now. Someone's bound to find out that's not true."

"I don't care what you tell them." She could never seem to make herself care as much about what everyone else thought as the Cunninghams did, though she'd tried. "I have every right to spend Christmas with my family. My sisters and I haven't been in the same room for well over a year, and I'm not going to miss this chance to spend Christmas with them." Who knew when they would all be together again? Besides that, she'd noticed Dahlia seemed...off. Tired, maybe? Or stressed. And last night she'd noticed Magnolia's smile hadn't been as broad as it used to be. Her sisters had changed. *She'd* changed. And this was the perfect chance for them to get to know each other again.

"Fine. I'm sorry." Gregory's audible sigh stole the authenticity from the apology. "My mother is stressing me out, that's all. I don't want to face the next few weeks without you here."

The comment should've warmed her but instead her shoulders tensed. "Maybe you should stand up to your mother," she murmured. It wasn't the first time she'd made the suggestion, but she always did her best to tread carefully. "You could come here for Christmas too, you know." She tried to make the invitation sound sultry. "Skip all the craziness and stay at the inn with me. It would be so cozy and quiet..." It very well might be the last cozy, quiet days they would have together before she joined his family for good.

"I can't leave. You know that. I have obligations here."

He could leave, but he wouldn't. His loyalty to his family was one of the things she'd admired most about him. Almost all the time. But there was also this side of her that wished he would choose her. Choose them. She let herself dream for a few seconds. Maybe he would show up at the front door of the inn with a beautiful red poinsettia. He'd tell her he couldn't bear to spend Christmas without her—that he'd told his mother where she could stick all her holiday events and had commandeered the family's jet to sneak away and be with her. They could sit in front of the fireplace wrapped in a blanket, sipping spiked hot chocolate. They could share boisterous meals with her sisters and aunt, and he could get to know the people she loved most in the world.

Rose shook her head at her inner romantic. That would never happen. Gregory would stay in Savannah because that's what was expected of him. She glanced around the room again taking in the various fairy-tale images. For some reason she had a hard time envisioning her and Gregory's happily-ever-after without Evaline sneering in the background like one of the Disney villains.

"Listen, I have a meeting." Her fiancé suddenly sounded distracted again. "I'll have to call you later."

She said goodbye and hung up the phone, deciding to leave it on the nightstand as she got out of bed. She needed time away from the phone calls, time away from disappointing people, time away from the potential guilt trips she would get when she talked to Gregory, or her mother, for that matter. Rose couldn't wait to hear what Lillian had to say when she heard her estranged sister wasn't dying after all.

Pushing off the bed, Rose shoved her feet into the Ugg slippers she'd packed in one of her four suitcases and padded across the wooden floor to the window. The cold temperatures had fogged over the glass, but she could still make out the frozen pond farther down the hill. Her heart swelled thinking about how she and her sisters used to ice-skate down there. They would dress up in tutus and pretend they were part of the *Ice Capades*. Sassy would bring them down a tray of steaming hot chocolate with extra marshmallows and marvel over their spins and fake jumps. Sassy had always done that—doted on them, indulged their girlish dreams and wishes.

It wasn't only creating the princess room or gushing over how smart and creative they were, Sassy simply had this way of bringing out the best in everyone. She had this miraculous ability to care about the people who crossed her path. And her spirit had been infused into this place. Whenever she had come to visit Sassy at the inn, Rose had been free to simply be who she was without worrying it wasn't enough. Now that she knew about her aunt's past—that she'd been separated from the man she loved— it made sense. Her aunt had learned to open her heart. Sassy had so much love to give that she made everyone her family. There was no better gift than that acceptance.

Here Rose didn't have to exercise at five o'clock every morning to keep herself toned and on the lower end of a size six. Heck, she didn't have to take a shower and spend a half hour straightening her hair and another twenty minutes applying face products and makeup. She didn't even have to change out of her flannel pajamas. No siree, she could wear them right downstairs to the breakfast table and no one here would think a thing of it.

Reveling in that freedom, Rose threw open the door and padded down the hall to the rickety old staircase. Something smelled absolutely divine—like the buttery, gooey inside of a cinnamon roll. Homemade. Dripping with frosting. Suddenly all that sugar sounded like the best breakfast she could imagine. She hurried down the rest of the stairs and careened into the kitchen where she came to a sudden stop.

Sassy was pulling a tray of her famous cinnamon rolls out of the oven, but it seemed they also had company. Two men sat at the kitchen table, and one of them needed no introduction. She'd recognize those intense dark eyes from a mile away, flannel or no flannel.

"Rosie! You're finally up." Sassy set the pan of cinnamon rolls on the stovetop and rushed over to usher her into the kitchen, flannel pajamas and all. "You girls must've stayed up late last night. I hope you slept well?"

"Uh, yeah." Why, oh why had she decided not to change out of her pajamas? Or at least to glance in a mirror to smooth down her hair? She tugged out of Sassy's hold and drifted to the other side of the kitchen island, as far away from the Christmas tree Grinch she'd met in the park as she could get.

"Since you girls slept in, I decided to enlist some help for our sprucing up efforts." Sassy left Rose's side and carried the tray of cinnamon rolls to the table. "This is Ike." She pointed to the man Rose hadn't had the pleasure of meeting.

"Nice to meet you." He stood immediately like he wanted to shake her hand, but Rose stayed where she was. She did, however, manage to summon a small smile. "Nice to meet you, too." It wasn't nice. It was downright embarrassing being in her pajamas and all.

"And this is Colt." Her aunt gestured to the Christmas tree Grinch.

"Colt," Rose repeated. The name seemed to suit him. Wild and untamed. "Yes, we've met." And, as seemed to be her luck, she was humiliating herself in front of the man yet again.

A look of recognition passed over his face, which didn't appear nearly as imposing without the hat and menacing scowl. "You're the tree lady. Didn't recognize you."

He might as well have said he didn't recognize her because she'd just rolled out of bed. Good Lord. What was Sassy thinking inviting people over before any of them were up? Rose hadn't even bothered to put on a bra!

"The tree lady?" Sassy started to set plates around the table.

"He thought I was stealing ornaments off the town's Christmas tree," Rose said hotly. Bra or no bra, she wasn't going to let this man think she was some lunatic. "When I was simply trying to rearrange them for better placement."

"Ah yes." Her aunt chuckled. "You always did have an eye for putting things right." She brought a pitcher of orange juice to the table. "Colt's hardware store let the kids decorate this year. It was so cute when all those little ones hung up the ornaments wherever they could reach. They thought it was the best thing ever."

"Oh." Rose let out the gasp of surprise. "I didn't realize the kids decorated the tree." But now the disorganized appearance made more sense. "Had I known—"

"No matter, no matter. You were only trying to help." Sassy started to fill glasses with juice. Six glasses, so these men were likely staying for breakfast. "Ike and Colt have graciously offered their services to help us fix up this old place for the holidays, so I thought it would be helpful for us all to sit down and discuss the details."

Sure, helpful. At lunch, maybe. Or dinner. But not when she was dressed in her pajamas with her hair all bent out of shape. Rose refused to even look at Ike and Colt. "Um, you know, I have some things to take care of upstairs." She started to back away. "I can come down later. After breakfast, and—"

"You'll do no such thing." Sassy rushed over and guided her to the chair across from Ike. "Since you're already down here, whatever you need to do can wait. This won't take long. Dahlia's on a walk but I expect her back shortly. And I heard Mags up and about, so I'm sure she'll be down any minute." Her aunt's face beamed with a genuine happiness. "Then we can all enjoy a nice breakfast together the way we used to."

Nice? Rose could think of a few other adjectives to describe having to sit across the table from the man who'd accused her of being a criminal…and not one of them involved the world "nice."

Chapter Ten

Dahlia

Dahlia tromped through the freshly fallen snow in her knee-high Sorels, a layer of sweat burning beneath the beanie she'd pulled down over her forehead. A good half-hour walk around the property hadn't seemed to clear the nervous energy that had been buzzing inside of her since she'd woken up before seven.

Back home, her day always started much earlier than that—Ollie had been born an early riser and was usually bright-eyed by six o'clock. It took a couple of hours to get the kids ready for school, between packing lunches and making a big breakfast with the right balance of carbs and protein that would hold them over until their noon lunch hour. Then there was the whole getting dressed issue. Based on what Ollie chose out of his closet every morning, she'd come to suspect he might be color-blind. No matter what he said, his orange shirt most definitely did not match the neon green pants his father had bought him.

Maya didn't have the matching clothing issue; hers happened to be more of an indecisive issue, especially now that she'd gotten a little older. She'd come down in at least three different outfits every morning and then end up lamenting that she had absolutely nothing cool to wear. On the really tough mornings she'd dissolve into tears and swear she was never leaving the house again, or at least not until she got a whole new wardrobe from a tween-approved store. Dahlia would spend precious minutes each morning talking her off the ledge, coaxing her back up to her room where they would choose an outfit together since no stores were open before eight anyway.

An emptiness seemed to spread straight out of her heart in a consuming ache. God, she missed her children. Pausing, she let go of a sigh, trying to keep her heart from sinking into sadness. Since she'd left Minnesota, this restlessness had followed her around, and it had really hit hard when she'd woken up and realized she had nothing to do today. Well, nothing tied to the schedule that had kept her afloat for the last year during the divorce anyway. She didn't know how to do nothing, how to be alone with her thoughts. They kept drifting back to the kids. What were they doing now? Were they eating right? Why hadn't they called her this morning?

She lifted her head and tried to focus on the view laid out in front of her. On the trees' frozen pine needles. On the frosted surface of the small pond. It was true that the inn appeared more run-down than it once had, but in the early morning snow, with the layer of fresh sparkling powder and the sun trying to break out from behind the gauzy clouds, beauty seemed to gleam off every surface.

The world around her had frozen, from the tree limbs to the wild grasses but it wasn't nearly as cold as Minnesota felt this time of year. Here there was no humidity. You didn't feel the heavier air that seemed to seep right into your bones. She'd never gotten used to it, and, despite growing up in Minnesota, neither had Maya. And there went Dahlia's thoughts again, drifting away from her, centering on her babies. Was Maya warm enough in France? Dahlia had been obsessively checking the weather every day, and Paris was going through a cold snap right now...

Walk. She had to walk and think about something else. The problem was, she had no idea what that something else could be. Her PTA duties were over for the semester at school. Usually, this time of year she didn't have one spare second to think... between the baking and the gift buying and the preparation for meals— Christmas Eve dinner with their good friends, Christmas brunch with her ex-in-laws, Christmas dinner with whatever family could make it all the way to Minnesota to celebrate. Then there was the wrapping and the cleaning and the classic wintry memories she always felt pressured to create with the kids... sledding and ice-skating and building snowmen. This year there would be no Christmas memories with her kids. They were busy building new memories without her—images from their childhood she wouldn't get to be a part of. And she was here... wandering aimlessly through the snow trying find the right path to follow.

Dahlia plowed a trail up the small hill that led back to the Juniper Inn's main house, pausing at the crest where the old camping Shasta trailer they'd named Betty came into view. A smile snuck up on her as she walked toward it, edging her way through a small stand of aspen trees that had seemed to grow in a circle around it, hemming it in. Snow fell from the tree branches as she brushed against them, slipping down into the back of her coat, but she kept moving closer, drawn in by the memories.

She and her sisters used to spend so much time in old Betty, playing dress up and having tea parties and camping out in the summer. It felt like the trailer had been their own secret hideaway. Rose had even sewed some curtains and pillows for the trailer. Dahlia had tried to help but had failed miserably, as she did in most creative pursuits.

Like the rest of the resort, the trailer had seen better days. Rust crept up the fenders and the pretty turquoise color she'd loved so much back then had faded into a mint green. She might be older and a bit shabby, but with those shiny chrome fenders and the black eyelashes Sassy had helped them paint around the windows, Betty still held her charm.

Dahlia crept around to the other side and tried the door, but it was locked. She hoisted herself up onto the small step and cleared snow off the window so she could peer in. She couldn't see much through the dingy glass, but there were still toys in there. More clutter than she remembered…

"There you are."

The sound of Sassy's voice nearly made her topple off the steps. Dahlia carefully climbed down and turned to find her aunt cutting through the aspen trees. "You kept Betty." She didn't know why it surprised her. Judging from the amount of old trinkets and magazines in the house, her aunt didn't get rid of much.

"I had to keep her." Sassy patted Betty's siding like she was an old friend. "She's a piece of history around here. Every time I see her, I picture you girls in your spinny dresses, as you used to call them."

Dahlia laughed a little. "Yes, spinny dresses." The fancy dresses that used to flare when they would twirl in circles. "And you kept our toys?" They'd stashed countless stuffed animals and tea sets and books in there. Most of which they'd bought with Sassy at garage sales around town over the years. "You haven't used her for anything else since then?"

"Just storage. I didn't have much use for Betty after you girls quit coming to see me." She smiled sadly. "Living here, it's not like I need to go camping or anything. I've got all the wilderness I need."

Dahlia smiled too, but she couldn't get past her aunt's first statement. "I'm sorry we stopped coming to see you, Sassy." She'd never considered how lonely it must've been for her aunt after their mother walked away from their relationship. They'd all been so close. Sassy had been like a second mother to them, and then one day their mother told them they wouldn't be going back to Colorado. Dahlia had wondered why, but that was also when life had started to get much busier. She'd become part of the theater group at school and was wrapped up in her honors classes. The questions and wonderings about Sassy and her mother had simply drifted away until she hadn't thought about them much. "What happened?" she asked now. She'd asked her mother before, but Lillian had simply said she and Sassy didn't get along and had nothing in common.

"Did you and Mom have a fight?" She couldn't imagine what it would've been about. They'd never even argued as far as she remembered. Sure, sisters drifted apart, especially when they lived so far away. She'd be the first to admit she'd gotten wrapped up in her own life and rarely remembered to call Mags and Rose. That's one reason she was here—to reconnect with them. But what could possibly have happened to tear two sisters apart? Especially when Lillian had to know her sister was sent away from the family simply for falling in love. Sassy needed her sister. She needed her nieces.

Her aunt's gaze shifted away as though searching for something far in the distance. "It was all so long ago," she murmured.

"It doesn't matter anymore. Now that you're here we can simply enjoy our time together. There's no sense in dwelling on the past."

Dahlia recognized an evasive maneuver when she saw one.

"It seems our friend Betty here could use some sprucing up, too." Her aunt ran her gloved hand over the faded paint. "A little elbow grease and she'd be as good as new."

Challenge accepted. "I'd love to see the inside." If only the kids could be here to see it, too. Wouldn't Maya love all those clothes? And Ollie would be in heaven surrounded by all the books.

"That can be arranged." Her aunt turned and started to walk away, shuffling through the snow. "I'll have to find the key, but I know it's around somewhere." She peered back over her shoulder. "After breakfast, though. That's why I came out to look for you in the first place. We have some company joining us, and there's a lot to discuss if we're going to pull off this event in only a few short weeks."

"Right." Dahlia fell in step behind her. "A project is good. I need something to focus on. I need a project." If they discussed the details about the Christmas extravaganza this morning, she could spend the next several days lost in the details. Add in the work on Betty and she wouldn't have time to miss the kids, to think about the emptiness that seemed to consume her when she was away from them.

Together, she and Sassy marched back up the hill to the main house. Dahlia had to slow down as they approached, thanks to the altitude. Dr. Ike had obviously been right about her aunt's health. The woman seemed to be in tip-top shape. She could hardly keep up with her. They walked around to the back door that led into the kitchen. Sassy opened it for her. "After you my dear."

"Thank y—" The second Dahlia stepped inside, she froze.

Rose and Mags were seated at the table with two men. They had their backs to her, but her sisters were still in their pajamas, their hair all rumpled and looking out of sorts. There's something she never thought she'd see. Rose didn't usually leave her bedroom until every strand of that beautiful blond hair had been sprayed into place.

"Dally, I'd like you to meet my friends." Sassy slipped past her and nudged her around to the other side of the table. "Colt and Ike are two of the most eligible bachelors in—"

"Ike?" She nearly tripped over a chair leg. Now that she'd come around the table, she had a clear view of his face. And why did her aunt feel the need to announce how eligible he was? Sassy had better not get any big ideas about setting them up…

"Morning," he said, cheerfully lifting his coffee mug in a toast. "Nice to see you again."

A few awkward seconds of silence passed before Dahlia mumbled a quick "good morning" back. She'd never been good with surprises. They set her off-balance. Especially surprises in the form of a good-looking man who seemed to wear his confidence as prominently as he wore that plaid vest. It bugged her that she'd noticed his good looks. She hadn't noticed a man in that way since Jeff had walked out the door. In fact, she'd been set on never noticing another man's good looks again, but with Ike that was nearly impossible.

"Oh good." Her aunt clapped her hands seeming delighted. "You two already know each other."

"We don't *know* each other," she rushed to explain. Hopefully she wasn't blushing. "We sort of ran into each other on the road when I drove into town yesterday." And he'd turned on that very pleasant grin.

"She almost hit a moose," Ike informed everyone. "And then she almost hit me," he added, settling his gaze on hers.

Dahlia looked away. "I didn't almost hit you," she corrected, holding her post behind the chair. "You came out of nowhere. And you were walking in the middle of the road." She peeked over at him again, and yes, he was still staring at her. But that couldn't be genuine interest in his eyes. Nope. No way. She'd fallen for gazes like that once before.

His shrug didn't dispute the accusation. "I wanted to make sure she didn't hit Brutus." He offered the explanation to the man her aunt had introduced as Colt, as though he would understand.

The man nodded. "Sounds like Ike here saved you from a mess. Hitting a moose is no picnic, trust me. And Brutus is one big moose."

"He didn't save me exactly." She didn't need a man to save her. She'd been on her own for over a year now. Dahlia slipped off her coat and hung it on the back of the chair. "I'm surprised to see you here." Surely Ike wasn't part of the reinforcements Sassy had mentioned. Why would her aunt's doctor be helping at the inn?

He set down his coffee mug. "We're here for operation Christmas extravaganza."

"Ike lives at the inn too," Sassy chimed in. "On the other side of the pond."

"You live here?" Well, he certainly hadn't mentioned that when they'd met. It seemed like an important detail. Though she hadn't exactly given him much time to say anything after he'd dug her car out of the snow...

"He's renting one of the cabins while he builds his beautiful new home outside of town," her aunt explained. "It's perfect, really. He'll be available to pitch in day or night and do some of the heavy lifting as we get things ready."

Day or night. Wonderful. He would be around twenty-four/ seven.

"Happy to help." Ike leaned back in his chair all casual and relaxed. Gazing at him now, Dahlia realized he wasn't good-looking. He was downright gorgeous. Without the hat on his head, his thick dark hair offered the perfect frame for his playful eyes, which appeared a bit darker than hazel in this lighting. And now she was staring right back at him, which was probably what he wanted.

"Colt here owns the hardware store. He's real handy too," Sassy said, tugging Dahlia's attention away from Ike. "I figured we were going to need all the help we could get." She sat down at the head of the table, leaving only one seat for Dahlia. The one right next to Ike.

Great. Surprises were difficult enough but add an overly confident, handsome man who charmed with a simple smile, and she was guaranteed to fumble around in awkwardness while she did her best to appear unaffected. Well, she had to remain unaffected. She wasn't interested anyway. Not in dating. Not in giving her heart away. How could she when it was still in pieces? Jeff chose to abandon her. She'd begged him to come back. She'd told him she would change. And he'd said right to her face that she wasn't enough for him.

Ike filled her mug with coffee for her and pushed the creamer in her direction as though it was the most natural thing in the world for him to be thoughtful.

A softening rippled through her heart before she steeled it back up.

"Thanks." Dahlia purposely didn't turn her head toward him. Instead, she added a splash of creamer to her coffee and tensed her shoulders against the desire to look at Ike.

Her sisters didn't seem to be faring any better than her. Currently, Rose was scooping fruit salad onto her plate with a glower while Magnolia chugged coffee.

This should be a fun breakfast.

At least if there was one thing Dahlia could do in the face of an uncomfortable situation, it was eat. She'd been up for quite a while, and her morning walk had left her famished. While she filled her plate with a cinnamon roll and a helping of egg casserole, Sassy officially called the meeting to order.

"I'm thinking the best plan of action is to divide and conquer," her aunt announced.

"For sure," Mags agreed through a yawn. "We'll be a lot more efficient if we can each do what we're good at."

"Exactly." Sassy's head bobbed in a definitive nod.

"That sounds good to me." Dahlia tore off a piece of her cinnamon roll and shoved it into her mouth. Still not looking at Ike...well maybe a peek.

"You're the boss," he said to Sassy. "I'm willing to do whatever I can to help you after all you've done for me."

Okay, that was sweet.

"You're such doll," Sassy said to Ike. "Not to worry. Everyone will get their fair share of work. Mags, I would like you to handle all the dessert preparations. We need a variety of festive cookies and your famous cupcakes as well."

"Sounds perfect." Her sister seemed to light up at the prospect of spending the next few weeks in the kitchen.

"Rose, you will be in charge of the decorations." Their aunt handed her a small scrapbook. "Here's what we've done in the past. It doesn't have to be the same by any means, but we have to turn this place into a Christmas wonderland."

"Consider it done." Rose focused on the pictures, not making eye contact with anyone. Especially not that man sitting across from her. Dahlia took the opportunity to study Colt. Unlike Ike, he didn't seem intent on charming anyone. She wouldn't call his expression a scowl, but it did seem closed off somehow.

"Colt will be available to help with the outdoor decorations," Sassy went on. "Hanging up lights and wreaths at your direction, of course."

This time her sister's head snapped up fast. "Great," Rose muttered, giving the man across from her a good, long glower.

Yikes. Dahlia took another bite of cinnamon roll and washed it down with a swig of coffee. She must've missed something before she'd walked in.

If Sassy picked up on Rose's attitude, she didn't let on. "And Dahlia you'll work with Ike to get this place cleaned up. I desperately need your organization skills. We can hire out the cleaning, but you and Ike will be overseeing it all, from the exterior to the interior."

Whoa. Hold on. Sassy was partnering her up with Ike?

"Sounds like a plan." Ike served up a wink along with his grin this time. "We'll make a great team."

Would they? Dahlia couldn't seem to speak. It shouldn't be a big deal to work with him, but simply being around him gave her this unsettled, out-of-control feeling. Chalk it up to the fact that her confidence with men had taken a hit when her husband had decided she wasn't enough for him anymore. She cleared her throat to gain control over her voice. "I can handle the cleaning on my own. I'm sure there's something else Ike can help you with. Like you said, we should divide and conquer."

"Oh, trust me, sweetie." Sassy waved her hand in the air, her red nails glittering. "We're going to need at least two people on the cleanup crew." She reached over to pat Ike's hand. "You should see how nicely he's fixed up the cabin he's renting. He's the perfect person to help you spruce this place up."

Before Dahlia could protest again, Sassy moved on. "I'll be floating between all three of you, helping with everything I can. Oh, that reminds me." She jumped up from the table and hurried to her purse, which sat on the counter near the stove. "I have a credit card for each of you, so you can purchase the supplies you'll need. I've come up with a budget for supplies." She handed out a paper and a credit card. "But you let me know if you need more. This is only a start."

Dahlia peeked at her paper. It might be enough to rent a dumpster...

Ike leaned in and looked over her shoulder, bringing with him the scent of coffee and spice. "No problem. We've got this."

"Right," she agreed, her voice shaky. The money wasn't the problem at all. Years ago, she and Jeff had lived on a tight budget. She could make the funds stretch.

The real problem was, she couldn't seem to stop the telltale fluttering in her chest when Ike smiled at her like that.

Chapter Eleven

Magnolia

"So apparently you two have been holding out on me." Mags lifted the mug to her lips, sipping the richest, most decadent salted caramel hot chocolate she had ever tasted.

After the big breakfast meeting, she and her sisters had decided to take a trip downtown to start compiling the supplies they would need. They simply couldn't walk by Grumpy's coffee shop without stopping in. The man had served them himself. Even back when they were young, Grumpy had looked ancient with silvery white hair and thick woolly eyebrows, but he still had a quick smile and, aside from the slight arthritic hunch to his shoulders, he hadn't seemed to change.

"Do tell…" Mags licked remnants of Grumpy's homemade whipped cream off her lips. "There are likely only two hunky men in a town this size and you each know one of them already?" she teased.

"Hunky?" A testy grunt accompanied Rose's hearty eye roll. "Colt is not a hunk. He's surly and brutish and…well, he's flat-out rude."

"He didn't seem so bad to me." During breakfast, Colt hadn't said much, but to her he seemed to be one of those strong silent types. When Rose had made up her mind, however, she typically wouldn't be swayed, so Mags turned her attention to Dahlia, who was overly focused on sipping her skinny, sugar-free, coconut milk vanilla latte. Grumpy almost had a conniption when she'd ordered that instead of his hot chocolate. "You failed to mention that the man you met on the road yesterday bears a slight resemblance to one of those firefighters on the charity calendars I sent you two for Christmas last year."

"He's not that good-looking," Dahlia said, tracing the rim of her mug with her finger. "And anyway, I hadn't noticed his looks. I was too busy trying not to run him over and then I was too busy trying not get trampled by a moose. The man's looks weren't at the top of my mind." Dahlia had put her mask on...the one that hid her emotions. Mags had never mastered the mask, but Dahlia had it down by the age of ten. Maybe it was because she'd been the oldest, the one who always had to be responsible.

"Well, not only is Ike good-looking, in case you didn't notice..." Mags wanted to laugh. Dally *had* to have noticed. "He's also friendly and fun." He had a lightheartedness that made it seem like he didn't take things too seriously. If you asked Mags, her sister could use a little more lightheartedness in her life.

"Sure. He's nice." Dahlia delivered the words in a robotic fashion.

Rose glanced at Mags with a wicked grin. Uh-oh...

"Have you been dating anyone?" Rose asked with a raise of her waxed eyebrows.

"Ha. Very funny." Dahlia's stern glare got her sarcasm across. "When would I possibly have time to date anyone? I have two children. Well, three if you count my ex-husband."

Mags cracked up. "Good point." Not a phone call went by where Dahlia didn't mention she had to do something for Jeff. *Jeff needs me to pick up the kids early. Jeff couldn't take the kids this weekend.* Even after divorcing her, Jeff sure relied on Dahlia an awful lot.

Rose leaned closer to their sister. "Well maybe you should do something for yourself," she whispered slyly. "Sassy made sure to mention Ike is single. And I've seen the way he looks at you. He didn't fill up my coffee mug for me, honey. And anyway, you shouldn't have to worry about Jeff anymore. You're divorced. He needs to figure it out all by himself."

Mags was about to agree but the sadness filling Dally's eyes stopped her. "I don't care about dating. You two couldn't possibly understand the responsibilities that go along with having children. They're the most important thing in the world to me. I don't need anything or anyone else."

The words grated against that raw landscape of Mags's heart, the area that bore the marks of miscarriages and lost dreams. She flinched against the pain, holding her breath, gagging back the automatic sob that rose in her throat. She *did* know. She knew that a baby would be the most important thing in the world to her, too. If she could ever have one...

"All I'm saying is that your kids are growing up." Rose's tone gentled. "They're not babies anymore, honey. They're going to start finding their own lives, and you deserve to have a life, too. You deserve someone who'll take care of you the way you take care of everyone else." Rose looked at Mags for confirmation, but the tears had started to build. They were about two seconds from spilling over, and she didn't want to do this now. Not here in public.

"Excuse me." Mags pushed back from the table and wobbled her way across the café and into the small, two-stall bathroom. Bracing her hands against the tile countertop, she let her head drop, let the tears come. It was too hard to hold them off when the grief caught her by surprise like that.

The door creaked behind her. "Mags?" Dahlia sounded panicked. "Are you okay?"

"Oh my God." Rose rushed in and put an arm around her. "Are you crying?" She didn't wait for an answer. "What is it? What's wrong?"

"I'm sorry." One minute she and Rose had been teasing Dally and the next she was having a breakdown in the bathroom. She was so tired of being on this emotional roller coaster. For a long time, she'd blamed the tears on the IVF drugs that constantly messed with her hormones, but even after a few months of being off them, she still couldn't control her emotions. She couldn't hide the pain the way everyone else seemed to. "We should go. We still have a lot of shopping to do." She lifted her head and swiped a Kleenex from the box on the counter. She couldn't unload all of her problems on her sisters in a bathroom of all places.

"No." Rose moved to block the door. "We're not leaving this bathroom until you tell us what's going on."

"We've got all day," Dally added, moving in shoulder to shoulder with Rose. "So, spill it sister."

Mags closed her eyes. She didn't even know where to start. The infertility, the miscarriages had been her secret for so long. She'd guarded it closely. It had been too difficult to talk about, especially on the sporadic phone calls with her sisters. "Eric and I can't have a baby." That was the truth of it. No matter what they did, no matter how many treatments, how many supplements, how many relaxation and positive vibe techniques they'd tried, they couldn't. And every time it had failed, she'd felt like it was her fault. That she'd missed something. She hadn't done everything right…

"Oh, honey." Dahlia's eyes filled with tears, too. She rushed over and wrapped her arms around Mags. "I'm so sorry. So, so, so sorry. I didn't know. I never would've said that if I'd known."

"I know you wouldn't have." Magnolia's throat ached from crying. "You couldn't have known. It's okay." She shouldn't be falling apart over one statement, but she'd been holding it together for such a long time it was like her heart had finally cracked. Now the tears wouldn't stop.

Rose left her post at the door and laid her hands on Mags's shoulders. "There must be something that will work. I know it's harder for some people, but there are so many options these days—"

"We've tried them." Mags cut her off before Rose could go into her problem-solving mode. "We've tried everything. Every option. We've lost three babies. Had four failed fertility treatments." The crushing weight of it bore down on her heart again.

"Why haven't you said anything?" Dahlia stroked her hair, tears freely streaming down her cheeks now. "My God, Mags. You didn't have to go through that by yourself."

"What does Eric say?" Even the unshakable Rose had gotten choked up.

Mags sank back against the counter. She was so tired. "He said he's done trying. That it's not worth it. All the money we've spent." All the months they'd planned out their sexual encounters like they were business meetings. "He said he doesn't care if we ever have children."

That had been the moment when the last of her hope had

shattered. As long as he'd been in the fight with her, she'd been able to hold on, but once he'd let go, she'd lost her grip.

"I'm sure he doesn't mean that." Dahlia used the same hushed tone Mags had heard her use to soothe her children. "It must've been so stressful, but in time I'm sure he'll come around."

Rose seemed to pick up on the doubt that had rooted itself deep in Mags's soul. "Do you want him to come around?" Her younger sister had always been direct.

She could lie. That's what she'd been doing for a year. She could say of course she hoped he would come around, that even with all they'd been through they could save their marriage. But lying had started to take more effort than simply coming out with the truth. "We've been fighting a lot. I feel like I hardly know him anymore." Worse yet, he didn't seem to know her, to understand this consuming desire they'd once shared. Yet again, speaking the words out loud brought this overwhelming sense of finality. It seemed impossible to go back and find all the broken fragments of their love and somehow fit them back into place.

"That's why he didn't come with you." Rose leaned against the counter next to Mags.

"I don't know what's going to happen." Saying it to her sisters wasn't nearly as scary as she'd thought it would be. "I need some time to sort it all out."

"I needed time to sort things out, too." Regal Rose slumped back against the wall.

"What?" Mags turned to study her. What could Rose possibly have to figure out? "You're practically marrying royalty. One of the most eligible bachelors in the country. And he adores you." Gregory was always buying Rose gifts, surprising her with jewelry, and taking her on extravagant vacations.

Dahlia gasped. "You don't know if you want to marry Gregory?"

Rose stared down at her hands. "I don't know if I can."

Mags had to drag her jaw off the floor. This might be the first time she'd ever seen her younger sister look lost. She shared a questioning glance with Dally, not knowing what to say.

"Did something happen?" Dahlia asked, supporting her sister with an arm around her shoulders.

"Not necessarily. There're just so many expectations with his family. I don't think our life together will ever be about us."

Mags had met Evaline Cunningham one time and that had been enough for her. It wasn't that she was intimidating necessarily. It was more that she seemed so judgmental. The last time Mags had visited Rose, they'd gone with their mother and Evaline to interview a caterer for the wedding reception. The head chef had been sweet and quirky, not a five-star chef by any means, but clearly creative and professional. Until Evaline had grilled her for a good twenty minutes about her classical training, that was. Then the poor woman had been reduced to tears.

"If it makes you feel any better, I wouldn't want Evaline for a mother-in-law either," Mags offered. Eric's mom, on the other hand, had always been wonderful. She came for frequent visits, and she'd always treated Mags like a daughter. The pang in her heart deepened. Her and Eric's lives and families were interwoven. She loved his parents, his sisters. What if they weren't a part of her life anymore?

"I could stand her being my mother-in-law," Rose said. "That's not the issue. I could deal with her if I had to." A heartsick sigh slipped out. "It's more that Gregory can't seem to stand up to her. Even with the little things. What's going to happen when we have kids? She'll probably be in charge of raising them." Her eyes widened. "I'm sorry. I shouldn't have brought up kids."

"No, it's fine." Mags found her smile coming easier. "You can talk about kids. I don't want everyone to have to walk on eggshells around me. That's one reason I haven't said much." She didn't need people hushing away from conversations when she walked into the room. It wouldn't make her reality any easier. "Having kids is something you should consider when you're about to get married." She'd thought she and Eric were on the same page in that department.

"It sounds like you're asking all the right questions," Dahlia agreed. "I should've asked more questions before my own wedding. I was too swept up in the romance and excitement to think much. Look where that got me." Their eldest sister laughed. "You two are right. That's why I was so annoyed when we were talking before. Ike is very good-looking. And, judging from the way he talks to Sassy, he seems kind and friendly. And I think you may be right about him being interested in me too, which is why everything in me is telling me to stay away from him." She shook her head as though frustrated with herself. "I can't go through that again. What Jeff did to me. It shattered me. And I'm afraid I'll never be able to let someone love me like that again."

"So basically, we all have issues." Mags slung one arm around Dahlia and the other around Rose. "It sounds like we all needed an escape for the holidays this year."

"I know I did." Rose rested her head on Mags's shoulder.

"Do you think Sassy somehow knew that?" Dahlia asked. "I used to think that woman had magical powers. She's always seemed to know just what we needed."

Mags thought back to all the times Sassy had played with them, encouraged them, believed in their dreams. She'd brought them back together, and this was their chance to finally help her. "Maybe it's our turn to figure out what she needs."

Chapter Twelve

Rose

Rose couldn't remember the last time she'd enjoyed an afternoon so much. She walked in step with her sisters, each of them bundled in hats and scarves and their bulkiest coats while they made their way down Main Street, pausing to peer in the windows of the shops, which had been decorated so festively with garlands and red velvet bows and locally made candy canes of all different colors dangling from ribbons.

After they'd finally left the coffee shop's bathroom, they'd ventured to the market so Magnolia could start planning desserts—and they'd had to stop by every sample station, filling up on chocolate and popcorn and bits of fresh-made pastries from the bakery down the street. Now they were window-shopping, working their way down the block, and even with the frostbite on her toes, Rose could stay out here all day. Everyone they walked past seemed to greet them with a welcoming hello and a smile. The streets weren't crowded, but they were bustling, as if the whole town was in full swing with holiday preparations and anticipation. "I love it here," Rose said with a contented sigh. "It's so different than Savannah."

"Well, it's colder, that's for sure," Mags said, her teeth chattering. "I think we need to go back to Grumpy's for another round of hot chocolate. I'm not sure how much more of this cold I can take. I miss the beach."

Rose had never been much of a winter person either, but she wasn't ready to duck inside just yet. The festive downtown streets were joyful and, more important, made Rose feel joyful. And as much as she loved being warm, the snow only added to the merriment. "We can go back in a—"

Wait a minute. Hold the phone. Rose's gaze fixated on the sign hanging above one of the shops across the street: "Sew It Seams— Quilting, Sewing, Fabric."

Seriously? Could there really be a cute little fabric store in this small town? "I knew I loved it here," she squealed, making a beeline across the street without even looking both ways.

"Hey! Where are you—" Dahlia's voice faded behind her as Rose slipped in through the glass door. She couldn't stop herself, couldn't *help* herself. She hadn't been in a fabric store for so long, and this one was even bigger than it looked from the outside!

"Good afternoon." A grandmotherly woman standing behind the counter welcomed her with a warm smile. "Welcome to Sew It Seams. Is there anything I can help you find today?"

Rose could hardly tear her gaze from the rows and rows of colorful fabrics—paisleys and damasks and ginghams and beautiful chintz patterns. "I'm not sure what I'm looking for," she told the woman in awe. "But whatever it is, I'm pretty sure I can find it here."

Chuckling, the woman came around the counter and offered her hand. "I'm Eloise. Always fun to meet a fellow fabric junkie."

"Rose." She shook the woman's hand as she continued to scan the store. "You have an incredible collection here. I mean—"

The door whooshed open and in blew her sisters. "Next time you ditch us you might want to make sure there are no cars coming," Mags said crossly. "Oh wow." Her scowl lightened. "It's so warm in here."

"Sorry." Rose stepped aside so she could introduce Mags and Dally to Eloise, who, with her long white hair and heart-shaped face appeared to be her angel from above. "These are my wonderful sisters. Girls, this is Eloise, and she has one of the most wonderful fabric collections I have ever seen anywhere. Ever." She turned to the woman. "Seriously. I'm from Savannah, and it's hard to find a store that carries such variety."

"Well, it's our passion." The woman's blue eyes shone. "We have quite the large quilting and sewing community in the area, so I try to make sure we're always stocked."

"It's nice to meet you." Dahlia removed her glove and shook Eloise's hand.

"That's a lot of fabric." Mags seemed to take in the many aisles. "We should take our time looking through every shelf. Maybe my fingers and toes will finally thaw."

Eloise laughed. "Yes, please do take your time looking around. And let me know if you need anything." She gestured to a table on the other side of the counter. "And please help yourselves to a warm drink. We have hot water and tea bags, or a wonderful spiced cider mix, as well as some cookies I baked myself last night."

"Now we're talking." Mags thanked her and headed right for the refreshments, but Rose couldn't fight the pull of those fabric samples calling to her. She might never leave this place.

Another group of customers walked into the store, so Eloise hurried off to greet them. Rose wandered deeper down one of the aisles, almost not knowing where to start.

"You've always picked out the perfect fabric for your projects. Do you remember that skirt you made me for the eighties dance my freshman year?" Dahlia walked alongside her, but her sister didn't gawk at the different patterns and colors the way Rose did.

"How could I forget?" Rose laughed at the memory. "You said you'd never wear it." The fabric had been hot pink with black tiger stripes and Rose had slaved over that skirt for days, leaving a mess of fabric scraps and thread and discarded attempts in her wake. She hadn't been able to tell what Dally hated more—the skirt or the mess Rose had made. "But you did wear it." She slung an arm around her sister in a half hug while they walked.

"I knew I'd never hear the end of it if I didn't wear it," Dally muttered hugging her back. "And I got a ton of compliments at the dance." Her sister pulled her to a stop. "You've always been talented. And creative. Do you still sew?"

"No. I can't even remember the last time I wandered around a fabric store," Rose commented, running her hand over a bolt of a soft baby pink Paris chiffon. It felt like butter beneath her fingertips. She thought about the sketches she'd done before Evaline had shot down her dreams of making her own dress. "This would be the perfect fabric to make a wedding gown with." Soft and elegant…

"I have to say, I was surprised when you decided not to make your own dress." Dally felt the fabric, too. "You always talked about that when we were younger."

"I wanted to, but…" Well, it didn't fit Evaline's vision for the wedding. From the day they'd announced their engagement, Evaline had been talking about a royal affair. *Just wait until so-and-so sees this*, she'd kept saying. *So-and-so will be so jealous about that.*

"Let me guess." Her sister faced her. "Evaline didn't want you to make your own dress."

"Why would she care?" Mags asked, walking over to join them.

"It seems to me Evaline has been dreaming about her son's wedding since she was a little girl," Rose joked. But she couldn't quite find a laugh to back up the humor.

"Well it's *your* wedding. It's supposed to be about you and Gregory." Mags bit into another sugar cookie. "Oh Mylanta. You guys have to try these. They're absolutely amazing. I thought I had perfected the Christmas cookie. Now I'm rethinking my whole life."

Rose stole one out of her hand. She could go for a little sugar rush right about now. "It's not *just* Gregory's and my wedding." She slowly wandered farther down the aisle, unable to keep herself from touching almost every bolt of fabric. "Not really." She didn't need to explain. Both of her sisters had met Evaline.

"Well, the wedding's not nearly as important as everyone thinks it is." Dally sighed. "What happens after is way more important."

That was exactly what Rose had started to worry about.

"You guys should elope!" Mags slipped in front of them, her eyes alight with excitement. "You could come to Florida! Have a beautiful ceremony on the beach right at sunset!"

"As romantic as that sounds, it will never happen," Rose assured her. "The wedding will be the way Evaline wants it or there won't be a wedding. Gregory won't disappoint his mother."

Dally pulled Rose to a stop. "Do you love him?"

"Yes." She'd thought she loved Gregory with her whole heart. She'd always believed that would be enough, that true love could conquer anything. "But it's starting to feel more complicated than that."

"Oh, it's complicated all right," Mags agreed, pulling a cookie out of her pocket. "Love is so much harder than I ever thought it would be."

"So much harder," Dally agreed.

Rose studied her older sister. "Do you still love Jeff?"

Dally didn't hesitate. "I think a part of me will always love him, love the life we had together." Sadness filled in her smile. "We'll always be connected through Ollie and Maya. And I'll always appreciate him for giving me those two. But I'm not in love with him anymore."

The revelation made Rose's heart skip. Was it possible to fall out of love? No, that wasn't the question that scared her the most. Was she falling out of the love with Gregory? She pushed the thought out of her mind. Things had been intense, that was all. She still loved him, and he still loved her.

Rose and Dahlia walked in silence, turning to go down another aisle.

"So, how's the design business going?" Dally finally asked.

Her sister was always so good at picking up on when Rose didn't want to talk about something, but this topic of conversation brought up yet another sigh. "I haven't had time to do much lately. Everything has been so busy with the wedding plans."

"You haven't been working?" Mags sipped something out of the insulated cup she was holding.

Rose inhaled. Cider with real cinnamon. It smelled like Christmas. "Not really." She'd done a few consults for friends who had moved, but nothing significant. "Evaline suggested I put things on hold until after the wedding." And Rose couldn't help but wonder if she would ever be able to take things off hold.

Mags rolled her eyes but seemed to bite back any choice words about Gregory's mother. "You love to work." Mags did, too. They'd always been the same that way. That's how it was when you did something you were passionate about. It didn't feel like work.

"I miss it." After their bathroom confessional, Rose had decided she wouldn't hold anything back from her sisters anymore. If she couldn't be honest with them, she couldn't be honest with herself. "Evaline doesn't understand why I want to work. And I'm starting to wonder if Gregory does. He keeps telling me I won't need to. He keeps telling me I don't need to now."

"Financially, maybe," Dally said. "But you're so creative and artistic. I can't imagine you ignoring that side of yourself."

She *had* been ignoring that need, that craving, and now that she stood in this store, she couldn't imagine why. Rose rested her hand on yet another bolt of fabric, a pink chintz that almost looked vintage. "Doesn't this remind you of the upholstery in Betty?" They'd spent hours curled up on the floral-patterned benches inside the old trailer. She and Sassy had made the curtains and covers for the cushions themselves.

"Yes." Mags pulled the bolt off the shelf and studied it. "Wow this brings back memories."

"The trailer is still around." Dahlia took a turn admiring the pretty pattern. "I saw it this morning. Sassy told me she hasn't done a thing with it. Poor old Betty has simply been sitting there neglected all these years. I think we should fix her up."

Rose gasped. "That's amazing. That's perfect."

Mags looked at them like they'd both lost their minds. "Don't we have enough going on right now?"

"No." Rose couldn't hold back a squeal. "I've been dying to find a project like Betty." Taking something old and decrepit and giving it new life. That was exactly the kind of thing she loved. "I seriously need to redecorate something! Something where I can do all the work, the sewing and the painting. Everything." And there was no one here to tell her she didn't have the time.

"That sounds like a ton of work." Mags glanced at Dally like she was hoping their older sister would shut the idea down, but instead Dally grinned. "You're right. It's perfect."

"Yes!" Rose squealed right at the same time Mags said, "Seriously?"

"Come on." Dally linked her arm through Mags's while Rose pulled every bolt of the pink chintz fabric off the shelf.

"Wouldn't you love to see that old trailer restored?" Dally purred.

"It would bring back so many memories from our childhood," Rose added, though she didn't know why she was trying to convince Mags. They were totally doing this, and she'd have to get on board eventually.

Mags pulled her arm away from Dally. "I think you two must've forgotten how much work we already have to do with the whole Christmas extravaganza."

"But for the next two weeks, I have no kids to take care of," Dahlia said with a lost look. "I could use another project."

"And I have no wedding tasks to do," Rose added, feeling so light her feet could've levitated off the floor. "We basically have at least fourteen hours a day for the next two weeks to pull this off." Seeing the uncertainty on her sister's face, she added, "It'll be just like old times. Us hanging out in Betty, drinking hot chocolate and eating cookies, giggling and talking about boys. We'll make it fun."

For the first time since the renovation had come up, Mags smiled. "Well in that case, count me in."

Before she could change her mind, Rose practically sprinted to the checkout counter.

"Wow." Eloise's eyes went wide at the sight of all the fabric. "You girls must have quite the project in mind."

"We're going to completely restore my aunt's old Shasta camping trailer," Rose told her, digging her wallet out of her purse.

Eloise paused from ringing her up. "Well, you must be Sassy's nieces then. She mentioned you were coming for Christmas. She was absolutely delighted."

"We're delighted to be here." Rose hadn't been this excited about Christmas since she was probably ten years old. Not even hearing the total, she handed the woman her credit card.

"Well, I'm sure you'll need more supplies for that sad old trailer." Eloise ran the card and handed her the receipt. "On the bottom there's a coupon for the hardware store. We like to refer customers to other local stores around here. It helps us all out."

"That's nice." Rose shoved the receipt deep into her purse and handed a few bolts of fabric to Mags and Dahlia.

"We have to head over to the hardware store anyway," Dahlia said.

Rose clammed up. She had no intention of going to the hardware store. Not if Colt would be there.

"Wonderful." Eloise walked around the counter and escorted them to the door. "We all certainly appreciate your business around here. I hope to see you again."

"You will." Rose had a feeling she would be making frequent trips to Sew It Seams, if only to be surrounded by all the colors and textures. "Thanks so much." She bid Eloise farewell and stepped out into the cold.

Mags lingered inside the door, pulling on her gloves and hat again, zipping up her coat all the way to her nose, but she finally stepped outside, too. "Should we head to the hardware store?" The fabric from her bulky coat muffled her voice.

"No." Rose headed in the opposite direction.

"Um…" Dahlia quickly caught up to her. "Then how do you suggest we'll find the supplies we need to complete the renovation? Not to mention to decorate the inn for Christmas?"

"I'll order things online." Yes, that would work. She had connections with a variety of different online retailers—

"We need supplies ASAP," Dally reminded her. "We don't have time to order them online."

Rose kept walking, the hardware store getting farther and farther behind her. "Then I'll drive down to Denver."

Mags laughed. "You're going to make a three-hour drive one way—across the snowy, icy mountains—simply to avoid a man you're going to have to spend time with while we fix up the inn anyway?"

Rose finally stopped and turned to face her sisters. "There's something I don't like about him." Mainly the fact that he didn't seem to like her. She wasn't used to people not liking her. She was pretty laid-back, easy to get along with, but Colt looked at her like she was an insect he might want to squash under his shoe.

"You two just got off on the wrong foot," Dahlia said. Spoken like a true mother. "I'm sure once you get to know him things will be different."

"He can't be all bad," Mags added. "He did offer to help with the work at the inn, after all."

"Or maybe Sassy offered to pay him. Did you ever think of that?" Maybe their aunt knew the three of them couldn't handle all the work, so she'd gone out and found the only two able-bodied men in town.

Mags and Dally shared a look and then crowded either side of her, turning her around and nudging her along to the hardware store. "Showing up at his store will be a nice gesture," Dally insisted. "You can start building the bridge. You heard Eloise. They all appreciate it when people shop local. That probably includes Colt."

"Fine." She drew out the word in a long, disgruntled sigh, but it *was* fine. She could be the bigger person here. "He probably won't even be there." He owned the place. He'd never said he worked there or anything.

But when they strolled through the door five minutes later, Colt was the only one behind the checkout counter. He didn't offer them the same greeting Eloise had, more of a grunt and a head nod instead.

"Hi Colt," Mags called, waving to him. "We need some supplies for our big projects."

"Sure," he mumbled. "Lemme know if you need help. Sassy always gets a fifty percent discount around here."

Dahlia looked at Rose and raised her eyebrows as if to say, *See? He's not all bad.*

She'd never said he was all bad. Her sister was right, though she wasn't about to say that out loud. She and Colt had gotten off on the wrong foot, but in time he would come to see how likable she was. In fact, she'd start showing him right now. "Thank you." She waved too, but Colt had already turned around. If he heard her, he didn't let on. She spun to look at her sisters. *See?* The man obviously didn't want to give her the time of day.

Dahlia shrugged as though his lack of acknowledgment had been no big deal. "Since I'm in charge of cleaning and organizing, I'm going to check out the cleaning supplies. We can meet up in a few." She veered down an aisle and disappeared.

Well, at least she had Mags to help her sort through the huge display of Christmas lights and lawn ornaments up ahead.

"I need to use the restroom." Mags's face had suddenly gone white.

"Are you okay?" Rose pulled a water bottle out of her purse and handed it to her sister. "Here, have some water."

"I don't know." Mags pulled off the cap and took a sip. "Maybe too many cookies or something. I'll be back in a few minutes." She quickly hurried toward the restroom sign at the back of the store before Rose could ask if she wanted her to come. Knowing Mags, she wouldn't want to be crowded or fussed over when she wasn't feeling well, so instead of following her sister, Rose moved on to the Christmas display set up in the center of the store. *Whew.* She eyed the variety of light boxes that had been stacked in a pyramid. When had Christmas decorating gotten so overwhelming? Living in a high-rise condo meant she and Gregory didn't put up outdoor lights. Who knew they had so many varieties? There were colorful lights, LED lights, white lights, big retro bulbs, snowflakes, icicles—

"Need help?"

Rose whirled and lost her balance, stumbling sideways into the pyramid of cardboard boxes. *No, no, no!* She tried to catch herself, but there was nothing to hold on to. Her flailing arm hit the pyramid, sending the boxes crashing over. Down she went right on her butt, squashing one of the boxes and probably all of the lights inside.

Colt stood a few feet away looking as unimpressed with her as he had when he'd caught her rearranging his tree. "You okay?" he asked calmly.

Did it look like she was okay? Her tailbone wasn't the only

thing that was bruised. Rose scrambled to her knees, crunching at least three more boxes of lights in the process. "Oh God, oh no." She wobbled to her feet but couldn't avoid stepping on one more box. It stuck to her boot and sent her stumbling again.

"Easy." Colt caught her shoulders and stood her back up straight.

"I'm sorry." Waves of heat rolled over her cheeks. She backed away, trying to kick the smashed cardboard box from her boot. Once she'd freed her foot, she picked up a box. "I can clean it up—"

"Not necessary." He stepped in to block her from touching any of the other boxes like he was afraid she would do more damage. "I'll take care of it. Really. Please."

"Whoa." Mags came rushing over to the display. "I thought I heard a disaster in progress. I just didn't realize you were involved."

"I lost my balance." Tears stung Rose's eyes. Because for some reason she had to make a fool out of herself every time he was around.

Colt said nothing. He simply knelt and started to restack the boxes.

Mags wrapped an arm around her stomach. "I think I need to get out of here. Get some fresh air."

Wow, Mags must really not be feeling well if she wanted to voluntarily step out into the subzero temperatures. Rose tried not to look too grateful as she rushed to her sister's side. "I'll take you. We can wait for Dahlia out there." She almost made it out the door when Colt's voice stopped her. "Did you want to buy those lights now or pay for them later?"

Ugh. She'd been so humiliated she'd forgotten she was holding a box of lights. The icicle lights, which would never work for her vision of what she wanted to do with the inn's Christmas deco-rations. "I wasn't going to steal them," she announced, marching back to Colt. "I forgot I was holding them." She added them to the top of the pyramid he was building.

"Okay." The disinterest in his eyes made her feel like she was two inches tall. "By the way, I wanted to talk to you about the tree in the park."

Not this again. She almost groaned. "Can we forget the tree? Please? I didn't mean to—"

"We had some wind last night," the man interrupted. "It needs to be fixed. And since you seem to have ideas, I thought maybe you would want to fix it up."

"Uh…" She blinked at least three times, trying to make sure she hadn't imagined the words that had come out of his mouth. "You want me to fix the tree? In the park? The same tree you didn't want me to touch?"

"If you don't want to—"

"Oh, I want to." She just couldn't believe he wanted her to. "Yes, I'll do it," she added before he could change his mind. "I can work on it right now if you want."

"Fine by me." Colt gestured to a stack of boxes by the door where Mags was waiting for her. "I've got some ornaments packed up over there if you want to take a look. I can haul them to the park for you."

More blinking. Was this really happening? Was Colt asking for her help with something? "Great." Judging from his typical frown, he wasn't trying to pull one over on her. "I'll go take a look then." She walked to the stack of boxes and peered inside. They were the same style as the ornaments that had been on the tree before, except now there were more colors—silver and turquoise and magenta. If she hadn't been trying to play it cool she would've squealed. This was going to be so fun!

"Wow." Mags peered into one of the boxes. "Sure seems like you're winning over Colt."

"I don't know about that." He still hadn't dropped the scowl that seemed to be a permanent fixture on his face when she was around. "Feeling better?" Rose asked, refocusing on her sister.

"Not really. I really gotta lay off the sugar." She peered over Rose's shoulder. "I'd love to stay and watch you work a miracle with the tree, but I think I'll go find Dally so she can take me home." Her sister's cheeks had started to pale. "I think I need a nap. This mountain air must be getting to me."

"Sure. I'll see if Colt would mind dropping me off after I'm done with the tree." It would give them a chance to talk about the inn's Christmas decorations anyway.

Mags hurried off, and Colt sauntered over with a ladder. "About ready?

"Sure am!" Whoa. That sounded a little overeager. "I mean, I'm ready if you are." She tried to calibrate her smile somewhere between polite and marginally enthusiastic. According to her sisters, she sometimes got carried away and she didn't want to overwhelm the poor man.

Colt nodded in response and led the way out the door. While he loaded boxes in the truck, Rose climbed into the passenger's seat, taking a look around as she buckled her seatbelt. The cab was pretty clean with only a stainless-steel coffee cup in one of the cupholders and a bulky flannel draped over the seat, and it smelled a lot like the pine forest outside of town.

Colt climbed in right as her sisters came out of the hardware store. They waved and made faces, which Rose pretended to ignore. "Don't you need to lock up?" she asked as he put the truck in reverse.

"Nah. Brett is in the back room watching television. He'll hear if anyone comes in."

Ah, so he had an employee. "How long has Brett been working for you?"

"A few years." Colt pulled the truck into a spot in front of the park. "He's a retiree. Works a few hours a day."

"That's ni—"

The man hopped out of the truck before she had a chance to finish. Okay, so he wasn't big on conversation. Duly noted.

Rose zipped her coat up to her chin and climbed out of the truck. He'd already hauled off the boxes, so she followed him down the sidewalk to the tree. Colt hadn't been joking. The Christmas tree was a mess. Most of the ornaments that had hung on the branches had been scattered in the snow. Now the tree was a blank slate.

"You're smiling." He set the boxes next to the tree and walked over to her.

She quickly evened out her expression. "Was I? Huh." She couldn't help but smile. She had the chance to decorate the most beautiful Christmas tree she'd ever seen in the most beautiful mountain town she'd ever been in. Standing out here in the park made her feel like she was worlds away from Savannah. This tree would be nothing like the extravagant display with the golden bows and glass ornaments in the Cunninghams' home. It would be homey and simple. Still elegant, but also unpretentious. She couldn't wait to get started. "I'm really glad you asked me to do this. It'll be—"

The sound of Colt's footsteps crunching away in the snow stopped her. Right. He didn't like to chat. Well, then. They'd simply have to get to work.

It took a good hour and a half of Colt holding the ladder and handing her ornaments, and her placing and assessing and standing back to admire the branches, but finally, she hung the last silver ball.

"Great job with the tree. It looks amazing," a woman's voice called from behind her. Holding on to the ladder carefully, Rose peered over her shoulder. A small crowd had gathered on the sidewalk. She climbed down.

"It's so pretty!" a little girl squealed. "I love the pink ornaments! They're sparkly!"

Awwww. Rose walked over to meet the tree's admirers. "I love the pink ones too," she said, gazing at the tree. It really had come to life.

"I think it's the most beautiful tree we've ever had in this town." An older woman who had been walking by stopped. "The colors are brilliant. Very eye-catching."

Rose nearly cried. Since the engagement had taken over her life, she hadn't had the chance to design anything. It had been a while since someone had appreciated anything she'd done. And complete strangers, no less. They'd actually stopped to thank her. That would never happen back in Savannah. "Thank you." Rose peeked over to see if Colt was listening, but he was busy folding up the ladder. "I was happy to help out." More than happy. She loved it here. Loved the mountains hemming in the town. Loved this park and how it seemed to be a gathering place. She loved the smiling faces and the chitchat on the street corners. And she especially loved how she felt like she was part of it all.

"I wish you could come decorate my tree," the little girl said shyly. Her mother laughed. "I'm afraid we don't have any pink ornaments at home."

"Well, here." Rose walked to the tree and pulled one off, but then paused when she noticed Colt watching. She wouldn't want to steal anything from the man.

Wait...

Was that a hint of a smile on his lips? She swore it was...

He nodded as though telling Rose to give the girl the ornament.

"Thank you, thank you, thank you!" The little girl's eyes got almost as round as the pink shiny ball when Rose handed it to her.

"Merry Christmas," the girl's mom said warmly.

"Merry Christmas." Something told her this would be the merriest Christmas she'd had in years.

Chapter Thirteen

Dahlia

Some people exercised to ease their nerves. Some people meditated. But when Dahlia started to fret, she always made spreadsheets.

There was something calming about those rows and columns all lined up and perfectly symmetrical. The order, the complete visual organization always put her at ease. It had taken her a good hour to revive Sassy's ancient printer, but finally—*finally*—she'd been able to print off her Christmas extravaganza project and supplies list. And actually, tinkering with the printer had distracted her from Ike's impending arrival.

"Ah-ha. I've found you." Sassy scooted into the office from the living room. "Glory be. What in the world happened in here?" She looked around at the decluttered desk and shelves, which had all been shined up with a healthy dose of wood polish. Spreadsheets and cleaning—that was how Dahlia de-stressed.

"I cleaned up a little." Dahlia folded up the printed spreadsheets and tucked them into her pocket before her aunt got the idea that she might be neurotic. "I figured I would get as much done on the inside of the house as I could before we head outside." If it was up to her, she would handle the cleanup detail herself, but Ike was due to arrive at the house in just a few minutes to help her.

"You cleaned *a little?*" Her aunt opened and closed the desk drawers. "Honey, you completely overhauled the office. I don't think it's ever been this organized."

"Well, it's what I do." She'd woken up at six o'clock that morning feeling utterly useless, so she'd decided to make herself useful. "I thought Ike and I would start out in the old barn when he gets here. I'm assuming we'll be using that as the hub for the sleigh rides again?"

"Yes." Her aunt closed the desk drawer and took a seat in the chair. "Colt has graciously agreed to bring his horse team to pull the sleigh. His father was the one who used to do that, you know."

"Really?" She thought back, but the memories were fuzzy. "I don't remember ever meeting Colt before."

"Well, he's a few years older than you girls, but he was around." Her cheeks turned a shade of pink Dahlia didn't often see on her face. "His mother passed away when he was young, so it was just him and his father."

"I remember the sleigh rides. They were always a highlight of the extravaganza." But she didn't remember much about the man driving the sled. "Will Colt's dad be coming to the extravaganza then?"

"I'm afraid not." Her aunt stood abruptly. "He passed away a few years back." She turned, and Dahlia had to wonder if Sassy was trying to hide tears.

"I'm sorry to hear." Dahlia walked around the desk so she could get a peek at her aunt's expression. The woman smiled but sorrow seemed to dull her bright eyes.

"Yes, well, I promised I would help Mags with the baking prep in the kitchen." Sassy paused on her way out the door. "I have to admit, I'm a little worried about her. She doesn't seem to be herself today."

"I noticed that, too." At breakfast, Mags had hardly touched the delicious strawberry waffles their aunt had made. "She wasn't feeling well a few days ago when we were out shopping either. We'll keep an eye on her." Hopefully it was some kind of short-lived virus.

"Yes, we will." Sassy patted her shoulder. "You've always been good at taking care of people, Dally. Even when you were young." She leaned closer like she wanted to share a secret. "Just don't busy yourself so much with taking care of other people that you forget to take care of yourself."

"It might be a little late for that." When she'd woken up this morning, the first thing on her mind was what she could do. She didn't know how to simply be. Somewhere in the midst of listening to the kids and listening to her husband and listening to all the things others needed from her, she'd forgotten how to listen to herself. And now... she didn't know what she needed.

"It's never too late, my dear. Remember that." Sassy wrapped her in a hug the way she used to and then let go. "Look at us, standing here together after all these years." Oh, that smile. Sassy had the most unique smile. It seemed to wedge itself into her cheeks, and it made Dahlia smile, too.

"If there's one thing I know, this is the perfect place to come and reflect," her aunt went on. "When you're not so busy, when you're not occupying yourself with taking care of others from morning until night, you start to find yourself again. Trust me." It was as if Sassy had known that Dahlia needed a time-out from her life. But how could she have known? Dahlia was about to ask when Ike walked into the living room beyond the office's French doors.

"Hello?"

"We're in here!" Sassy waved him over to where they stood. "You're just in time. It appears my darling niece has finished quite the thorough cleaning in my office and is now ready to tackle another project."

Ike whistled as he looked around the room. "I'll say it's a thorough cleaning. Last time I was in here you couldn't even see the desk."

Well, what could Dahlia say? She had become more than comfortable with making things look shiny and clean. Unfortunately, she was less comfortable spending the day with a man who clearly had a way with women, so whatever her aunt was trying to pull by matching her up with Ike would most likely backfire.

"Well, I'll let you two get to it." Sassy scurried away. "I'll catch up with you later this afternoon!" She disappeared around the corner, leaving Dahlia staring blankly at Ike. He hadn't shaved that morning, but the stubble only enhanced his well-formed jawline.

"Where should we start?" He scrubbed his hands together like he couldn't wait to get out there. Dahlia, on the other hand, had nerves churning through her stomach. How ridiculous was that? She'd talked to plenty of Maya and Ollie's friends' fathers with no problem. Though none of them were single or ruggedly handsome. The prospect of spending the afternoon alone with this man felt very different than hanging out at a playdate. The fact was she was too used to hiding behind her kids. She'd used Maya and Ollie as an excuse for why she couldn't put herself out there when what she really feared was having her heart broken again. Was it worth the risk?

Instinctively, Dahlia dug the spreadsheet out of her pocket and carefully unfolded it. "I thought we would start in the old barn." She didn't have to look at the paper to formulate the plan—she pretty much already had it memorized—but she stared at it anyway.

Ike leaned over to have a look. "Is that a spreadsheet?"

His amusement automatically made her defensive. "Yes. With so much to do, I thought it would be best to plan and prioritize. This covers all the details. The areas that need cleaning up, the supplies we'll need in each location, and the specific tasks that need to be accomplished in each different area."

"Wow." He eyed the rows and columns with an impressed smirk. "Are you looking for a job? I need to hire you down at the office."

"I live in Minnesota," she said, quickly tucking the spreadsheet back into her pocket.

"I know." He laughed a little. "I was joking. I mean, I'd hire someone with your organizational skills in a second, but you'd be way overqualified to be a receptionist."

Of course, he'd been joking. Her face heated. "I don't know about that." Dahlia slipped out of the office and they walked to the entryway where her winter gear was hanging. To her surprise, Ike helped her on with her coat. She might as well add "thoughtful" to his list of positive qualities. "I stayed home with my kids, so I haven't worked in a long time." She pulled on gloves and her hat as he opened the front door and gestured for her to go first.

The sun was out but that woodsy heavy scent in the air promised more snow would be on the way soon. Dahlia led the way down the porch steps and started to walk on the plowed part of the driveway.

"Staying home with your kids sounds like work to me." Ike fell in step beside her. "How old are they?"

"Ollie is five and Maya is eight." Her heart settled a bit talking about the kids. They were always an easy topic of conversation—the thing she knew most about in the world. "And it is a lot of work. But I love it. It feels like the most important job I could be doing right now." Now that they were both in school, she'd considered going back to work, at least part time. Jeff had tried to talk her out of it, though. He seemed to like that she could be on call to pick them up from school whenever they were sick or to help with projects like the Christmas cookies. *I don't mind paying you alimony all the way until they're ready to leave the nest*, he'd said in his good-natured way.

At the time it had felt like a gift, a relief when she was overwhelmed with everything else the divorce entailed—dividing up everything into two separate households, drawing up custody agreements, preserving the kids' sense of family—but now it felt more…oppressive. Why shouldn't she find an outlet for herself? Why shouldn't she pursue something that would give her financial independence?

"My mom stayed home with us too," Ike said, pausing outside the barn door. "And I've never known a harder worker."

Dahlia let the last bit of nerves go. Ike didn't seem to be trying to charm her now. He was easy to talk to. Yes, he was good with words. But they seemed to come from a genuine place. Not like Jeff who was always trying to impress people with his wit and charisma. "Did you grow up around here?" Had she met him at some point during her childhood?

"Nope." He opened the barn door for her and followed her inside. "I grew up in Arizona. But I've always been obsessed with snow."

Dahlia laughed. "I supposed you didn't see much of it there?"

"None." He walked over and flipped on the light switch, illuminating the exposed bulbs that hung overhead. "I didn't see snow for the first time until my parents brought me out to Colorado for a ski trip when I was twelve. And after that, I was hooked. I did my undergrad and medical school in Boulder, and then did my residency in Denver."

A glimpse inside his story piqued her curiosity. "But you didn't want to stay in Denver?" As a doctor he'd likely make more money in a larger city. Then again, Ike didn't seem to be the type who cared much about money. Every time she'd seen him he'd been dressed casually. And his truck certainly wasn't fancy.

"I wanted more snow." He grinned, that playful glow coming back to his eyes. "And I wanted to be in a small town where I could get to know my patients as people outside of the office." He laughed again, a low deep rumbling sound that brought rivulets of warmth cascading through her. "Basically, I wanted what I never had—the freezing-cold, small-town life."

Dahlia found it easy to laugh with him. "I'm in the same boat. I was born in Savannah, but I ended up in Minnesota."

"I guess we have something in common then." He glanced around the cluttered space. "So where should we start?"

Oh, right. She'd been so into what he was saying she'd forgotten all about their project. "I guess the first thing we need to do is sort through the junk and make a trash pile." At least that's what she'd outlined on the spreadsheet. Not that she wanted to pull it out again and highlight her idiosyncrasies. He likely already recognized her extreme anal retentiveness, but luckily it didn't seem to bother him. Not like it had Jeff. Even though her ex had always relied on her to organize their lives, he'd always complained about her obsession with details, too. He'd complained she wasn't fun or spontaneous.

She did her best to shake herself out of the past, but that was much more difficult to do at the Juniper Inn. Sassy was right. She had more time to reflect here, and, while she'd made sure to cover up the wounds her divorce had left behind, they were much more difficult to hide when she didn't have to worry about keeping up a front for her kids. It was tempting to blame the problems in their marriage on Jeff, but she couldn't pretend Jeff wasn't right about her. She didn't know how to be spontaneous. She never veered away from the plan. But maybe she should start…

"A trash pile sounds like the perfect place to start." Ike drifted over to the stacks of stuff outlining the wall. On her walk earlier, Dahlia had stopped in to see what they were dealing with, so she already knew there were scraps of wood and old lawn maintenance tools and half-broken lawn ornaments scattered around. The old sleigh they'd used for the Christmas extravaganza years ago was still parked near the back of the space, and thankfully it seemed to have been protected from the elements and any rodents that happened to be residing in here.

"Looks like a lot of this can head right into the dumpster." Ike lifted a few broken boards off the stack, checking both sides before starting a new pile closer to the door.

"That's what I was thinking." Once they had the space cleared up and cleaned out, Rose could figure out what she wanted to do for decorations. Well, Rose and her best friend Colt. Dahlia had to smile. "Sassy has an old truck parked up at the house. Maybe we should drive it down here so we can load everything up and bring it over to the dumpster." Lord knew, she wouldn't be carrying all that scrap wood. Who knew what types of critters they would find. She'd already seen three spiders and Ike had only started going through things.

"Sure." He lifted some rusted sheet metal and dragged it over to the trash pile.

Dahlia moved in to help sort through Sassy's collection of old gardening tools and broken flowerpots, glad she had on some heavy-duty gloves. "What's this?" She pulled a few cracked two-by-fours off a huge log sign. "Oh, wow." Though grime covered the surface, she could still read the words:

The Juniper Inn

Breathe in the Magic

"That's quite the sign." Ike knelt and brushed away some of the dirt that had marred the words.

"It used to hang on a post right where you turn off the highway." Dahlia crouched next to him. "I wondered what had happened to it." Seeing it now brought memories flooding back again. "It was always the first thing we would see when we were a half mile down the road. The three of us would argue over who spotted it first." She distinctly remembered elbowing her sisters so they'd be distracted, and she could point out the sign before anyone else saw it. "I wonder why Sassy took it down." Sure, it had gotten old, but with a little work it could be restored.

"I'm guessing it's just like other things around here." Ike stood. "The time, the weather, things tend to wear out after a while. This place would be a lot to manage on your own."

"I wish I would've gotten in touch with Sassy years ago," Dahlia admitted. "I mean, we loved her. She was so important in our lives when we were young, but the older we got, the busier we got. And…she had some kind of falling out with our mother. So I guess I always felt like it would be disloyal somehow to reach out to Sassy." She'd also figured her aunt didn't want anything to do with them. Her mom had said as much on more than one occasion.

"I always wondered about her family." Ike studied the sign again. "She never said much but I figured she had to have some family somewhere. Although she does seem to make everyone she meets her family."

"Did you meet her at the office?" Instead of continuing with the cleanup, Dahlia faced the man she'd been so unsure about.

"No, actually." Ike dragged the sign to the wall and stood it up. "When I moved to town two years ago, Sassy was the first person I met." He went back to sorting through the stack of wood. "I'd just bought the practice, but I hadn't found a place to live, so I was staying in my van."

Okay, that was a little creepy.

Upon looking at her face, Ike laughed. "I know. It's a really nice van, if that helps. A Mercedes Sprinter. So more like a camper than a van."

"That does help." Was she smiling too much?

"Anyway, your aunt was doing some volunteer work on a trail near where I was camping."

That sounded like Sassy.

"When she wandered into my camp, she gave me the third degree, and when she found out I was the new doctor in town, she demanded I come and stay at the inn. She said the town couldn't have a doctor living in a van."

"Camper van," Dahlia corrected. A Mercedes at that. "Yep, that sounds like my aunt. She's always been openhearted and generous."

He grunted out an agreement as he hauled more trash to

the pile. "At first she wouldn't let me pay rent, but she came around."

"I'll bet." Something told her Ike could be quite convincing when he wanted to be. "Do you still have the camper van?"

"Oh, yeah." He walked back over and stood across from her. "I take it touring every once in a while. Just hop in when I have some vacation time and see where I end up."

"That sounds awful." She slapped a hand over her mouth, but Ike only laughed again.

"I take it you're more of a planner."

That was one way to put it. "I don't think I've ever gone anywhere without having the place mapped, without having everything scheduled down to the second." Part of that was how she was wired, but it only got worse after she had babies. Her life had changed fast, and it didn't take long for her and Jeff to drift apart. Maya had been colicky and she'd had reflux. Then there had been the allergy issues with Ollie. With the long hours Jeff had worked, she'd been on her own to take care of the kids, to keep them healthy, to make sure they hit every developmental milestone. And, yes, admittedly she got swept away in those roles. So much so that hadn't made much time to take care of her marriage.

"Well, you should try it sometime. Just getting in the car and seeing where you end up. I highly recommend it." His gaze held hers, and Dahlia was sure something passed between them. Only she couldn't decipher what.

"I have an idea…"

Uh-oh. "Okay…" She did her best to keep an open mind.

"Why don't we restore the sign for Sassy?" He led Dahlia to where it stood, propped up against the wall. "We could repaint it, make it look more modern and inviting. And sand it down some."

"You lost me at repaint." He clearly didn't know her, but she would clue him in. "I don't have one artistic bone in my body." That was all Rose. Even Mags had been bestowed with a creative spirit, but somehow it had completely skipped her.

"I don't believe you." Ike posted his hands on his hips looking all doctorly and serious. "Everyone has some spark of artistry inside them." His grin teased her. "Even if it's buried way down deep."

"I don't think—" Her phone rang, cutting off the protest. She quickly dug it out of her back pocket and saw Jeff's name flash on her screen. "I have to get this." Backing away, she brought the phone to her ear eager to hear an update from Maya or Ollie. "Hi—"

"You need to talk some sense into your son." Jeff's voice had a tight, annoyed undertone that always signaled impending disaster.

Great. Dahlia turned away and ducked into a corner where Ike hopefully couldn't hear what was about to transpire.

"What's the problem?" she asked, keeping her voice low.

"Ollie is being completely unreasonable," her ex-husband barked. "We're out to dinner and he's throwing a massive fit right in the restaurant."

Dahlia calculated the time. It would be late in the evening there. "Why are you eating out now?" Seriously, Jeff should know by now that Ollie had to be in bed before eight or he turned into a Gremlin.

"People eat dinner late here," he snapped. "And everyone else in this restaurant is acting civilized and reasonable. Everyone except for him."

"He's five." Dahlia could count the number of times they'd had this conversation. Jeff had never wanted kids he had to teach and nurture. He'd wanted kids who were already adults. But having that conversation wouldn't benefit either one of them right now. "What am I supposed to do about it?"

"Talk to him." There was a shuffling sound, which meant Jeff hadn't waited for an answer.

"Mooommmeeee," Ollie wailed through the speaker.

"Hi, sweetheart." Dahlia peeked over her shoulder. Ike had busied himself with resuming their trash-sorting chore.

"I hate it here! I hate it!" her son lamented. "I hate this yucky food and I hate how it smells and I hate that you're not here!"

"I know, honey." The familiar sadness cracked her heart open again. With as many times as that had happened over the last year, it was a wonder she hadn't fallen completely apart. "I don't like that I'm not there either." Though she had gotten more okay with not being Jeff's wife, it still weighed on her that they were no longer a family. "Daddy said you're at a restaurant," she said in her most soothing tone. "What are you having to eat there?"

"All they have here is stinky cheese!"

Dahlia squeezed her eyes shut. "You're eating cheese?" Seriously? She'd given Jeff a complete list of Ollie's allergies before the trip.

"Cheese is all they eat here," she heard Jeff growl in the background.

Immediately, her jaw tightened. "Can you please put Daddy on the phone?"

More shuffling and then Jeff started in on her. "What am I supposed to do—"

"You need to stop feeding him dairy," she interrupted. "He's lactose intolerant, in case you forgot. It's no wonder he's acting up." The reaction in his body had always made Ollie high-strung and anxious. "You feed him more dairy and acting out will be the least of your concerns." It wouldn't be long before her ex-husband and his newer model girlfriend were up to their elbows in diarrhea.

"Fine." Jeff sighed. "I won't feed him any more dairy."

"That will help." This trip was his chance to finally step up and be what his kids needed him to be. As much as she hated being away from them, they needed to start relying on their dad. "I have to go—"

"Wait." Her ex's voice softened. "I need you to talk him down, Dally," he begged. "He always listens to you. This is a nice restaurant and I think they're about ready to kick us out."

She almost hung up on him. Almost. But how could she punish Ollie for his father's poor decision-making? "Put him on the phone," she said instead.

"Thanks. I owe you one." Actually, he owed her more like five hundred, but she didn't say so.

"Mommy?" The anger in Ollie's voice had collapsed into sadness.

"Hi, sugar," she soothed. "I know it's hard, baby. And I know you're not feeling good, but do you think you can do something for me?"

"What?" he whined.

"Do you think you can look all around that restaurant and remember every detail?" Tears sprang to her eyes. This was the longest she'd ever been away from her children, and she'd give anything to pull him into her arms right now. "I want to know what it looks like, what kind of people are there, what kind of music is playing. Because I've never been to France, sweetie, and I need you to tell me everything about it."

"It's not a very nice place," he grumbled. "It's so boring. We have to walk around and look at stuff all day. And when I say my feet hurt, Daddy yells at me."

"No, I don't," she heard in the background.

Dahlia's throat ached with unshed tears. "I know that's how you feel now. But maybe you'll feel differently when you get to tell me all about it. It'll be like you're sharing the adventure with me." Ollie loved a good adventure. He loved a good adventure story even more. "I know! You can make up a story. Right now, sitting in that restaurant." That would distract him.

"What'd you mean?"

"Well…" Dahlia glanced around. "What if a mouse bungee jumped into the restaurant through the window on a noodle or something? What do you think would happen?"

"Hmmm." Her son considered the idea. "That would be kind of funny. Or what if it was a pigeon? A pigeon could fly in the window!" The idea seemed to excite him.

"Yes, that's perfect," she agreed. "That would make a great story."

"And then the pigeon could get stuck in Jade's hair!" Ollie exclaimed.

Dahlia pressed a fist against her mouth to keep from laughing. "Maybe you should change Jade's name in the story though," she suggested.

"I really miss you, Mom," Ollie said abruptly.

This time she couldn't stop a few tears from slipping out. "Oh, honey. I really miss you, too." Her throat ached she missed him so much. "But I want you to collect all the details and pictures and stories you can so you can bring them home to me. Can you do that?"

"I think so." At least he wasn't whimpering anymore. "I'll really try."

"Okay, baby. Finish thinking up that story and you can tell it to me when you call tomorrow. How does that sound?"

"That sounds good." He gasped. "Oh! Maybe the pigeon could steal a spaghetti noodle from that funny old man's plate over there!"

Dahlia pictured the embarrassment that was likely on Jeff's face right about now. "That would be so funny. Just make sure you keep your voice down while you make up the story, okay?"

"Okay, Mommy! I can't wait to tell you tomorrow! It's going to be a good one!"

"I can't wait either," she murmured. "I'll talk to you real soon."

"Okay! Bye!"

The line clicked, and Dahlia turned around, stuffing the phone into her pocket. The pile of junk seemed to be miraculously sorted. She walked over just as Ike dusted off his gloves. "You weren't totally honest with me earlier," he said, eyeing her with what appeared to be disappointment.

"What?" She thought back through their conversation. "I'm so sorry. I don't know—"

"You definitely have a creative bone in your body." A smile broke through his serious expression.

He must've heard her whole conversation. "Oh, no. My son is creative." And she'd learned how to encourage that in him. "But I've got nothing to offer in that department."

Ike seemed to take that as a challenge. "We'll see about that," he said, handing her a paintbrush.

"I'm not kidding." She went to hand the brush back to him. "Painting totally stresses me out." Anything creative stressed her out, and Ike didn't need to see her obsessing over paint lines and symmetry.

"But you've never painted with *me*. I promise it won't be stressful at all." He waved her over to an old table set up in the corner where he'd already laid out the sign and a few cans of paint. "All we have to do is fill in the spots where the color is chipped or faded."

All they had to do? "You clearly don't know me at all."

"Maybe not, but I'd like to know you." His gaze intensified on hers.

I'd like to know you, too. She couldn't find the courage to say the words out loud.

Ike stepped up to the table and dipped his brush into the red color, but she kept her distance. Without even seeming to pause, Ike started to flick the brush over the wood.

"Oh, be careful." His lack of precision with the brush moved her to the table. "You can't go out of the lines…"

The man stopped abruptly and grinned at her, seeming to take that as a challenge. "Oh yeah?" He refocused on the sign and slashed a big red line right through the middle.

"Hey!" That flick of the brush had gone way outside the lines. "You messed it up." She looked around for a paper towel or anything she could use to clean off the red paint. Ike set down his brush and walked around the table, standing directly across from her. "It's easy to fix." He nodded toward some sandpaper. "Once it dries, we'll sand it down and try again."

That made her feel a little better. "You can do that?"

"Sure." Ike put his hand over hers and guided the brush into the red paint. "It's okay to make mistakes. It's okay to go outside the lines." His hand moved hers down to the sign. "Go ahead. Try it."

A drop of red paint landed smack dab in the center of the wood. Dahlia glanced at Ike's face, her heart pounding a little harder.

He nodded his encouragement but let go of her hand. "Go ahead. No one's gonna care if you make a mess."

On a wild impulse, Dahlia swooshed the paintbrush over the wood, drawing a thick red line directly through the center. Straight lines were her specialty. This time she raised her eyebrows at him. "Is that what you had in mind?"

Laughing, Ike reached up and touched the paint. "Not exactly. But I have a feeling you're full of surprises," he said. And somehow, he made that sound like a good thing.

Chapter Fourteen

Magnolia

When Dean Martin came over the loudspeaker singing "Silver Bells," you knew it was going to be the perfect shopping trip.

Magnolia pushed her cart into the produce section, wandering aimlessly from the bins of apples to the pomegranates to the stacks of bananas, grabbing a selection of each as she went. Sure, she'd come in for baking supplies, but this beautiful display of ripe fruit seemed to stir up a craving. Maybe her blood sugar was low or something. Probably, since she'd been fighting off some weird stomach bug lately.

Ohhh, look at those red pears. She paused next to the bin and picked one up, instantly caught in the memory of when she'd made Eric spiced red wine poached pears for dessert on their fourth anniversary. They didn't have money to go out—not with all of the funds they'd spent on the latest treatment, but it hadn't mattered. They'd both been hopeful starting a new round of IVF. Instead of going out for a fancy dinner, she'd made him filet mignon and herbed butter lobster tails. They'd spread a blanket out in the living room and had a romantic picnic right there on the floor, and when she'd brought out the pears, Eric had fed her a bite telling her it didn't matter where they were—if they were on the floor at home or if they were at a three-star Michelin restaurant—as long as he was with her he would be happy.

Longing pressed in against her heart, somehow sneaking past the numbness that had shut down her feelings for so long. Her eyes filled with tears and she couldn't stop them from falling. She must look so ridiculous standing here staring at a pear, but she didn't care. Eric had always said things like that to her. It doesn't matter as long as we're together. But they weren't. Not now.

Still holding the pear, she dug her phone out with her other hand and opened to the last text he'd sent earlier that morning. I miss you. That was all it said. I miss you too, she typed back, realizing it was true. She missed him. She missed *them*.

As if it would help her hold on to the memory, she took one of Sassy's reusable produce bags out of her purse and picked out more pears, then stashed them carefully in the cart. Thankfully this small-town market didn't have the same crowds as the grocery store back home. No one seemed to look at her strangely for taking a moment to reflect on a pear. Everyone else appeared to be taking their time too, smiling as they passed, humming along with Dean Martin. Mags inhaled deeply, embracing the emotions. The longing for her husband, the hope that maybe her heart had started to thaw. It felt good to feel something.

Magnolia steered the cart past the bakery section—because none of those cookies would be as good as her own—and veered into the baking aisle. She paused to pull out the list of what she would need to get started on the first batches of cookies—old-fashioned molasses made with browned butter, the stained-glass cookies Sassy had taught her to make the year she'd turned eight, and the chocolate-mint snowballs that would conclude round one of her baking. *Let's see…*She perused each item on the list. She'd need more baking soda—

"No! No, Mommy!" a toddler screamed nearby. "I want that one!"

Trying not to be too obvious, Mags peered toward the teeny voice. At the other end of the aisle, a young mother knelt down to speak to what looked like a three- or four-year-old little boy. "We can't use that mix, honey. It has gluten. That'll make you sick. Remember?"

"I want this one!" the boy howled stomping his foot. A tiny wail sounded from an infant car seat sitting in the cart.

"Oh, no." The mother scrambled to stand up. "Hold on, honey. Sissy's awake." She fussed with the car seat and lifted a pink bundle into her arms.

As per usual when she saw a baby, Mags succumbed to the distinct squeeze of her heart. Oh, how she wanted to feel that weight and warmth in her arms. How she wanted to pull her crying baby in against her chest, gently shushing him or her like the young mother was doing now. Mags bent her head as though looking over her list, but really her gaze kept drifting back to the mother. The woman who was part of a club Mags so desperately wanted to join.

"I want this cake for my birfday!" the little boy yelled, as though trying to compete with his sister's cries. "This one! Mine! Mine! Mine!" Now he started to jump up and down, his winter boots clomping loudly on the tiled floor.

"Honey, we can't." The mom's voice had grown more frantic as she tried to sway and soothe the baby.

Between the boy's shouts and the baby's heart-wrenching cry, Mags could no longer hear Dean Martin. Other people had started to stare—stopping at the ends of the aisle and then making a quick turn to avoid coming any closer. Mags, however, pushed her cart over and knelt next to the boy. "Your birthday is coming up?" she asked.

He instantly stopped screaming and stared at her with the largest pair of blue eyes she'd ever seen.

Finally, he nodded.

"How old are you going to be?" Mags asked, smiling up at his mom. The young woman smiled back, still bouncing the baby.

"Free." He held up four fingers and then quickly adjusted them back to three. "Free days after Christmas I'll be free."

"Wow." She widened her eyes. "You're going to be a big boy then, aren't you?"

He nodded again, and then looked at the cake box he held in his hands as though he'd forgotten about it.

Mags studied it, too. It was one of those confetti cake mixes—bland and run-of-the-mill. She could do so much better. "So, you need a really cool cake for your birthday, huh?"

"This one has sprinkles." The boy held out the box for her to see.

Yes, sprinkles and food dye and gluten and also a ton of preservatives.

"Well, buddy, I happen to be a baker, and I would love to make you a very special gluten-free birthday cake." She'd always dreamed about making kids cakes and had even taken a few custom orders for friends over the last few years.

"For real?" The boy's face lit up.

"Oh, I'm not sure we could afford that." His mom stepped forward, still bouncing the baby. She was maybe a few years younger than Mags, her blond hair tied back into a ponytail and a happy tiredness settled in around her eyes.

"I won't charge you anything." Mags stood and faced her with another smile. "I love to make kids' cakes." She glanced at the boy. "I could easily make you a super-duper sprinkle cake. Or even cupcakes so everyone could have their own. Would you like that?"

The boy's nose crinkled. "Would there be red sprinkles?"

"For sure," Mags promised. "And we could get some blues ones and green ones…"

"Wow." He started to bounce as if the excitement was too much for him. "Can I have her sprinkle cupcakes, Mama? Please? Please? Please?"

"I couldn't ask you to do that." The mom had snuggled the soothed baby against her chest. "Not for free. It's too much."

"I want to." It would help to fill the emptiness she'd lived with since the last failed attempt at in vitro. "I happen to have a lot of extra time on my hands this week. It would be fun. Really."

"Are you sure?" Tears brightened the woman's eyes. "Thank you so much. That's incredibly kind of you."

Mags smiled. "I'm Magnolia," she said, holding out her hand.

"Jess." The young mom shifted the baby so she could shake Mags's hand, and then she uncovered the little bundle's lovely face. "This is Lola."

"And I'm Patrick," the boy said proudly, edging in between Mags and the baby. "Patrick Flemming."

"Nice to meet you Patrick Flemming." Mags reached out and shook his little hand. "I'm going to make you the most amazing birthday cupcakes you've ever seen." They were already coming together in her mind. She'd frost them with a thick white buttercream and she could make the sprinkles herself with egg whites, powdered sugar, and organic food coloring.

"I can't wait to see it!" The boy threw his arms around her

waist, hugging her tight. "Thank you, thank you, thank you! Wait till my friend Thomas sees!"

Both laughing and fighting off tears, Mags hugged him back. "You're so welcome."

"You have to let me pay for the ingredients, at least." Jess settled baby Lola back into her car seat and reached for her purse.

"No, don't worry about that." She reached down to ruffle Patrick's hair. "Think of it as a birthday gift."

He stared up at her, his mouth gaping. "But I don't even know you," he whispered. Then his eyes brightened. "Are you my fairy godmother?"

"Yes." Jess knelt down in front of her son and planted a kiss on his nose. "I do believe we've both just met our fairy godmother." She stood back up, leaning closer to Mags. "I couldn't bake my way out of a paper bag."

"My mom's cookies feel like they're going to break my teeth," Patrick confessed sadly.

Mags chuckled along with Jess.

"It's true." The woman shook her head. "No matter how hard I try they turn out like hockey pucks every time."

"Well, it's all about the flour and baking powder," Mags explained. "Sometimes baking soda too, depending on how the dough is looking. The altitude makes it more challenging."

The boy gasped. "You can teach my mom how to make cupcakes and maybe cookies too!" He tugged on the hem of Mags's coat. "Please, please, please! You have to teach her so she can keep making me stuff!"

Jess laughed again, shaking her head. "I'm sure Magnolia has better things to do than to teach me how to bake."

Actually... "I'm pretty open at the moment." Minus planning

the desserts for the extravaganza and working on Betty with her sisters. "I'll tell you what. We can make the cupcakes together and then you can even help me decorate them."

Patrick narrowed his left eye and looked up at her. "Really?"

"Yes." Mags knelt down to his level again. She couldn't get over those darling eyes. "You can help put the frosting on and all the sprinkles."

"Please, Mom." He folded his hands together in front of his chest like a little angel. "Please, please, please."

"If you're sure..." Jess almost looked like she was afraid to believe, too.

"I'm more than sure." Mags stood back up with purpose. "I'm staying at the Juniper Inn with my aunt."

"Sure. I know right where that is." Jess's smile hinted that she might be fond of the place. "It's beautiful. Everyone says Sassy is the cornerstone of this town, but I haven't met her yet. We've only just moved here, so we don't know many people. We haven't gotten out much with the baby. It's been hard to make friends."

"Perfect, this will be a great opportunity for you to get acquainted with her." Sassy would have the young woman acquainted with everyone in town in no time. "Why don't you three come over on the twenty-third?"

"Yes! We can! Right, Mom?" Patrick launched himself at his mother. "We can come on Thursday!"

"Sure, honey. That should work." She rested her hand on Patrick's shoulder. "This move has been so tough for us. I don't know how to thank you."

"No thanks necessary," Mags told her, meaning every syllable. "I love to bake. Especially for someone who will appreciate it so much."

"I 'preciate it!" Patrick hugged her waist again, and Mags got all teary despite herself. Kids were like little packages of joy leaking out happy feelings wherever they went.

"All right, Patrick. We should get your sissy home." Jess peeled him away from Mags and gave her one more grateful smile. "We'll see you on Thursday."

"I'm looking forward to it." She hoped her voice didn't sound as watery as her eyes felt.

After a final wave, Patrick reluctantly followed his mother down the aisle and Mags went about her shopping. She found everything she needed to make Patrick's epic birthday cupcakes, including the gluten-free flour blend and the food coloring. As she rounded the corner to the checkout stations, her legs suddenly felt like lead. Good God almighty she was exhausted. Normally she could spend an hour in the grocery store and leave still feeling like she was ready to run a marathon...okay not a marathon. She detested running, but shopping and thinking about baking usually gave her energy. Right now, though, she could climb into bed and take a long winter's nap.

Yawning, Mags unloaded her cart and went through the checkout, making polite conversation with the clerk.

On the drive home, she had to open the chocolate chips she'd bought so she could munch on something to keep herself awake. After she'd parked the car in front of Sassy's driveway, she loaded up her arms with groceries, making sure she would only have to make one trip, and stumbled her way into the house.

"Oh goodness!" Sassy met her near the front door. "Let me take some of those, dear girl." She freed up Mags's right hand and led the way into the kitchen. Mags all but dropped the bags onto the table where her sisters were sitting and collapsed into a chair.

"Gluten-free flour?" Dahlia pulled the package out of a bag.

"It's a long story." Mags rubbed her temples. The warm glow that had engulfed her when she'd met Patrick and Jess still smoldered but the rest of her felt bone-weary tired. And she'd started to get a headache.

"Whatever is the matter?" Sassy asked, stashing the flour and sugar in a cabinet. "You don't look well."

"I don't feel well." That flu bug she'd been fighting off didn't want to leave her alone.

"You haven't been feeling well a lot lately." Dahlia seemed to assess her from across the table. "I wonder if you should go in and see Ike—I mean Dr. Songer."

Mags didn't miss the rosy pink hue that appeared on her sister's cheeks. Forget the headache, she wanted to know more about that blush on her sister's face. "How is Ike?" she asked, propping her chin on her fist.

"Dahlia painted with him," Rose blurted.

Mags nearly fell out of her chair. "I'm sorry, you *painted*?"

"With Ike," Rose confirmed before Dahlia could say a word.

Mags blinked at her sister. Dahlia loathed anything that had to do with the creative arts. She always said she appreciated seeing others' creativity, but she didn't have any herself. Sure enough, though, the evidence was all over the red paint flecks splattered on her hands.

"You really did paint!" She had to blink a couple times.

"With Ike!" Sassy sang from the stove. She set a teakettle on the burner. "And I couldn't imagine a more wonderful man to paint with."

Mags laughed. Suddenly the word "paint" had become quite the metaphor. "He's very good-looking," she murmured, watching Dahlia's face for a reaction.

"We painted a *sign*." Her sister huffed, wearing a mask of indifference. But if you asked Mags, her cheeks still seemed rosier than normal. "It's not like we were painting a romantic portrait of the Eiffel Tower in Paris together or something."

"Today it's a sign, tomorrow you're painting a portrait of the Eiffel Tower together. Maybe even in Paris," Mags teased. She couldn't resist encouraging her sister the tiniest bit. Dally had been divorced over a year now, and her sister deserved to have some fun.

"We're not talking about me." Dahlia straightened her back against the chair. "We're talking about your virus. You should get it taken care of before you infect the rest of us."

Mags didn't react to the irritability in her sister's tone. Dally always bristled when she got defensive. "I'll be fine. I'll go to bed early tonight and be good as new in the morning." She'd said that to herself the last three nights, and it still hadn't done any good.

"I brought a bunch of herbs with me," Rose started to rifle through her purse. "Some zinc. Oh! Here's some elderberry lozenges…"

"Tea will be a much better remedy than all that," Sassy insisted, joining them at the table with a tray. "I've added in some honey and cinnamon."

Mags inhaled deeply. She'd always loved her aunt's tea. Sipping from the warm mug, she glanced across the table at Rose. "I noticed we don't have any exterior decorations up yet." She'd wondered how things were going with Rose and Colt. From the looks of things, they didn't exactly seem to be jiving, and they didn't have much time to turn the inn into a Christmas wonderland.

Sure enough, her sister's face steeled. "We agreed through texting to divide and conquer."

Dahlia laughed. "Basically, Rose is drawing up a plan and Colt is responsible for doing all the work."

"But you were supposed to work together." Sassy cast a disapproving frown in Rose's direction. Mags remembered seeing that look directed at her a time or two during her childhood when they would bicker. It was a rare show of disappointment from her aunt. "That was the deal."

"He doesn't like me," her sister muttered.

Well, she had knocked over his display at the hardware store, but Mags decided not to bring that up.

"Colt has always been shy," Sassy said. "I can't believe you don't remember him. He spent so much time here when you were all young."

"I thought I recognized him." Mags still couldn't quite place him in her memories, but there was something about him that seemed familiar.

"Well I have no memory of him at all," Rose declared dramatically. "And I can't think of anything I would've done to deserve his attitude."

"The past isn't important now," Sassy insisted. "What's important is that we get this place in tip-top shape for the extravaganza. And that's going to mean all of us working together. Even if it's a bit uncomfortable."

"I'm not uncomfortable at all." A subtle shift in Rose's posture betrayed the words. "If this is how Colt wants to work together, it's fine by me." Her sister regally lifted her tea and took a delicate sip. "Besides, I've already started to work on Betty, too. I thought the trailer could act as a beautiful warming station where we could serve some of the goodies and hot chocolate during the extravaganza."

"Oh, that's a wonderful idea!" Sassy's eyes sparkled as though she'd forgotten all about Colt and Rose splitting their duties. Mags hadn't though. Something about Colt niggled at her. A memory she couldn't quite bring into focus. Had something happened between her sister and Colt when they were younger? And why had Colt spent so much time at Sassy's place?

"It will be perfect," Aunt Sassy went on. "I have some small heaters we can run to keep Miss Betty nice and cozy warm." Her aunt targeted Mags with a curious gaze. "What are you thinking for goodies?"

"It's all under control," Mags assured her. "I'll get started on the first couple of batches of cookies tomorrow." She just couldn't seem to find the energy to do it now. "And we'll start stockpiling everything in the freezer so we're ready to go for the big night."

In the meantime, she'd do a little digging to figure out why Colt was so familiar.

Chapter Fifteen

Rose

Once again, Rose's love for spontaneity and enthusiasm for a project had come back to bite her in the derriere. "Perhaps I was a little optimistic," she said as she scanned the piles of clutter that had been crammed into Betty's every nook and cranny over who knew how many years.

"I tried to tell you." Mags scooted herself onto the bench at the dinette table with her thermos of hot tea. "But I believe your exact words were, 'It will be fun!'"

Rose ignored her and pulled down a box from the top of the stack. "I don't remember us stockpiling this much stuff in here." There had to be at least fifteen boxes crammed in with the stuffed animals and books and dress-up clothes that had once belonged to them.

"Sassy mentioned she'd been using Betty for storage." Dahlia took the box from Rose's hands and set it on the table in front of Mags. "And I think we're all going to have to help to get through this mess before Christmas comes."

Rose appreciated the show of solidarity, but…wow. "I don't know if we could get through all this before Easter." Seriously.

She'd already sewed the new covers for the cushions, but when she'd been in here measuring the other day, she hadn't bothered to evaluate how they would actually clean the space out.

"It'll be no problem," Dally insisted, moving another box to the table. "Mags can go through the boxes while she sits here, and we can get started with the cleaning."

"Perfect." Mags tore open the first box. "Oh! Look, it's some of our old clothes."

Her excited squeal drew Rose over to the table. "Wow." She pulled out a pair of purple satin gloves. "I used to love wearing these." The gloves, the costume jewelry, the old-fashioned hats they'd bought with Sassy at the local antique shop. She pulled out a flashy red velvet pillbox hat with black netting and set it on her head.

"Soooo fancy." Mags declared, peering into the box and then selecting one for herself. She stood and moved in next to Rose, pulling her phone out of her pocket. "Selfie time."

Rose hardly had a chance to put on her best selfie smile before her sister snapped the picture. "I need to see that picture," she said, trying to get a look at her sister's phone screen.

"Absolutely not." Mags stuffed the phone back into her pocket. "You always look so glamorous. Doesn't it get a little exhausting sometimes?"

"Okay you two," Dally interrupted before Rose could admit that, yes, always putting herself together did get a little exhausting. "We have to keep working or we're never going to finish this. I have to meet Ike soon to go over some ideas for how we can spruce up Sassy's sad front porch."

"Ohhh," Mags crooned. "Meeting Ike again today, huh?" She selected an obnoxious leopard hat and plunked it onto her older sister's head. "I think you should wear this."

"Yes," Rose agreed, snapping a picture on her phone. "And this." She reached into the box and pulled out a long string of hideous fake pearls, carefully putting the necklace over her sister's hat.

"Very funny." Dahlia might've sounded a little miffed, but she was smiling.

"Come on. One more selfie." Mags wedged herself in between Rose and Dally and snapped a few more photos.

"We don't have time for this," Dally reminded them both with the stern bossy look she'd perfected throughout their childhood. "Back to work."

"Yeah, yeah, yeah." Mags sifted through a few more hats while Rose brought down another box from the top of the stack. This one hadn't been sealed, so she peeked between the flaps. "Sassy must not throw anything away." She reached in and pulled out a handful of old letters and cards.

"Yeah, that's the one thing that I wouldn't look forward to if we decide to keep this place." Dahlia closed up the box of dress-up clothes and moved it off to the side. "Think of how much work it would take to clean it out."

Rose had been purposely trying not to think about the work. "We agreed to wait until after Christmas to talk about the inn," she reminded them. None of them wanted the extra stress of thinking about taking on something else right now. But she wasn't ready yet to tell Sassy she didn't want the place, either.

"We're not considering keeping it though, right?" Mags asked, ignoring Rose. "There's no way I could live here. I love you two, but seriously…it's too cold."

"I don't know how it would work," Dahlia said, but Rose was only half listening. Inside the box, she'd discovered an envelope that had come from their mother. While Mags and Dally went on debating the pros and cons of keeping the inn, she opened the letter and started to read.

Sassy,

I received your last letter, and I have to say, I am very disappointed in your decision. You know exactly how I feel, and yet you don't seem to care. I didn't want it to come to this, but I'm sure you will understand that I have to protect my daughters from certain influences. In light of your choices, we won't be able to come and visit you at the Juniper Inn anymore. In fact, I think it is best to go our separate ways. We certainly no longer share the same values, as evidenced by your willingness to move forward despite my protests. After everything we've talked about, I can't get past this. I'm sorry. Please take care of yourself.

Lillian

The words turned Rose's stomach as she read them again. Protect her daughters? What in the world did that mean?

"We don't have time to read every letter," Dahlia informed her.

Rose silently handed her sister the letter, still turning those words over and over in her mind.

Dahlia impatiently held the letter in front of her face, but immediately her eyes widened, and her lips parted with surprise.

"What?" Mags demanded. "What did you find?"

"It's from Mom." Dahlia handed the letter over to Mags and shared a look with Rose. They waited for Mags to read it.

"What was she trying to protect us from?" Mags turned the letter over as though looking for the answer on the back.

"I have no idea." Rose couldn't begin to imagine what choice Sassy had made that would've driven their mother to write that letter. "It makes no sense." All Sassy had ever done was dote on the three of them. Rose took the letter back from Mags. The words were so cold—especially the *I'm sorry*. Their mother hadn't sounded too sorry.

"What could possibly be so important that she would walk away from her own sister?" Dahlia sat across the table from Mags, but Rose couldn't sit. She knelt down by the open box and pawed through the papers, looking for anything else that could help them understand. All she found were Christmas cards and old letters from guests who raved about the inn. There were no other letters from her mother.

"Every time I've brought it up with Sassy, she's refused to talk about it," Dahlia said, staring down at Rose.

"Maybe she's embarrassed," Mags suggested. "Maybe she doesn't want us to know what decision she made. It must've been a pretty big deal."

"Not necessarily." Rose pushed off the floor of the trailer and began to pace. "You know how Mom is. If you don't agree with her—if you don't do what she wants she gets so upset. It sounds to me like Sassy stood up to her and Mom booted her out of our lives for it." They hadn't even gotten a choice. When their Christmas plans had come up that year, their mother had simply told them they wouldn't be going to see Sassy.

"We all know Mom can be pretty difficult," Mags said. "But, still, she didn't make that decision out of the blue. Something obviously happened."

"And we're going to find out what." Rose marched over to the door and pulled on her coat. "We deserve to know the truth, and we deserve to know it now."

"Whoa." Dahlia stood and followed her to the door. "We don't want to ambush poor Sassy. It's pretty clear she doesn't want to talk about it."

"It's time we know." She tucked the letter into her pocket. "I'm not going to ambush her. But I am going to ask her what happened. I want to understand." They were adults now, and Sassy had brought them back here. It was time. "Maybe if we figure out what happened we can get Mom and Sassy to patch things up."

Mags and Dahlia shared a skeptical look, but they didn't argue.

"You go," Dally said, reaching for another box. "We'll stay here and keep working."

"Chickens." But Rose didn't need their help for this conversation. And Dally was right. It shouldn't feel like an ambush. "I'll be back down after Sassy and I have a little chat." She slipped outside into the cold and slogged through the knee-deep snow up to the main house.

By the time she slipped in through the front door, she had a whole script planned out. She'd pull the letter out of her pocket, lay it flat on the kitchen table and ask her aunt why their mother had written it. Rose pulled off her boots and coat, and then wound through the living room where the murmur of voices stopped her before she could turn into the kitchen.

"You have to give her a chance," Sassy was saying. "She's changed a lot, you know. And so have you, for that matter."

"This has nothing to do with Rose."

Colt? Why were he and Sassy discussing her? She moved closer to the kitchen wall, trying to hear.

"I'm telling you, Sassy. They shouldn't have this place. They've ignored you all these years. Now they're back for one Christmas and you're just going to give it to them?"

The passion in Colt's voice took her back a step. For hardly speaking two words to her, he sure had a lot to say to Sassy. What business was it of his?

"Let me buy it from you," he went on. "Fair and square for market value. I'll make something out of it again. You know I will."

Rose's jaw dropped. The nerve of that man! Trying to buy the inn right out from under them.

"The past isn't their fault," Sassy said in a hushed tone. "They didn't have any say in what Lillian decided, and I won't hold it against them."

"But they obviously don't care about this place," Colt argued. "Not like I do."

Rose fisted her hands, ready for a fight. How could he possibly know that? He hadn't even spent time with her or her sisters. He hadn't tried to get to know them at all.

"I know," Sassy murmured sadly. "You and I will always have such a special connection."

Rose nearly tripped over her sock-clad feet. A special connection? What kind of special connection could her aunt possibly have with Colt?

"But those girls are my family too," her aunt went on.

Wait just one minute. Her family *too*? What did that mean? Rose strained to keep listening.

"And I want to offer them this place. Something tells me they all need it. If they decide they don't want it, you know it's yours."

"I understand." A rustling warned that Colt might be getting up from the table, so Rose retreated back into the hallway and quickly shoved her feet into her boots, her heart pounding. Without bothering to grab her coat, she slipped out the door and stumbled in a clumsy jog all the way back down the hill to the trailer. Throwing open the door, she stepped back inside, heaving out breaths.

Mags and Dally froze.

"What is it? What happened?" Mags finally asked.

Rose stared at her sisters, still trying to process what she'd heard. "What if Colt is Sassy's son?"

Chapter Sixteen

Dahlia

Dahlia took in the shocked expression on Rose's face and found it hard not to shake her head.

Ever since her youngest sister was old enough to talk, Rose had thrived on drama, drama, drama. In fact, that had probably been one of Rose's first words. Combine that with her wild imagination and you got cockamamie theories about aunts who had secret sons.

"That's crazy." She took down another box off the stack and started to rifle through more dress-up clothes and costume jewelry. This one had been harder hit by the years, so she set it aside in the trash pile. "Colt is *not* Sassy's son." She glanced at Mags for confirmation, but a thoughtful look graced her other sister's heart-shaped face.

"I'm not sure it's crazy," Mags said slowly. "I know I remember him from our past. Now that I think about it, didn't we used to play hide-and-seek with a boy? It must've been Colt. Sassy said he was around here a lot when we would visit."

Rose scooted onto the bench seat across from Mags. "I heard him talking to Sassy in the kitchen. He's not happy she wants to give this place to us. And the way Sassy was talking to him…he's family. He has to be."

"We would know if Sassy had a son." There is no way their mother or their aunt would have kept a secret like that from them all these years.

"Maybe that's why Mom stopped talking to her!" Rose gasped. "Maybe she found out Sassy had a secret son that she'd never told Mom about, and Mom got so upset she vowed to never speak to Sassy again!"

This time Dahlia laughed. Thankfully Mags joined in. "You're right," Mags said. "She's crazy. Colt is probably just a neighborhood kid who grew up nearby."

"Exactly. And anyway, we don't have time to do any investigative work." Dahlia shoved another box of dress-up clothes aside, turning her attention back to the task at hand. "There's no way we're going to be able to clean out this trailer before the extravaganza. Not with all the boxes we still have to sort through. Plus, what are we going to do with all this stuff?"

Rose pouted as though she resented the change of subject, but then she shrugged and sent Dahlia a mischievous grin. "I asked Ike to meet us down here so we can load up some of it into his truck. He offered to bring it to the dumpster for us."

At the mention of Ike, a distinct quiver skittered down the length of Dahlia's spine. She'd actually enjoyed working with him the other day. Maybe a little too much. And now her fears had started to boil over again. There was no use in denying her attraction to the man. But what would happen if she let herself feel something for him?

"He should be here in about ten minutes," Rose went on, carefully watching Dahlia's face.

"Great idea," Dahlia said dismissively, looking through another box to deflect her sisters' stares.

"He seemed more than happy to help." Rose walked over. "Especially when I told him you would be here."

"Mmm-hmm." Dahlia continued with her rummaging. Whew, was it warm in here? She looked into the box again. "I think most of this can go straight into the dumpster."

There were a few dress-up items and hats they could save, for sentimental value. Maybe she could bring them to Maya. "I'll bet we can whittle this all down to one box." Her brain started shifted into administrative mode again. "Maybe I should start documenting everything we're finding." She searched a drawer in the tiny kitchen for a pad of paper.

"Why do you always do that?" Rose demanded, watching her from the dinette.

"Do what?" Dahlia located an old notepad that seemed on the verge of falling apart but it would do. Now she only needed a pen…

"Why do you always make yourself crazy busy when one of us brings up Ike?" Rose came over and stole the notepad out of her hands. "You're not very good at pretending, you know. I can tell you totally have the hots for the man. And I don't blame you, by the way."

"Me neither," Mags agreed heartily. "He's so…"

"Vigorous," Rose finished for her.

Dahlia had to laugh again. "Vigorous?" Well, there was a word for you. "Really? I hadn't noticed," she lied.

"What she means is that Ike is hot. Manly. And yet he's easy-going," Mags mused. "At least that's how it sounds from the way you described the little moose mishap when you two met."

"He's laid-back all right." Maybe even a little too laid-back for her. Look how her relationship with Jeff had turned out.

"Come on." Rose stacked her hands on her hips the same way she used to when she was three years old. "Don't tell me you haven't noticed that he's absolutely gorgeous."

"Fine. He's gorgeous." She'd done her best to fight off the blush, but heat seemed to spill across her cheeks. "And yes. He's manly, too." Not because he went to the gym every day like Jeff, but because a person could tell he worked outside. And he probably hiked all the time and climbed mountains for cripes' sake. "But Ike is not my type." It had been so long since she'd been on the dating scene that she wasn't sure she even had a type. "I'm fine on my own." Even as she said it, the words mocked her. She wasn't on her own. Her ex-husband still occupied far too much of her time. "My life is complicated enough, I don't need—"

"Exactly," Mags broke in. "Your life is complicated. But Ike is not. He's easygoing. Fun. Right now, all of your complications happen to be out of the country, so..." She wiggled her eyebrows.

Dahlia ignored the way the insinuation made her palms tingle. Instead of indulging her sisters' suggestions, she picked up a box and opened the door. "Ike and I are not—"

She quickly snapped her jaw shut at the sight of the man. He stood a few feet away outside. Good God, had he heard them talking?

"Hi there." He walked over with his good-natured smile. "I heard you ladies needed a garbageman."

Was that all he'd heard? Dahlia jerked her head to stare at Rose, her face flushing with humiliation. These camper walls were paper thin!

"Yes!" Rose pushed past Dalia and rushed out the camper door. "Thank you for coming, Ike. As you can see, we have about fifteen boxes that we'll have to haul over to the dumpster."

"No problem." He smiled that smile at Dahlia, the one that made it seem like the two of them shared a secret.

"Why don't you stack the boxes outside the door, and I'll load them into the truck?" Ike removed a pair of gloves from his coat pocket and pulled them on.

Rose eyed the junk pile. "It might take five trips. Or more."

"Nah." The man shrugged off any concern. "I'll get it in one."

"Sounds perfect, doesn't it, Dahlia?" Rose climbed up onto the step and nudged her in the ribs.

"Right. Yes," she said quickly. Then she moved deeper into the camper so Ike wouldn't be able to see the red roses blooming on her cheeks. "We'll start with this one." She shoved a box into Rose's arms with extra oomph.

"Geez." Her sister shot her an amused glare. "What's your problem?"

As if she didn't know.

"Girls, girls," Mags chastised, standing up from the dinette table. "Let's not keep Ike waiting. Let's get this done so I can get in a nap."

"I thought you already had a nap." Dahlia examined her sister's face.

"That was my midmorning nap. This will be my midafternoon nap." Her sister hoisted a box off the stack and set it by the door. "I can't seem to find any energy."

Probably because her sister had spent the last few days baking to prepare for the extravaganza. The freezer was slowly running out of space.

"Well, there's no time for naps," Rose declared. "After we get this mess cleaned out, we have a family mystery to solve." Her eyebrows peaked with expectation, but Dahlia simply shook her head.

"You watch too much *Real Housewives*," she said, setting aside a box of jewelry and clothes for Maya. They couldn't throw all of these old treasures away.

"I love the *Real Housewives*." Ike appeared at the doorway, peering inside where they stood.

Dahlia couldn't hold back a laugh. "Do you now?"

"Yes." He effortlessly lifted two boxes into his arms. "It's a true anthropological study," the man said before he disappeared with the boxes.

He had to be joking.

"Which *Real Housewives* is your favorite?" Rose called through the open door.

From somewhere outside, Ike answered, "*Real Housewives of Orange County* all the way."

"Me too!" Her younger sister squealed.

Oh, good Lord. "Maybe we can talk more about the *Housewives* after we get these boxes out of here." Dahlia nudged Rose toward the back of the camper.

"Or we can talk about it while we load the boxes." Without waiting for an answer, her sister snatched up another box from the discard pile and traipsed outside with it.

Dahlia only heard snippets of the latest *Real Housewives* gossip. She mostly hid in the camper and organized boxes as they went, and by the time an hour had passed, the camper sat mostly empty.

Usually cleaning out a space gave her a swell of satisfaction but standing in the empty trailer brought on a twinge of sadness. "It looks so different." Back when they'd played in here all that clutter had made it seem cozy and safe somehow.

"Yeah," Mags said through a yawn. "It actually looks clean."

Clean and hollow. And yet...she supposed that's how it should be. In order to repurpose a space, you had to wipe it clean— leaving little reminders of the past, maybe. Like the tic-tac-toe marks they'd penned onto Betty's wall. But you had to make room for new things, too. New experiences, new memories. She'd tried hard to keep things the same, even through all the changes of the last year, but maybe the same wasn't what she needed.

"That's it?" Ike stepped into the camper, crowding in with her and Rose and Mags. "I thought we'd be here another few hours," he joked.

"You're very efficient." Rose glanced at Dahlia as though waiting for her to agree.

"We appreciate your help," she said instead, tingles erupting in her cheeks. Ugh. She had to busy her hands with something, to distract herself from the power of those eyes...

"No problem." Ike glanced around as though making sure they'd really gotten everything. "Since we're done early, I'm gonna head over to the country-western bar in town. The Crazy Moose. I've got a friend playing a set there this afternoon. Anyone care to join me?" He seemed to let his gaze linger on Dahlia.

"Dahlia is free this afternoon," Rose blurted. "I would love to come but I texted Colt about meeting up to finish the outdoor decorations in an hour."

Uh-huh. Sure. Rose really wanted to finish the decorations. Her text had nothing to do with trying to devise a way for Dahlia to spend time with Ike.

"But Dahlia loves music, don't you?" Her younger sister didn't give her a chance to answer. "She was always going to concerts when we were younger."

Was she? Interesting. Dahlia didn't remember going to that many concerts. "Uh..."

"Well I don't know how good the concert will be," Ike said with a laugh. "Poor old Clyde is a patient of mine. I'd call his sound..." He paused as though searching for the right word. "Eclectic."

"It sounds fun, but I have a lot to do here, I'm afraid." Dahlia's jaw tightened around the words. She wasn't about to let Rose force her to go out on a date with this man. She'd go on a date when she was good and ready. Maybe. Probably...

"What do you have to do around here?" Mags asked, calling her out. "You've already cleaned out every room in Aunt Sassy's house."

"Not every room." Mags was as bad as Rose. "I still haven't even been in Sassy's master bedroom." She couldn't begin to imagine what a mess that was if the office had been any indication.

"Well it might be good for you to take a break," Rose said with a harrumph.

"You work too hard," Ike agreed.

Yes, she worked too hard. Because work wasn't complicated. Work was familiar. Work was distracting in the best way. If she worked she didn't have to try to navigate this attraction she felt to a man she'd only just met. She didn't have to think about what to say to him. Heck, she didn't have to talk to him at all if she worked.

"It'll be fun," he said. "I promise."

In desperation, Dahlia turned to Mags. Mags who'd always been the one she'd gone to with boy trouble or friend drama. This qualified as a sister emergency. "I suppose *we* can go." She couldn't do it alone, but if her sister came, there wouldn't be the pressure of a date lingering over her. She let her eyes plead with Mags.

"I'd love to go." Dahlia was likely the only one who noticed Mags's lengthy sigh. "It's been a while since I've been to an eclectic concert. I guess my nap can wait."

"Yes, it can." Dahlia half hugged her sister. "We'll have a great time." This would be much better than her sister sleeping away the afternoon. With everything she'd been through lately, Mags could surely use an afternoon out. And Dahlia could use the moral support.

"Great." The man held out his arm. "Shall we?"

He obviously meant it as a casual gesture, but that didn't stop Dahlia's heart rate from spiking. "Sure. Yeah. Let's go." She scampered out the door and into the snow, hoping the chill would snuff out the blush on her cheeks. What was it about Ike that made her feel so unsteady?

She didn't have time to figure it out before he led the way to his truck. Dahlia made sure to climb into the backseat of the extended cab before Mags could. Her sister gave her a look on her way past the window, as though she knew exactly why Dahlia had literally taken a backseat in this scenario.

What could she say? Small talk had never been one of her skills with a regular person. Throw a good-looking, incredibly charming man into the mix, and she was at a complete loss. Luckily, Mags never seemed to be at a loss for words.

"So, Ike," her sister began as he put the truck into gear. "You're a doctor, huh?"

"Last time I checked."

She couldn't see his face at the moment, but Dahlia could hear his grin.

"You must be staying pretty busy this season." Mags groaned. "I swear, I feel like I've been fighting off some weird flu since I got into town."

"Actually, it's been a pretty light flu season so far." He turned to glance at Mags as though giving her a quick assessment. "Maybe you should come into the clinic, get checked out."

"I'm sure it's nothing serious." Her sister waved off the concern. "I've just been tired and queasy. Must've picked up some kind of stomach bug on the flight here."

Was it really a stomach bug? Dahlia leaned forward. It was easier to join the conversation when it was focused on Mags. "But like you said, it's been a few weeks. I can't imagine you'd still be fighting something off *now*." She peeked at Ike for confirmation. He had such nicely shaped eyebrows…

"Yeah, that's weird," he agreed. "I haven't seen as much stomach stuff as I have respiratory this month."

"And none of us have gotten it," Dahlia pointed out, her worries growing. Mags hadn't been herself the whole time they'd been at Sassy's.

"Fine," her sister grumbled. "If I'm not feeling better in a few days, I'll stop by the clinic."

It sure sounded like an empty promise to Dahlia, but she'd keep on Mags. As the eldest sister, nagging came naturally.

Mags turned her attention back to Ike. "I'd imagine things are pretty quiet for a doctor in a small town like this."

"That's the way I like it." When they got to a stop sign he waved for another car to go through first. Dahlia couldn't remember the last time she'd driven a car without rushing somewhere. Even though she was habitually early, she constantly felt like she was running five minutes late when she drove the kids around.

"How did you know you wanted to be a doctor?" Dahlia surprised herself by asking the question. Surely, he'd struggled and stressed at some point in his life. Maybe in medical school?

"My dad was a doctor." Ike eased the truck forward, waving at someone who passed by on the other side of the street. "He inspired me."

"I'll bet he's proud of you." Mags seemed to be intrigued by Ike as well, but she kept stealing glances that Dahlia pretended to ignore. Her sister was likely assessing what kind of couple they would make.

"I'm sure he would be proud," the man said, his eyes steadily gazing at the road. "But he passed away a month after I turned twenty."

Dahlia gasped. "I'm so sorry." She had no idea. In all their conversations, he hadn't mentioned his father. But to lose him so young… "That's awful."

"It was pretty awful." Those eyes that always seemed to spark and dance dulled just a touch. "He had a heart attack at the gym. And he was a heart surgeon." Ike shook his head as though considering the irony. "He lived under too much stress. Always on call, always living for his job. He was good at it—one of the best, but it came at a cost." The truck stopped, and for the first time in a few minutes, Dahlia looked away from Ike. They'd already made it to the bar, and she hadn't even noticed. She'd been too captivated by his story. She was too captivated to move now. "That's why you wanted the small-town life?" So, he wouldn't end up like this father.

"Yes." He turned to peer back at her. "I loved medicine, and I knew I wanted to be a doctor, but I didn't want to end up where he did. Always stressed out, practically living at the hospital. I want to help people, but I also want balance. In some ways he gave me a gift when he passed away. I realized I get to choose what my future looks like. I get to choose what I want, but also— especially—what I don't want."

Those words resonated deep within her. Choose. She could choose something different for her life, too. She didn't have to consumer herself with PTA work and committees and Pinterest projects. "That is a gift," she half whispered. The inspiration to choose wisely. To hold your life in your hands and fight to live it the way you want to instead of waking up one morning and wondering how you got there.

Being here, hundreds of miles away from Dahlia the PTA mom's world, she could choose. She could choose to live a little. She could choose to let go. Maybe Ike could show her how.

Chapter Seventeen

Magnolia

S he should've chosen the nap.

Mags stepped one foot in the Crazy Moose and had the notion to spin on her heel and walk right back out. She had never been a bar snob—at least she'd never pegged herself as one, but this place was already packed and a yeasty beer smell seemed to overpower the space. "Is it usually this crowded here on a Friday afternoon?" Sheesh, listen to her. She sounded like a cranky old grandma.

Ike started to edge them through the crowd. "No, but the closer it gets to the holidays the more people around here tend to excuse themselves from work. There's an open table over there." He gestured to the corner over by the window and led the way, parting the crowd and greeting people as they walked through.

"Hey, doc!"

"Good to see you! Better to run into you at the bar than at your office."

Mags lost count of the people who paused to shake Ike's hand on their way past them. He was obviously very popular in town. She eyed her sister. Dahlia looked at the floor shyly, but in the truck, Mags had noticed a spark of interest in her sister's gaze.

As they made their way to an empty table, an older gentleman stepped in to shake Ike's hand. "I knew you'd make it," he said, a big grin smoothing the wrinkles around his mouth. He looked like he'd walked straight off the mountain, dressed in fringed leathers, his long white hair blanketing his shoulders.

"Ladies, let me introduce you to this afternoon's featured artist." Ike swung an arm around the man. "Clyde, these are my friends Dahlia and Magnolia."

"Any friends of Ike's are friends of mine too," he said, first shaking Dahlia's hand, then Mags's.

"What're you going to play?" Mags checked out the set up on the small stage a few feet away. There was a guitar, a banjo, and keyboard set up behind a microphone.

"All Johnny Cash all the time." Clyde leaned in, the pungent scent of pot circling around them. "You want to join me up there? I could use a female backup vocalist."

"Oh, no thank you." Mags laughed. That was the first time anyone had asked her to sing anything. "I appreciate the offer, but I'm afraid my singing would empty the place out pretty quickly." She glanced at Dahlia for confirmation, and the ice seemed to break away from her sister's expression.

"You don't want Mags singing," Dahlia said with a laugh.

"You all can dance then." Clyde hurried away, glancing over his shoulder. "Get everyone else out on the floor with you. I like to see people enjoying my music."

"I'm afraid I don't dance," Dahlia called, backing away from Ike like she'd suddenly spooked.

"Yes you do." Mags edged in behind her so her sister couldn't get too far away from a little peer pressure. This was why she'd come. Mags and Rose agreed that Dahlia needed a little push when it came to putting herself out there with Ike. Though for the life of her Mags couldn't figure out why Dally hesitated. The man obviously had a thing for their oldest sister. His eyes got as sparkly as a Disney prince's when he looked at Dahlia. Exactly like they were now.

"You loved dancing back in the day," she reminded her sister. Then she turned to Ike. "And she's a much better dancer than she's letting on." Ignoring the murderous glare in her sister's eyes she nudged Dally toward Ike. "She won a square-dancing trophy once."

Her sister's face turned red. "That was in sixth grade!"

Ike laughed. "Tell you what...we'll settle in and enjoy a drink first, then we can dance if anyone's up for it."

Mags would be sure she wasn't up for it.

"I'll head to the bar." Ike draped his coat over the back of a chair. "What can I get you two?"

"I'll take a ginger ale." She didn't need another stomachache like the one that had been plaguing her on and off since she'd gotten here.

"Chardonnay for me," her sister said with a distinct squeak in her voice.

While Ike headed off toward the bar, Mags plopped down into a chair.

Dahlia sat stiffly across from her. "My hands are shaking," her sister whispered.

"What?" She gave Dally a visual assessment. She looked terrified. "What're you so afraid of?"

"I haven't danced with a man other than Jeff in well over ten years," Dahlia hissed. "I have no idea what I'm doing. My heart is racing. I can't even seem to think straight!"

"Because you like him." Dahlia liked Ike as much as he liked her. Obviously. Or she wouldn't be freaking out right now.

"I'm a mom." Her sister stared hard at the table. "I'm a frumpy mom who's obsessed with spreadsheets and schedules and home organization blogs." A look of desolation tugged at the corners of Dahlia's eyes, and Mags couldn't stand it. She couldn't stand to see what Jeff had done to her sister.

"That's not all you are," she said sternly. "You are also beautiful, Dally. And you're smart and resourceful and you're devoted and you're worthy of a good man."

Her sister's gaze shifted, peeking toward the bar where Ike chatted easily with the bartender. "What if he doesn't like me? After he gets to know me, I mean? What if he doesn't like what he sees inside of me?"

"If Ike doesn't like what he sees in you, then he's as blind and as foolish as Jeff is, and he doesn't deserve you anyway." Anger broke through the words. Back when they were younger, Dally had all the confidence in the world. But Jeff had spent so much time highlighting her flaws that now insecurity seemed to hold her back. What she wouldn't give to have a few minutes alone with her sister's ex-husband. How dare he make Dally question her value? Mags gazed steadily into her sister's eyes trying to infuse her with confidence. "You are a catch. And I'm not only saying that because you're my sister."

"Yes, you are." Her frown created worry lines in her forehead.

"No. I'm not. You love people well." That was a gift not many people had. "You always have loved people well. You were always there for Rose and me no matter what. You were always everything we needed you to be." She'd never had the chance to thank Dally for that, for being more nurturing than their own mother. It was long past time that she thanked her sister for everything she'd done for their family. "Now it's your turn. It's your turn to think about yourself. To embrace what you truly want in life." Emotion seeped into her eyes. No one deserved to be loved more than Dally.

"I'm not sure I know what I want." Her sister looked in the direction of the bar again.

"I know the feeling," Mags muttered. She thought by thirty she'd have everything figured out. She thought she'd be a mom. She'd pictured her and Eric walking along the beach hand in hand while they watched their little ones play in the sand.

"You and Eric will work things out." Dally covered Mags's hand with hers. "I know you will. You two were meant to be together. I've always thought so."

"I hope so." She'd feel more hopeful if they'd been able to talk at all. She hadn't heard much since the day he'd texted her that he missed her. He'd been working a lot of overtime, but still...

"Drinks are served." Ike presented the ginger ale and wine and sat down with his beer just as Clyde started to strum his guitar.

"Thank you." Dahlia picked up her wineglass in one hand and reached for her purse with the other. "How much—?"

Ike shook his head. "My treat."

Geez-o-Pete, when the man flashed that grin, even Mags got all gooey inside. She snuck a look at her sister. Dahlia was sipping her wine while she watched Clyde play. She wasn't pale anymore, and she didn't keep looking down at the floor either. Well, good. In another half hour, maybe Mags would call Rose and tell her to come pick her up so this could turn into a real date for Dally.

Clyde finished the first song and leaned into the mic. "I'd like to invite the doc to the dance floor," he said with a mischievous smile. "There ain't no one who can dance as good as the doc."

A murmur of agreement went around, and people started to whoop.

"Get on out there, doc," a woman called. "Break the ice for us!"

"Nah." He waved everyone off. "I'm enjoying a drink with these lovely ladies."

And he was obviously too much of a gentleman to leave one of them alone at the table. Which meant Mags would have to give him a little push.

"Dally was just saying how much she'd love to dance."

Her sister's eyes went as wide as the rim of her wineglass.

"That so?" Ike turned his attention to Dahlia.

"Yep," Mags answered for her. "And my ankle has been really sore lately, so I can't dance anyway. You two should get this party started."

Her sister rolled her eyes, but she was smiling, too.

"You up for a dance?" Ike asked Dally, with that tempting grin of his.

"I suppose so." A lovely shade of pink colored her sister's cheeks.

As the two of them walked to the dance floor to the sound of cheers, Mags sat back, quite satisfied with herself. Her love life might be a mess right now, but at least she could help Dally move forward.

As soon as the whoops and hollers from the crowd quieted, Clyde started to sing "I Walk the Line." Within seconds Ike had Dahlia two-stepping around the dance floor, expertly leading her while they talked and laughed.

Dally's whole face came alive when she laughed. Mags hadn't seen the expression on her sister's face in a long time. A sigh built in her chest. She remembered when she and Eric had looked at each other like that. When they'd laughed like that. She remembered when their love had been so new and exhilarating and seemingly indestructible. How had it dulled over time?

Other couples started to join Ike and Dally out on the dance floor, but there seemed to be this glow of happiness surrounding those two. A yearning brought an ache under Mags's breastbone. She missed Eric. She didn't miss the fighting or the uncertainty that had seemed to stretch between them lately, but she missed *him*. Missed the way his hand felt in hers. Missed how he always paused when they were kissing, looking deeply into her eyes. She missed the teasing way he'd touched her butt, the growl in his throat when she used to lead him into the bedroom before their intimacy had been ruled by a calendar.

"Excuse me, would you like to dance?" A good-looking cowboy approached her table. Mags glanced behind her to make sure he was actually talking to her.

"I don't like to see a pretty lady sitting at a table by herself," he went on.

She peered up at him in disbelief. He had to be younger than her by a good five years, and he was adorable. Dark brown hair stuck out underneath his cowboy hat, and he had dark shy eyes with long, thick lashes. She let the invitation sit for a second. It had been eons since she'd been hit on at a bar.

"Or I could just buy you a drink," he offered.

She didn't know where these cowboys learned how to smile, but they all seemed to have mastered the skill. And yet that charm did nothing for her. There was only one man she wanted to be smiling at her right now. Only one man she wanted to dance with. "Thanks for the invitation, but no. Sorry. I'm married, actually."

"Ohhh." His eyes went wide. "My bad. I didn't see a ring—"

"I forgot to put it back on." With all the baking she'd been doing lately, she'd taken to leaving her ring in a dish by her aunt's kitchen sink. "But I really appreciate the offer. If I wasn't married, I would've said yes."

He simply tipped his hat and told her to enjoy her afternoon as he walked away.

She wasn't sure she could enjoy her afternoon. That ache inside had grown deeper, hollowing her out. She checked on Dahlia and Ike again. Clyde had started crooning out a slower song and Ike pulled her sister closer, gazing down into her eyes. Dahlia peered back up at him, no longer looking shy and nervous, but smiling softly.

Yeah, they wouldn't miss her. She scooted out of her chair and pulled her phone out of her back pocket, quickly making her way closer to the door. Zipping up her coat, she stepped outside onto the frozen sidewalk and hit Eric's number. The rings echoed in her ear, making her feel even lonelier.

Just as she was about to shut off her phone, a click sounded.

"Mags?" Eric sounded out of breath.

"Hi." Tears pricked her eyes. She would've liked to blame it on the cold air, but emotion churned through her at the sound of his voice.

"Are you okay?" he asked gruffly.

No. She wasn't okay. She hadn't been okay in a long time. A gust of wind blew against her cheeks, chilling her to the bone. "I needed to hear your voice."

"You did?"

The disbelief in his voice made her tears spill over. "Yes." Didn't he know how much she loved him? "We've hardly talked at all."

"You left." There was an edge to his voice. "I didn't think you wanted to talk." He paused briefly. "I didn't know what to think, Mags. I still don't."

"I didn't leave. Not forever." She turned her face away from the wind. "I...I took a break. I needed space." What else could she say? How could she reach across the dry wasteland of pain that seemed to stand between them?

Background noise echoed through the speaker. "I have to go," Eric said quietly. "Sorry. I'm at work. We've got a call coming in."

Desperation flooded her. "Wait. When can we talk?" They couldn't keep doing this. Shutting each other out.

"I don't know." He sounded far away. "I'll try to call you later."

Before she could tell him she loved him, the line clicked, and she lost him.

Chapter Eighteen

Rose

Getting information out of Colt was proving to be more difficult than hacking into the nation's top-secret database.

Rose watched him up on the ladder where he was nailing a string of colorful globe lights to the white trim on the barn. For the last half hour, she'd tried to make polite chitchat while they worked to beautify the main barn where the Christmas extravaganza would be held, asking him about his family and growing up here. His answers consisted mainly of grunts and short begrudging sentences, and, so far, she hadn't gotten any closer to figuring out how he was connected to Sassy.

It was time to change tactics.

"Looking good up there," she called. Oh, wait. "I mean, the *lights* are looking good. I didn't mean *you're* looking good. Not that you don't look good…"

The man didn't even turn to acknowledge her babbling. He simply kept the steady pound of his hammer going and pretended she wasn't talking. She should be grateful. For some reason, this man had the ability to make her feel awkward and unsure. Which was ridiculous. She was a grown woman, and she'd dealt with plenty of difficult men in her day.

"So how long have you known Sassy?" she called up to him, trying again.

"Years," he muttered, pounding in another nail.

Sighing, Rose tromped a few steps to the left so she could get a better look at his face. He certainly didn't *resemble* Sassy, but that didn't mean he couldn't be her son. "How—"

A low rumbling bark sounded somewhere behind her, cutting off her question. Rose whirled just in time to see a huge white dog tearing out of the woods and barreling right for her.

"Woof! Woof!"

"Oh my God!" That thing was going to kill her! She darted forward and threw herself at the ladder, climbing halfway up just as the dog reached the first rung.

"What the hell are you doing?" Colt demanded, steadying the ladder.

Down below, the dog yipped and jumped around as though it, too, wanted to climb the ladder. Probably to eat her...

"What'd you mean, what am I doing?" she gasped and sputtered. "There's a dog down there!" Rose scrambled up another rung so that she was right below Colt's boots.

"I can see that." His flat tone informed her he wasn't stupid.

"Dogs don't like me." Fear inflated her heart, pressing it in tightly against her ribs. "One bit me when I was ten years old. And I didn't do anything to deserve it." She'd simply been walking down the street in her neighborhood, and the thing had attacked her from behind.

"This dog isn't gonna bite you." His gaze looked past her. "I'd say she looks pretty harmless."

Rose peeked down at the dog again. Its front paws were still up on the ladder's fourth rung.

"Woof! Woof, woof, woof!"

"It has huge teeth," she whimpered, remembering exactly how it had felt when that stray dog had sunk its teeth into her back. She still had a big scar.

"All dogs have big teeth," Colt informed her. "But listen to her bark. It's friendly. She wants some love."

Easy for him to say. He was still up higher than her. "I'm not going to risk it." She held on to the ladder so tight her knuckles had to be white underneath her gloves.

"What do you plan to do then?" the man asked impatiently. "We can't stay up here all night."

"We could," she argued. It would beat getting bitten by a dog. "I had to get stitches. And a shot. It was all very traumatic." And she hadn't been able to pet a dog since. She'd wanted to—she'd wanted to see the creatures as sweet and furry and lovable—but instead, all she noticed when she saw a dog approaching were their scary big teeth.

Colt sighed and glanced around as though looking for a way to get around the crazy woman below him. "Look, we have to get down. I have to move the ladder in order to finish hanging the lights you insisted you wanted on the barn."

Rose stared up at the half he'd already finished. "Looks great the way it is." No need to move the ladder. No need to move her off the ladder. "I'm sure the dog will go away soon."

As if it wanted to argue, the dog plopped down onto the ground and stared up at them with a whimper while its tail swooshed through the snow.

Colt shifted his weight. "What if I promise you she won't hurt you?"

"You can't promise that." Dogs were unpredictable. "Do you know the dog? Have you ever seen it before?"

"No," he admitted. "But I can tell with animals. Look at her eyes."

Rose frowned up at him.

"Come on," he prompted, and she couldn't help but notice his tone had gentled slightly. "Look down at her. Her teeth aren't showing anymore."

Securing her arm around the rung, Rose leaned back slightly and looked down at the dog. Okay, so it had a cute face. Fluffy grayish white fur stuck up around its floppy ears and bristly old-man eyebrows hovered over large dark eyes.

"Woof!" Its tail started to sweep again, whipping up a cloud of snow.

"See?" Colt bent closer to her. "She's friendly. I can tell."

"Then you go down first." Rose held her grip firm on the ladder. "If she's friendly with you, I'll come down." Maybe. Most likely.

"How do you suggest I get down with you in my way?" Colt nudged her shoulder gently with his boot as though teasing her.

"Go around me." Even as she said it, she knew that would involve a difficult maneuver.

The man leaned his forehead against the ladder and muttered something under his breath. "I can't believe you don't like dogs. You of all people. The woman who's trying so hard to be everyone's friend. You and that dog down there likely have a lot in common."

Rose huffed but decided to let the snark go. "I never said *I* don't like *them*. They don't like me." What if she went down there and it tackled her? "I suppose you're not afraid of anything. You've probably never been afraid of anything in your whole life."

"That's not true," Colt said thoughtfully.

"Really?" She raised her head, but she couldn't get a look at his face. Was he actually going to open up about something?

"I have fears." He paused dramatically. "I'm terrified of nosy interior designers who go around redecorating Christmas trees without permission."

Despite herself, Rose had to smile as she swatted his boot with her glove-clad hand. "Now I'm really not moving." She would make him stay up here for hours. Though she had to admit, even in her Uggs, her toes had started to get a little frosty.

"I'm joking." A rare grin hiked up one corner of his mouth. "I'm not *that* scared of you."

"Ha." Suddenly, Colt was a jokester. "You might not be scared of me, but I'm terrified of that dog." Rose peered down to where the dog had put its front paws back on the fourth rung of the ladder. Sure, it was fluffy and cute and probably very nice. But it was also big and unpredictable. And it had sharp teeth. Her heart raced again.

"I have an idea." Colt bent so she could see his face. "If you can carefully move to the back of the ladder, I can climb down first and tame the beast, so she won't hurt you."

She was about to hesitate, but her toes were moving past the cold stage all the way to numb. "I guess we could try it." She judged the distance from the ground. That would be a hard fall...

"Move an inch at a time," Colt coached. "One hand on the back of the ladder, then one foot. Take your time."

"Right." Rose shuffled her feet and shifted, reaching one hand around to secure a hold on the back of the ladder.

"That's it." The man almost sounded like he was talking to a child. "Easy."

Easy. Right. Nothing about this was easy. She looked down past her feet and the movement seemed to get the dog all excited again. Or angry?

"Woof! Woof!" The thing bounced as though trying to make its way up the ladder.

Yeah, she wasn't going down there. "Okay, here goes." She wound one leg around the frame of the ladder until she found a secure place to set her foot on the inside of the rung. With one foot and hand on each side of the ladder, she shuffled her way inch by inch to the back of the ladder, her hands clutched in a death grip. "There." She was breathing so hard she may as well have run a marathon.

"All right. I'm coming down." Colt moved slowly, keeping his eyes on her. "Watch your hands."

Legs shaking with the effort, Rose moved her hands to the outside of the ladder's frame so he could work his way down past her. When he'd reached her level, he paused, smiling a little. "Don't worry. I've got this."

The man's face changed when he smiled. His eyes warmed and his jaw relaxed. For some reason it put her at ease. "I'm not worried." Much.

"Good." He continued down the ladder, and the closer he got to the ground, the higher the dog jumped. "Hey there, pup." Colt took the last few rungs slowly while the dog jumped all over his back.

"Be careful!" Rose watched in horror as the dog reached its paws all the way up to Colt's shoulders.

"Good girl," the man cooed. "Sit. Can you sit?"

The dog immediately dropped its butt to the ground and smiled up at Colt, its tongue hanging out the side of its mouth

"Good dog," he gushed, scratching the dog behind its ears. "See?" he called up to Rose. "Nothing to worry about."

"Okay." Heat flashed across her face as she carefully made her way down the back side of the ladder until her boots met the ground.

Colt had knelt to keep a hand on the dog so it wouldn't maul her, but still she kept a healthy distance. "Where do you think it came from?"

"There's no telling." He glanced in the direction of the woods. "No collar but it's possible she has a chip." He stood to his full height. "Do you want to pet her?"

"Oh. No. That's okay." Rose stepped back. The dog was pretty cute, especially up close. Those eyebrows...

Whimpering, the dog lay down, stretching out its front legs and inching toward her with the most hopeful look. She finally understood what people meant by puppy dog eyes.

"Just a quick pat on the head," Colt coaxed, kneeling next to the dog. "I'll keep a hand on her just in case."

"I guess a quick pat couldn't hurt." The dog seemed to listen to Colt. It was probably his deep commanding voice.

"Hi there." Fear swelled, but Rose pushed through it, easing one foot closer.

The dog's tail went into hyperdrive again, but she stayed on her belly while Colt scratched her ears. "Stay," he murmured soothingly.

A little shaky on her legs, Rose removed her glove and reached out her hand, holding her palm just beneath the dog's cold nose. Her mom had tried and tried to help her get over her fear of dogs, and this was as far as she'd ever gotten.

"Good puppy," she murmured, mostly trying to calm herself.

She reached her hand to the dog's head and swept her fingers over the soft fur.

The dog leaned toward her, its nose tipped down as though begging for more.

"She likes you." Colt stood while Rose continued to pet the dog, inching closer and closer.

"She *is* pretty sweet." Rose couldn't deny that. And soft. Her fur was like silk.

"She looks like a mix." Colt seemed to give the dog a good inspection. "I'm guessing she's got at least some golden retriever in her. Maybe some terrier, too."

"You're good with dogs." Rose held her hand underneath the dog's nose again and she licked Rose's fingers happily.

"Most dogs are easier to deal with than people." When Colt moved a few steps away, the dog sat taller.

"I wonder where her owner is." Rose knelt down to the dog's level. No creature with eyes like that could be vicious. "Hi, baby." She moved her hand to the dog's back.

"Looks like someone's not afraid of dogs anymore," the man commented, watching her with a smile.

Rose found herself smiling, too. "What are we going to do with her?" she asked, standing up. Who knew how long the dog had been outside. "Should we bring her into Sassy's to warm her up?"

Colt seemed to consider the idea. "I guess that would be good. We can give her some water. Maybe feed her and then take her to the vet to see if she's chipped."

"What if she's not chipped?" Rose started up the hill toward Sassy's house with the dog following right on her heels.

"I don't know." Colt walked alongside her. "I guess we could make posters and put them up around town. Someone might recognize her."

For the first time since she'd arrived in Juniper, Colt wasn't trying to get away from her. Maybe this dog situation would give her the opportunity to ask him about his connection to Sassy. "Great idea." She could take a picture of the dog and print it out in Sassy's office. "I'm sure someone is missing her."

"Hopefully." Colt didn't seem convinced. "We get a lot of strays around here though, being so close to the highway. Seems some people thinks it's easier to abandon their dogs in the mountains than it is to take them to a shelter."

"What?" Rose stopped, dropping to her knees to pet the dog again. "How could anyone do that?"

"I don't know." Colt reached his hand to the dog's snout. "Like I said, in my opinion, most dogs are easier to deal with than—"

A shiny black SUV turned into the driveway, following the tracks in the snow up to the house.

"Who's that?" Colt asked, watching the car.

"I don't know." Rose started walking to meet the car. "If they're here for Sassy, they'll be disappointed. She told us she had a lot to do today and wouldn't be around."

The dog bounded ahead of them barking, seeming excited about the prospect of another new friend.

After the car had parked next to the front porch, the driver got out and hurried to open the back door. The dog rushed to greet the mysterious visitor, but the woman who got out of the car pushed her away.

Hold on a sec…

Rose jogged closer.

"Mom?" Even with Lillian buried under a thick fur coat, she recognized her right away. "What're you doing here?"

"I came to talk some sense into you." Lillian shooed the dog away with a wave of her hand and teetered through the snow until she stood across from Rose. "I came to bring you home."

Great. She really should've anticipated this. "I'm a little busy right now." And she didn't need her mother to make a scene in front of Colt. "Do you have suitcases? We can go into the house and get you settled…"

"I'm not staying." Her mother shifted her gaze to Colt and slipped off her sunglasses. "You." She pointed in his direction. "I know you."

Colt's face had turned stony again. "I should take the dog to the vet. See what I can find out." He ducked away and hurried to his truck, whistling for the dog to follow him. "See ya around." The dog jumped into the car, and Colt was right behind her. The truck peeled out before Rose could figure out what was happening.

"What're you doing with him?" her mother demanded.

"With who? Colt?" What on earth was Lillian going on about? "Wait. How do you know him?" If he really was just some neighbor boy like Mags had thought, there's no way her mother would remember him.

"I can't believe it. I can't believe he's still here," her mother snipped. "That boy is part of the reason I haven't spoken to your aunt in over eighteen years."

Chapter Nineteen

Dahlia

Dahlia couldn't remember the last time she'd laughed like this. Ike twirled her again, slipping to the opposite side and then reeling her back to him and moving effortlessly back into a two-step.

"You really are a good dancer." She couldn't tell if she was breathless from the dancing, or the laughing, or the fact that the last half hour had chipped away at some of the loneliness that had walled off her heart.

Ike dazzled her with his grin. "You're making me look good," he said, dipping her as the song came to an end.

"Right." She giggled again. She couldn't help herself. Rose had been right. Dahlia had forgotten how much she used to love dancing. Jeff had always hated dancing. Even at their wedding, he'd only danced with her once—when he'd been forced to during the bride and groom's song. He'd never had even an ounce of rhythm, and he only wanted people watching him when he could impress them. According to him, dancing made people look stupid. But for the last half hour, she hadn't cared if she looked stupid, and Ike hadn't seemed to care either. She'd forgotten how light music made her feel. Or maybe she'd never felt quiet as light as she did in Ike's arms. He smelled good—clean and spicy, and for once she didn't have to think too hard about her next move. Instead she relied on his expert guidance.

Everyone started to clap for Clyde, and the older man stood up from his stool, taking a bow.

"Wooh!" Ike whistled loud, leading the applause. Dahlia joined in as she scanned the crowd. She'd seen Mags slip out while talking on the phone a few minutes ago. Now her sister ducked back in through the door, and she wasn't smiling. "I'm going to go check on Mags," she said to Ike.

"Sounds good." He leaned in, his hand brushing the small of her back. "Can I get you ladies another drink?"

"I'll let you know in a minute." She remained close to him for an extra few seconds, feeling the warmth of his touch rise through her body. After being numb for so long, she'd like to stay longer and explore the flutterings he made her feel. Except her sister needed her. "Be right back." She drifted away from him and pushed through the crowd until she made it to the table where Mags sat with a blank expression on her face.

"Hey." She sat across from her. "Are you okay?" Silly question. Mags's eyes were red. She'd obviously been crying. Dahlia leaned forward, reaching for her. "What is it? What happened?"

"I called Eric." Her sister swallowed hard. "He didn't even want to talk to me. He sounded so far away. I feel like I don't even know him anymore."

"Oh sweetie." Dahlia scooted her stool around so she could sit next to her and slip an arm around her shoulders. "I'm sorry. What did he say?"

"Nothing." Mags dabbed at her eyes with a napkin. "That's the thing. He didn't know what to say. I'm afraid he doesn't want to try anymore. I'm afraid we'll never be able to fix our marriage."

Dahlia closed her eyes. She remembered that feeling of desperation when Jeff had started to drift away from her. The fear. All along she'd known what was coming, but she had still done everything she could to keep it together. It had been such a lonely lost time in her life.

Jeff was different than Eric though. Mags's husband had always impressed her. He'd had a rough upbringing after immigrating to the US as a young child, and he'd had to tough things out most of his life. As far as she'd heard, he'd never taken the easy way out of anything. "I'm not the authority on fixing marital issues," Dahlia said with a humorless laugh. She'd proven that with the implosion of her own relationship. "But I always felt like you and Eric had something Jeff and I didn't have." That grit in their commitment. That toughness. The feeling that they would always fight for each other. "You need to find it again, that's all."

Tears brightened her sister's eyes again. "Do you think we can?"

"I do." She would believe that enough for both of them right now. As wounded as Mags had been by Eric's refusal to continue trying for a baby, Dahlia could see how much she still loved her husband.

"Hey." Ike sauntered over but slowed when he caught sight of Mags's face. "Can I get anyone a refill?" He hovered a few feet away. "Or some food maybe?"

Dahlia's heart warmed all over again seeing him stand there with concern tugging at his expression. "Actually, I think Mags is ready to go home." She stood with an apologetic smile. As much as she would love to stay and dance with him all night, she knew Mags wouldn't have fun sitting here any longer.

"It's okay." Her sister jolted to her feet. "I can call Rose to pick me up. I don't want to ruin your fun."

"You're not ruining our fun," Ike insisted. "I'm happy to give you a lift home." Dahlia had never seen so much kindness in someone's eyes.

"Yes, let's go," she agreed, lifting her purse off the chair. "We can snuggle up on the couch and have some tea. Maybe we can watch a good old-fashioned chick flick."

"Or the Hallmark Channel," Mags said wistfully. "I could use some escapism right about now." She dabbed at her eyes again. "Thank you both so much. I'm going to run to the restroom and then I'll be ready to go." Hurrying away, she kept her head down, likely embarrassed by the tears.

"Is she okay?" Ike asked as soon as she was out of earshot.

"She will be. Eventually." The emotion her sister had shown only proved she still loved Eric. Her heart still longed for him. And Dahlia had to believe they would find their way back to each other.

Ike moved in closer, peering down into Dahlia's eyes. Instead of shying away or darting her gaze to something else, she stared back, completely transfixed by this man.

"Anything I can do?" he asked.

Now that he mentioned it. "I don't like the way she keeps downplaying the symptoms she's been having." If Mags's facial expression on the car ride over was any indication, she wasn't serious about getting checked out. Yes, she was sad about Eric, but something else had to be going on.

"Keep encouraging her to come to the clinic," Ike said. "I'd be happy to do a simple checkup. We could run some blood work and see what comes back."

"That would be great." Mags likely wouldn't think so, but it was time for an intervention.

Ike stepped in closer, bringing that spicy scent with him. "Speaking of dropping by…would it be okay if I dropped by to pick you up for dinner tomorrow night?"

Dahlia's heart seemed to double in size, making it difficult to breathe. "You mean like a date?" Oh Lordy. She shouldn't sound so shocked. And excited. And nervous…

Ike simply grinned. "Yes. Like a date. I like you, in case I haven't made that clear."

Forget playing it cool. It was impossible to control the smile that rose on her lips. "I like you, too. And I would love to go on a date." A date! She was going on a date!

"Yeah?" The man leaned in closer, and everything in her seemed to pause. Would he kiss her—?

"Okay. I'm ready." Mags hurried over, and the moment passed. "Thanks for waiting."

"No problem." Dahlia cleared her throat, trying to inhale without a gasp. "Yes. Well. We're ready. Let's go." The quick pound of her heart made her legs shaky, but she managed to lead the way out to Ike's truck. He opened the door for both of them, and this time, Mags snagged the backseat before Dahlia could.

On the way back to Sassy's place, she couldn't stop sneaking peeks at the man sitting next to her. The man who was taking her on a date. Tomorrow night.

"You two should really go back to the Crazy Moose after you drop me off," her sister said from the backseat. "You looked like you were having a great time and then I had to go and ruin it all."

"It was getting late anyway," Ike said with a wink at Dahlia.

"Exactly." Dahlia peered over her shoulder, unable to keep a straight face. "We're going out to dinner tomorrow night so it's okay."

She could tell her sister wanted to squeal, but instead Mags remained silent. "Good. That's good," her sister murmured with a false calm.

Ike turned the truck into the Juniper Inn's driveway, slowing as they maneuvered through the trees. "Huh. Wonder who that is."

Dahlia glanced over to the house where a dark SUV sat parked next to the porch. "Sassy didn't mention having company." She'd said she'd be out all day, but surely, she would have told them if she was expecting someone.

"It looks like one of those car services from Denver." Ike pulled the truck up behind it and cut the engine.

"That's weird." Mags climbed out of the truck, and Dahlia followed, trying to get a peek inside the car as they passed. It sure looked expensive.

Ike got out of the truck, too. "I promised Sassy I'd take a look at the leak in the kitchen faucet, so I'll come in with you, if that's okay."

It was more than okay with her, but she simply peered back at him with a smile, already dreaming of dancing with him again.

"Thank goodness we have you," Mags commented as they made their way up the front porch. "I wouldn't know the first thing about fixing a leaky faucet."

"Yes, thank goodness," Dahlia echoed.

"Fixing a faucet is the least I can do for Sassy." Ike hurried to open the front door for them.

Dahlia stepped inside and froze.

Loud voices echoed from the kitchen, and they needed no introduction. She and Mags stared at each other. "Is that Mom?" her sister whispered.

"It sure sounds like it." Lillian's voice carried out into the foyer in an intense, one-sided discussion much like it used to when she would lecture Dahlia on the importance of keeping a close eye on her sisters so they wouldn't get into trouble.

"Maybe I should wait here." Ike stepped aside into the living room, and she was mighty tempted to wait with him, but Mags waved her down the hall.

"Whoa boy," her sister muttered.

"I don't understand," Rose was saying. "How could you do that? How could you let a man come between you and your sister?"

"It wasn't my fault—"

Dahlia gathered in a breath. Whatever was happening in there, it sounded like their sister needed backup. "Hi, Mom," Dahlia interrupted, walking into Sassy's normally cheerful kitchen. Right now, tension sat heavy in the air. Rose and Lillian were sitting at the kitchen table facing off.

"What're you doing here?" Mags hung out on the other side of the room by the sink as though she was afraid to go any closer.

"She's here to drag me back to Savannah," Rose said with an angry crack in her voice. "My future mother-in-law sent her. Evaline let her use the private jet and everything." Their sister jumped up from the table and began to pace in front of the window.

"Seriously?" Dahlia didn't know why she was surprised. Their mother had always admired Evaline Cunningham.

"Don't be so dramatic." Lillian rolled her eyes and stood regally, holding out her arms. "I came to see all of you. I've missed my girls."

Dahlia stumbled forward to give her an obligatory hug since she hadn't seen her in months, but Mags didn't move. "Rose can't go back to Savannah. She has to stay here through Christmas. We all have to stay here together through Christmas."

"That was our deal with Sassy," Dahlia explained.

"Well Rose has obligations with her fiancé and his family." Lillian walked over to where Rose stood. "He's getting impatient, and quite frankly, I don't blame the man. This is the most important time of year for the Cunninghams' foundations. Gregory needs his future wife by his side."

For a second, Rose looked torn. Oh, no. No, no, no. Rose had always been the people pleaser, especially when it came to Lillian, but she would not let it happen this time. Dahlia slipped between Rose and their mother. "Gregory's family will survive one Christmas without you." This was their sisters Christmas, their escape in the mountains, and their mother would not ruin it. "Sassy is the one who needs us."

"You're right." The stubbornness returned to her younger's sister's features. "I'll come home when I'm good and—"

"Hey." Ike stuck his head in through the doorway. "I think I'm going to head out. I can fix the faucet later."

The interruption broke through the tension in the room, diverting their mother's attention. "Who is this?" she asked, looking Ike over with interest.

Uh-oh. The last thing Dahlia wanted to do was introduce Lillian to the man she was going on a date with. Her mother had been constantly texting her with the names of eligible bachelors back in Savannah.

When no one said anything, Ike stepped forward and introduced himself. "Ike Songer."

"He's the doctor in town." Dahlia didn't know why she felt the need to justify him.

"Oh, lovely. A doctor." Lillian smiled that big fake smile she remembered so well from their childhood.

"Nice to meet you." He shook their mother's hand, but then caught Dahlia in a hopeful gaze. "See you tomorrow night?"

"Yes. Let's say six o'clock." Dahlia walked him to the hallway. She could feel her mother watching, but she refused to acknowledge her.

Thankfully, they stepped out of view. "I'll pick you up here." Ike leaned down and brushed a kiss across her cheek.

"Can't wait." One small kiss and she was almost breathless.

The man turned to go, and she floated back into the kitchen on a cloud. Who cared that Lillian had ambushed them? She was going on a date with a man who could *dance*...

"Tomorrow night?" Lillian started in on her the second she sat down at the table. "You're dating that man?"

The euphoria started to evaporate under the coldness of her mother's judgmental stare. "No. I mean, yes. We're going on a date, but it's not a big deal. It's only dinner." She had to change the subject before her mother gave her the third degree. "What were you two talking about earlier anyway? What man came between you and Aunt Sassy?"

"Oh." Rose bolted back to the table like she couldn't wait to share. "Apparently, Sassy was in love with Colt's father when we were younger."

"What?" Mags finally came over and joined them.

"It wasn't love," their mother said bitterly. "It was misguided affection. The man was a criminal. I knew it from the first time I met him. He was a deadbeat."

"So, you were right?" Dahlia addressed the question to Rose. "Colt is Sassy's son?"

"Heaven's no." Their mother scoffed. "But she treated him like her son. He practically lived here. Both him and his dad." Their mother raised her chin the same way she did when she disapproved of something. "That's why we stopped coming to visit. I didn't trust that man or his son for one second. I recognize a loser when I see one." She gloated at Rose. "And I was right, too. The man ended up in prison."

"Colt's dad?" Dahlia shared a look with Rose. It was so tragic. Sassy had lost another man she loved when he went to prison?

"What happened to his mom?" Mags asked.

Lillian shrugged. "I'm not sure, exactly. I think she died after he was born. That's not important. What is important is that I had a bad feeling about the man, and Sassy didn't care."

It was just like their mother to see only one side of a story— her side. But Dahlia couldn't imagine Sassy falling in love with a monster. "What did his father do? *Why* did he go to prison?" Maybe it wasn't as bad as it seemed.

"How would I know?" Lillian obviously didn't care enough to get the whole story. "He got arrested a few years after our last visit. Sassy wrote me a letter to tell me. I called her up and asked her if she was done with him then, and she said no. She told me she still loved him." Their mother didn't even have the decency to look defensive. She fully believed she'd done the right thing. "I'm sure you can see why I had to cut everything off."

"I can't see it," Dahlia told her. "She's your sister."

Her mother gave her a wounded look. "And she chose someone else over me."

That would be exactly how Lillian would see the whole situation. Forget sympathy or empathy.

"Oh, and now I know why Colt hates me," Rose fumed. "Mom reminded me that he gave me flowers once. A bouquet he'd picked himself when we were here the summer I turned eight. And she threw them in the trash! He probably thought I'd done it."

"I had to throw them in the trash," Lillian snapped. "I knew that boy would never amount to anything. How could he with that man for a father?"

Rose let out a frustrated grunt and glared at Dahlia as though asking for a little assistance.

But nothing they could say would change their mother. Lillian was who she was. Dahlia had learned a long time ago to let her be. It wasn't worth the fight.

"Well, I'm not going back," Rose announced. "Not until after Christmas like I planned. I'm a grown woman and I can make my own decisions."

Exactly. They were all grown women, and they all had decisions to make. Decisions Lillian couldn't dictate for them. Dahlia gave their mother a placating smile. "You should stay, too." She'd always played the part of the peacemaker in the family, and she couldn't stop now. "This is your chance to make things right with your sister. I can't imagine my life without my sisters." Being here with them had revived her…

"I'm not staying here." Lillian buttoned her fur coat and pulled on her gloves, displaying the same stubborn frown as Rose. "My car is waiting." She glared at Rose. "If you refuse to come home, you're risking everything with the Cunninghams. I hope you know that. Evaline doesn't have patience for this kind of disrespect."

"Evaline Cunningham doesn't run my life," Rose shot back. "She might run Gregory's, but she doesn't run mine."

"Fine." Their mother started to walk away. "But you're being selfish. If I were you, I would think long and hard about how you're treating your fiancé." She shook her head with disappointment. "After all he's done for you. It's disgraceful." Lillian went to make a dramatic exit, but Dahlia followed her to the foyer.

"Wait, Mom, don't go." It would mean so much to Sassy if they could work things out. "All that stuff with Colt's dad happened years ago. It doesn't matter anymore. Not now. You're both getting older. Maybe it's time to let it all go."

"My sister made her choice years ago," she said on her way out the door. "I have nothing to say to her now."

Chapter Twenty

Rose

I can't believe Evaline sent her out here." Rose paced in front of the fireplace in the living room, where she and Mags and Dahlia had retreated after their mother had left. "Actually, I can't believe a lot of things." She didn't even know where to start with unpacking what their mother had told them about Sassy.

"You're really surprised?" Mags sank into the old leather couch cushions and wrapped a blanket around her shoulders. "Evaline obviously wants you back in Savannah, and I have a feeling she's used to getting her way."

"You did the right thing by staying," Dahlia told her. She'd settled herself on the brick hearth next to the fire. "This is our Christmas. A sisters' Christmas. No one can take that away from us."

"Exactly." And yet…there was still this seesawing inside of her. Was she being selfish? Did she owe it to Gregory to be back in Savannah for Christmas? She was about to commit her life to the man—

"Want to know what I can't believe? That Sassy had another secret love we never knew about." Mags propped her feet up on the coffee table. "How did we never notice? I mean, sure, we were kids, but if Colt was around, his father must've been, too."

"Mother probably kept us away from him." She clearly hadn't wanted Rose anywhere near Colt. She wedged herself on the couch next to Mags. She'd seen the disdain in Lillian's eyes when she'd gotten out of the car. "Colt remembers everything though. He knew who Mom was right when she stepped out of the car." That's why he'd kept such a distance. "He probably thinks I'm as stuck-up as Mom always has been."

Dahlia reached into the bin by the fireplace and added another log to the fire. "How sad that his dad ended up in prison."

"I wonder what he did," Mags said. "It must've been something pretty terrible. Maybe Mom was right to put some distance there."

The front door clattered, opening with a whoosh of wind. Sassy stumbled through with a beautifully wrapped stack of packages piled up in her arms. "I'm home!"

"We're glad you're back." Rose jumped up to help her with the boxes so Sassy could see over them.

"I spent the whole day shopping in Denver." Their aunt traipsed into the living room and started to set packages under the Christmas tree in the corner. "Remember how excited you girls would get when I would put the presents under the tree? You would squeal and dance, and—" She turned around and stopped the second she saw their faces. "Whatever is the matter with you three?"

For some reason Dahlia and Mags both looked at Rose. As usual. After all, she was the reason Lillian had made the trip. "Mom came to see us," she said, watching Sassy's face for a reaction.

A look of utter hopefulness widened their aunt's eyes. "Lillian is here? Oh, that's wonderful—"

"She didn't stay." It hurt Rose to say it, to deliver the news that brought a sad slant to Sassy's mouth. "She flew out here because wanted me to come home with her. So, I would be with Gregory over Christmas."

"I see." Sassy backed to the overstuffed chair across from the couch, sitting with a slump in her shoulders. "But you didn't go."

"No." Rose reclaimed her seat next to Mags. "I promised you I'd stay. I promised my sisters I would stay." Selfish or not, no part of her wanted to go back to Savannah right now. She needed to be here. It was time for them to hear Sassy's story, to make up for too many years of silence. "Why didn't you tell us about Colt's father?" she asked gently.

"Mom said he went to jail," Dahlia added. "That he's the reason we stopped coming to see you."

"Was he dangerous?" Mags asked.

"No." Sassy shook her head sadly. "Oh, dear. I should've told you. Especially after you met Colt. But I suppose I didn't think it was important anymore. Robert passed away a few years ago, after all. And I didn't want to relive all of the pain again."

The revelation sunk Rose's heart. "It is important though. The man must've been a big part of your life." No matter what he'd done, she could see the strength of Sassy's feelings for him welling up in her aunt's eyes.

Sassy looked at each of them in turn and then inhaled deeply. "Robert moved here shortly after his wife passed away. Colt was only five years old at the time." She looked down at her hands as though the memories were pressing in. "They came to the inn for a place to stay while they looked for a home to buy. I didn't know it, but Robert was running from his past."

Rose shared a look with Mags and then Dahlia. She'd assumed Larry had been the love of her aunt's life, the reason she'd never married anyone else, but the emotion in her aunt's eyes, the waver in her voice made it clear how much she cared for Robert.

"Your mother never liked him," their aunt went on. "She refused to let you girls be around him, but Colt…well, he spent a lot of time here and you girls played with him sometimes."

"I knew it." Mags scooted to the edge of the couch. "He looked so familiar."

"Yes." Sassy's sad gaze landed on Rose. "He loved playing with all you girls, but he especially liked you, Rose." She laughed a little. "I think he was drawn to your imagination, if you want the truth. The poor boy had had such a difficult reality. And you were always coming up with games and stories that helped him escape."

"Mom told me about the flowers." The words left a bitter, metallic taste in her mouth. It must've crushed him to see flowers he'd picked dumped in the trash like that. A kind gesture completely disregarded like it was worthless.

"Lillian has never had much grace for anyone," Sassy said, staring into the fire.

That was putting it mildly. Once again, Rose forced herself to keep her mouth shut so her aunt could continue.

"Why didn't she like Colt though?" Dahlia asked. "Heck, if you didn't even know the details about his past, why didn't she like Robert?"

Their aunt gave a helpless shrug. "They weren't her kind of people. Robert did odd jobs around town. He didn't have any money. She thought he was freeloading while he lived here, I guess. But he always paid rent. And he helped me keep things up around here. He had a good heart." She closed her eyes as though seeing him again. "He used to hike miles up in those hills just to pick me a bouquet of the mountain bluebells I loved. And at night we'd take long walks up to a stream a mile past the pond. Colt would fish and Robert always brought his guitar so he could sing to us."

"His past caught up with him though," Rose prompted. Patience had never been her virtue. She had to know. She had to understand how their mother could've cut Sassy out of their lives for so long.

After a pause, Sassy seemed to collect herself. "Robert robbed a bank. It happened a long time before he moved to Juniper Springs. There were a few others in on the robbery with him. More seasoned criminals. One of them shot and killed a teller." Her eyes pleaded with them to understand. "But Robert never intended for that to happen. His wife was sick, and they couldn't afford treatment. The medical bills were stacking up, and he was desperate." A tear trickled down her cheek. "He finally told me. Five years after they'd moved here permanently. By then, I was already in love with him and his mistakes didn't matter to me."

For once, Rose couldn't speak. The world she'd grown up in had largely been black and white, thanks to their mother. Bad people robbed banks. But there was no room for empathy in that worldview. Since she'd left home, Rose had learned to see the gray areas. If one of her sisters was dying and they had no money, no options, she could see herself robbing a bank.

"He always regretted what he'd done," Sassy murmured. "And he made me promise that I would take care of Colt if anything ever happened to him. I don't know how the police finally found him. Colt was fourteen when they came knocking." A tear slipped down her cheek. "Sometimes I wonder if he didn't call them outright and tell them where he was. The more time passed, the more the guilt got to him."

Mags and Dahlia sat in a stunned silence, seemingly as captivated as Rose. "You never married him?" she asked with a breath of disbelief.

"No." Sassy used a blanket hanging on the back of the chair to dab her eyes. "Robert was afraid it would ruin me if they ever came for him. I knew they'd take him away if they ever found him, so I went through the process to become Cole's foster parent. And he lived with me until he left for college."

"What happened to Robert?" Mags asked tearfully.

Even Rose had started to feel the thickness of emotion in her throat.

"He passed away serving his sentence." Sassy's voice hardly hovered above a whisper. "Heart attack. He was only in his sixties." Their aunt seemed to sit up straighter, fortifying herself with strength. "I know it might not seem like it, but Robert was a good man. We wrote letters every week the whole time he was in prison, and I knew his heart. We used to dream about the things we would do together once he'd served his time. We had a bucket list. He would research places he wanted to visit and write to me about them. I think it gave him something to focus on."

Rose wiped away a tear. How tragic. Her aunt had lost the love of her life twice. "I'm so sorry." She couldn't imagine what Sassy must've gone through. And not having her sister—her family— to go through it with her must have only made it more devastating. "I can't believe Mom would let that come between you. All those years."

"I suspect she thought she was protecting you girls," Sassy

said kindly. "But Robert never would've hurt a soul. He may not have had money or a big beautiful home like your father, but he had a kindness about him. A thoughtfulness. Lillian never saw it in him, but I always did."

Anger built a rising pressure in Rose's chest. "Looking past the surface isn't exactly one of Mom's strengths." That's why Lillian was so desperate for Rose to marry Gregory. Because on the outside they would have everything that seemed to make up the perfect life—money and prestige and luxurious things.

Except she didn't want that. Not any of it. She wanted the kind of love and passion and devotion she saw in her aunt's eyes right now. She wanted a kind of love that changed her, that made her a better person. That wasn't what she had with Gregory. And she didn't know if they ever would.

"Do you have pictures of Robert?" Mags asked.

"Why, yes." Sassy rose from the chair and hurried to the old trunk underneath the window. She carefully opened it and withdrew a photo album. They all squeezed onto the couch to get a look.

"He was quite handsome," Dahlia murmured, resting her head on Rose's shoulders as they looked through Sassy's memories.

"He was," their aunt agreed, brushing her finger over one of the pictures. "And he could sing, too. His voice…" She smiled and sighed at the same time. "He sounded like John Denver."

Rose studied the pictures of the man standing next to her aunt. Colt had his father's features. The three of them looked like a family and their love for each other was evident in the photographs. "I'm sorry we didn't know Robert."

Sassy squeezed her hand. "I am, too. He would've loved you girls. He always said he wanted more children, but he was too afraid of what would happen." Their aunt turned the page. "Oh, this was one of the letters he wrote me. About going to the Grand Canyon. Neither of us had ever been, and he dreamed of seeing it in person."

"Oh my God." Rose stared at the magazine clipping. "That's what you have to do." She clasped her aunt's hands in hers. "You have to go to the Grand Canyon! And to the other places he wrote you about." She flipped through a few more pages in the book. There were more magazine clippings included with his letters. "Banff! Denali! New York City!" There was no reason Sassy couldn't go to all those places. "That could be your next adventure."

Sassy studied a picture of Times Square, a slow smile taking over her face. "Why, yes. I guess it could be. All these years I haven't even touched the inheritance my parents left me. Maybe it's time…"

"I love it," Dally sang. "What a perfect way to honor his memory."

"Yes," their aunt agreed. "And maybe Colt would like to go with me to some of those places. It means a lot to share him with you."

"I'm sure he would." Rose had seen his care toward Sassy. He'd likely go to watch out for her. "How did Colt handle it all back then?" She couldn't imagine what it must've been like for him to lose his father twice. First to prison and then permanently.

Their aunt seemed to think for a moment. "Colt has always had a certain strength about him," she finally said. "If you want the truth, I think he puts his head down and just marches through. He never said much about his father after he left, even to me. But he did always make sure to tell me how grateful he was for everything I did."

Rose nodded, thinking back to the look on his face when he'd seen their mother step out of the car. His memories of her family likely weren't fond ones. But they'd had a moment together on that ladder, her and Colt. And when she'd redecorated the tree. There'd been…a connection. Maybe they could build on that. "I need to run out for a bit." She stood. By now, Colt had probably taken the dog to the vet and figured out whether she was chipped. She could try to catch up with him at the hardware store so she could clear the air with him after her mother's impromptu visit. Now that she knew his history, she understood why he'd been so skittish with her.

"Yes, my dear." Sassy stood, too. "I should get some dinner going for us anyway. I'm making stew tonight."

"Mags and I will help." Dahlia scooted past them while Rose put on her coat.

"I won't be long," she promised.

Sassy simply smiled. "Tell Colt I said hello, will you?"

Her aunt was too sharp for her own good. "I will." She slipped out the door into the frigid night and crunched through the snow to her rental car. While she drove to the hardware store, she admired how the Christmas lights lining the shops on Main Street glowed beneath a new dusting of snow. It had been so long since she'd felt a glow inside of her during the holiday season. There was always too much to do—the parties and the shopping and the events. But here things were simpler, quieter. There were more opportunities to pause and enjoy the little things.

At the edge of Main Street, she slowed the car, finding a prime parking spot in front of Colt's store. Letting the engine run, she sat and watched him through the windows. He stood behind the counter next to the cash register while the dog lay on a cushy pillow a few feet away. Zipping her coat all the way to her chin, Rose climbed out of the car and ducked inside the hardware store. "Hi there."

Colt turned as though surprised to see her. "Hey."

She walked to the counter. As far as she could tell there were no customers in the store, which was just as well. "I see you still have our friend with you." She leaned over to pat the dog's head.

"Yeah." Colt busied himself with something on the laptop in front of him as though he didn't want to look at her. "I took her in to see the vet. She's not chipped, unfortunately."

"So, you think she was abandoned?" Rose pushed off the floor. "Right before the holidays?"

"Not sure yet." He continued to stare at the screen. "I already posted some signs around town, but so far everyone I've talked to doesn't recognize her or know where she came from." Judging from his grim frown, he didn't expect to find the owner.

Poor thing. "I guess I can keep her until we know more." Rose stood up and leaned into the counter.

That seemed to catch his attention. He finally looked away from the screen. "You?"

"Sure. Thanks to her I'm warming up to the idea of spending more time with dogs." At least the adorable white fluffy dog variety. "I'm sure Sassy won't mind. I can take care of her, let her sleep in my room." The dog rubbed her head against her leg as though she understood everything Rose had said. "I think I'll name her Marigold."

"Marigold." Colt gave the dog a critical look as though he wasn't sure it fit.

"All the girls in my family have flower names," she informed him. "So, Marigold it is."

"You know we still might find her owner, right?" He shut the laptop, giving her his full attention.

"I know." But, in the meantime, it would be good for her. "I'm sure it's a lot of work, but I'd like to take her." She'd never been afraid of hard work and, besides, her heart broke for Marigold. Being abandoned right before Christmas? That shouldn't happen to anyone.

"Okay." Colt was giving her a thoughtful look. "If you're sure."

"I'm sure." Now that they had that out of the way, Rose changed the subject. "Based on how quickly you left the inn earlier, I'm assuming you remember my mother." She couldn't pretend she didn't know what happened all those years ago. It would be better to get it all out.

Colt simply stared at her as though trying to gauge how much she'd heard. He had to realize she would find out the history sooner or later.

"I'm not like her, you know," Rose said. Looking into his eyes, she understood so much more about Colt. "I never would've thrown away flowers. I love them too much. The truth is, my mother has never been all that nice to me either."

His lips hinted at a smile. "So, not much has changed then."

"Not a whole lot." At least on her mother's side. Rose would like to think she was changing though. "I'm sorry I don't remember hanging out with you back then. Sassy said we were friends."

"I guess we were." His eyebrows shot up. "Even back then you were pretty nosy though."

That made her laugh. She would never deny that she was interested in the details of people's lives. She preferred to think of it as caring. "Well, maybe we could be friends again someday."

"Friends." Colt seemed to consider the word carefully. "Maybe."

There you had it. They were making progress. "Did you recognize me that first day I was in town? In the park?"

Amusement flickered in his eyes. "Not at first, but then you got this look on your face. Just like you used to when you were eight years old and someone tried to boss you around. Your nose got all scrunched. That's when I knew it was you."

What could she say? She'd never been able to hide her feelings well. Rose checked the clock on the wall. "Looks like it's about closing time."

Colt scanned the streets outside. "I guess so."

"Sassy's making us dinner. You should come." She hesitated. "Unless you have something better to do."

"I don't, but that's okay," he said awkwardly. "I'm not gonna crash your family time."

"Come on," she pushed. "You're part of Sassy's family. Besides, we can introduce Aunt Sassy to Marigold. Maybe she knows who the dog belongs to."

Colt might be strong and silent and a little grumpy sometimes, but he needed family, too.

Chapter Twenty-One

Magnolia

M ore sprinkles! We need more sprinkles!" Patrick shook the jar of crystallized sugar over the frosted cupcakes.

Mags leaned over the island in the center of Sassy's kitchen. "Ohhh, those look perfect." Sure, they might have a good two inches of sprinkles layered on, but the pride in the little boy's eyes was unmistakable. "You're a natural," she told the boy. "If becoming a race car driver doesn't work out, you could always be a baker."

The boy's eyes grew rounder. "Really? You fink so?"

"You're better than me and I'm a grown up," his mother insisted, watching from the other side of the island. Baby Lola was neatly swaddled against her chest in a brightly colored carrier that looked complicated, but if Lola was any indication it was also comfortable. She turned to Mags. "I'm not exaggerating when I tell you that you've saved his birthday. This is all he's been talking about since the day we met you in the store."

"Well you two saved the day for me, too." She wasn't exaggerating either. After the disastrous phone call with Eric, and then the confrontation with their mother yesterday, she'd been walking around with a rock sitting dead center in her chest. Typically, she needed days to prepare for a visit with Lillian but she hadn't even had five minutes to brace herself. Shockingly, her mother's disapproval had been directed at Rose for once. That honor usually belonged to her, the wayward daughter who had little in common with the woman who gave her life. She'd never been quite pretty enough or polished enough or interested in the debates and school theater productions her mother wanted her to pursue.

She'd wanted to play soccer and wear her hair short and dress in sweats for school. *I don't understand you, Magnolia* had been one of Lillian's favorite phrases. As a teen she'd worn those words like a badge of honor, but now that she was older, now that she'd walked through such heartbreak, she couldn't deny that she wanted her mom to understand, to offer her comfort. That's what she would do if she ever became a mom. She'd be like Jess, doting on Patrick and chuckling at his cute mistakes instead of trying to fix them all.

When Patrick and Jess and Lola showed up two hours ago, she'd gotten lost in the baking, in the sweet smiles that boy kept directing at her, and her heart didn't ache quite so much.

"We should get out of your hair." Jess smoothed over baby Lola's beautiful silky black curls.

"Don't be silly." Panic suddenly struck in Mags's chest. They couldn't go. Not yet. They'd had so much fun, and once they left, she'd go back to stewing in her own problems. "You can't leave until we've tested our work." Gazing down at Patrick, she raised her eyebrows. "How would you like to sample a cupcake?"

"Yes!" He jumped off the stool and continued to bounce with the ferocity of a real-life Tigger. "Please, Mama! Please! Please can we try one?"

Jess laughed and shook her head at the same time. "If that's what the professional says we should do." She leaned in close to Mags. "I have a feeling this might go down as one of the best days of his entire life."

Mags smiled and hurried over to a cupboard and pulled out three plates. "Well if we don't test them out, how are we going to know if these cupcakes are any good?"

"Because they look sooooo yummy." Patrick eyed the rows of decorated cupcakes with an intensity that made both Mags and Jess giggle. "I want this one." He reached for a heavily frosted cupcake on the end. "No, this one." His hand reversed course going to grab from the middle. "Oh. Does that one have more frosting?" He pointed.

"That'll do just fine," his mother said sternly. She picked up the cupcake for him and set it on a plate.

"Let's sit at the table and rest our feet," Mags suggested, choosing her cupcake. It had to be the one with the least amount of frosting—which was hard to come by.

Jess picked out a cupcake too, and then joined Mags and Patrick at the table.

"It's good all right!" The boy had already ripped off the paper and taken a huge bite. He grinned at Mags with a colorful frosting mustache. "We did great! Try it!"

"I can't wait." Mags unwrapped hers and took a bite, but when she sunk her teeth in, that sugary smell suddenly overwhelmed her, sending a hard lurch through her stomach. She chewed slowly, willing the sudden bout of nausea to subside. "Mmmm," she murmured, hoping to satisfy that expectant look on the boy's face.

"It's good? Right?" Patrick stuffed another bite into his mouth. "This is the best cupcake I ever had!"

"It's very good," Jess agreed. She seemed to study Mags from across the table.

"How come you're not eating the rest?" Patrick asked her, licking remnants of frosting off the wrapper.

"Oh." Mags set the cupcake on her plate. She couldn't. Not without making a quick run to the kitchen sink. "I might save it. It's almost too good to eat." Even the thought of the frosting in her teeth made her gag. She cleared her throat and quickly stood to fill a glass with water.

"Hey, Patrick," Jess said behind her. "Remember that bathroom down the hall? Why don't you go wash your hands and get cleaned up?"

"Okay." On his way past Mags he paused. "I can help you finish that cupcake when I get back if you want." The offer was so sincere that Mags held back her chuckle.

"We'll see." She cast a look at Jess who was shaking her head with horror. "Or I can send it home with you and you can have it after you eat a healthy dinner."

"Yes!" Patrick bounded out of the kitchen celebrating the whole way.

Mags trudged back to the table with her glass of water and plopped down with a groan.

"Are you okay?"

"It's my stomach. I don't know what's wrong with me. Sometimes I feel great and then other times I suddenly feel like I'm going to lose my lunch. I never know what'll set it off."

"I was the same way." Jess finished off her cupcake and dusted the crumbs off her hands. "It'll get better though. My nausea completely went away in the second trimester. It was like magic."

Trimester? A pained gasp escaped her lips and the weight

came barreling back in to crush her heart. "No. I'm not—" She couldn't be...

"What?" Jess's hand flew to her mouth. "Oh geez. I'm so sorry! I thought—I didn't mean—I just saw you have a wedding ring on and you're so good with kids, and then with the nausea I assumed..." Her whole face turned as red as Sassy's checkered tablecloth.

Heat filled Mags's cheeks. "Don't feel bad. Please." Jess had no way of knowing the struggles they'd endured. "We... um...haven't been able to get pregnant." *Don't cry. Do not let one tear out.* Too late. That emotion spilled over and trickled down her cheek.

And now Jess looked like she was about to burst into tears. "That's even worse. I shouldn't have said that. I shouldn't have said anything! Oh, I'm so sorry."

"What is that divine smell?" Sassy traipsed into the room from the hallway and gasped. "Cupcakes! They're finally done! I just love your cupcakes, Mags." After coming in to meet Jess and Patrick earlier, Sassy had disappeared to her office to wrap presents, but Mags had fully expected her to come sniffing around sooner or later.

Her aunt swiped a cupcake off the counter but froze when she caught sight of Mags and Jess sitting at the table.

Those damn tears wouldn't stop rolling down Mags's cheeks, and now Jess was crying, too.

"My goodness." Sassy rushed the rest of the way to the table and pulled out a chair. "You two look sadder than a kid the day after Christmas."

"It's my fault," Jess blubbered. "I thought Mags was pregnant, so I opened my big mouth..."

"Pregnant?" Sassy turned to look at Mags, her eyes wide.

"I can't be," Mags reminded her aunt. But her heart suddenly seemed to be beating faster and louder.

"You've been dealing with a mysterious illness on and off," the woman murmured, hope lighting her eyes.

No. Mags was afraid to hope. No. It was impossible. Hope had been too painful. "I'm not..." She couldn't seem to say the word. Instead she gazed at Jess, seeing only a blurred version the woman's face. "You said that's how you felt when you were pregnant? Nauseous on and off? Like you were suddenly going to throw up at the most random times?"

Jess nodded, dabbing at her eyes with a napkin. "It was the smells that got to me most. They seemed so much stronger in the beginning. Even good smells—smells I liked—might send me running to throw up in the bathroom."

"Oh my God." Mags had never known. She'd never made it far enough along in any of her pregnancies to have symptoms.

She laid her palms flat on the table, trying to stop the trembling that overtook her.

"Mommy! My hands are clean!" Patrick shot back into the kitchen showing off his clean hands. "See?" he said to Mags. "I washed 'em just like you taught me before we did the frosting."

She tried to smile. Maybe she was smiling? She couldn't tell. Tears built a curtain of blindness in her eyes again, spilling over with a vengeance. "They look amazing," she blubbered. "You're amazing, Patrick, do you know that?" What she wouldn't give to have a little boy or a little girl like him. Someone to love and to teach and to give the world to.

"What's a matter?" Fear quieted his voice. "Why are you sad, Miss Mags?" His chubby little arms came around her.

"I'm not sad," she assured him, hugging him back. "Sometimes tears can be happy," she said, even though caution had already raised its flag. Mags pulled back and peered down at him. "Did you know that?"

He nodded solemnly. "Mommy and Daddy cried when Lola was born. I didn't though. I wasn't that happy."

Laughter bubbled up, mingling with the range of emotions growing inside of her.

"We should go. Give you two some space." Jess stood. "What do you say to Mags?" she asked Patrick.

The little boy frowned, but he knew better than to argue with his mother, Mags had seen evidence of that. "Thanks so so so much Miss Mags."

"You're so so so welcome." She rose from her chair trying to find her balance on shaky legs. "Thank you for coming Patrick. And for being such a sweet boy. I'm happy we got to bake your birthday cupcakes together."

"Me, too." He threw his arms around her waist again.

"Gentle," Jess admonished him.

"He's okay." Mags ruffled his hair.

"You're going to come to my party, right?" He turned to Sassy. "You can come too, Miss Sassy. It's going to be so much fun! We're going to blow-up a bouncy castle!"

"That does sound fun," Sassy agreed.

"I'll do my very best to be there," Mags promised. She'd planned to fly home a few days after Christmas, but maybe Eric didn't want her to come home. She didn't know what her future held. Not for a baby, not for her marriage, not for a viable pregnancy. Anxiety tightened its grip on her chest.

"Keep me posted," Jess said gently, hugging Mags tight.

"Anything you need. Even to talk or something. You've done so much for us so please know I'll be there for you."

Mags nodded, her eyes filling up again. "I'll text you later." She didn't recognize the sound of her own voice.

A strange fog descended over her as Sassy helped Jess and Patrick cart the cupcakes out to their car. Mags eased a hand onto her belly and sank back into a chair, remembering the times she'd found out she was carrying a baby, and then the times she'd seen the blood in the toilet. Sobs rose up her throat, crashing through her with a force that bent her over the table.

Arms came around her, and that scent. Sassy's sweet rosy scent seemed to still everything. "I can't do it again," she moaned, letting her aunt hold her up. "I can't lose another baby." The possibility threatened to break her heart apart.

"I know," Sassy whispered into her hair. "I know, sweet girl. Everything's going to be all right. We're going to take one thing at a time. Just one thing." She smoothed her hand over and over Mags's hair. "First, I want you to breathe. Deeply. Calmly. That's all you have to do in this second, honey. Breathe."

Mags did as she was told, drawing in a breath and holding it before letting herself sigh out an exhale. Her racing heart started to slow its pace.

Sassy let go of her. "Now you need to lift your head, Mags. Lift your head and look at me."

It took effort to raise her chin, to stare into her aunt's vibrant eyes. "You're strong. You're so very strong."

She tried to believe that.

"We need to go see Ike," her aunt said, standing. She didn't let go of Mags's hand though. "None of this trying to decide if we've got two lines or none on some plastic stick. We need a professional's opinion right away."

"Okay." Deep breath. Just breathe. That's all she had to do in this second.

"Do you want to find Dahlia and Rose so they can come with us?" Sassy tugged on her hands, helping her to stand.

"No." It would take too long. Rose was out hanging lights with Colt and Dahlia had gone shopping. She let her aunt lead her to the coat closet. "Only you and me. We need to go now." She had to know.

"Come on, then." Sassy helped her pull on her coat and then led her outside, down the steps, and to her car. Mags said nothing on the drive to the clinic. She simply stared. Couldn't talk, couldn't think, couldn't let herself feel anything.

Once they reached Ike's clinic they slipped inside the door together, her aunt holding her hand.

"Well look who it is!" The receptionist stood up from behind the desk. "I didn't know you had an appointment today, Sassy." Like most other people in town, the middle-aged woman greeted her aunt with a hug.

"No appointment for me." Her aunt leaned in closer. "We need to see Ike as soon as possible."

"We'll get you right on back." The receptionist waved them toward a door and ushered them down the hall and into an exam room like they were VIPs. "I'll tell Ike you're here," she said before closing the door.

Mags slid into a chair next to her aunt and stared at the framed photograph of a glassy mountain lake reflecting the surrounding peaks, trying to soak in the peacefulness of the image. As much as she tried to ward off hope, it had still taken root in the deepest part of her, somehow outmatching the fear and the uncertainty with its weak but glowing light.

How could she be pregnant? Maybe she had simply wanted it so much for so long that her body was fooling her. "We've only had sex once since the last failed treatment." Before that, they'd done it every time there might've been a chance she was fertile. Every time the doctors told them it would be the perfect time…

"Once is all it takes." Sassy held her hand.

"Not for us." Mags's gaze bored into the photograph of the mountain lake. "The doctors told us we only had a five percent chance of getting pregnant naturally."

"Pshaw. What do doctors know?" Sassy said, just as the door opened.

Ike walked in laughing. "Not much."

"See?" Her aunt looked quite pleased with herself. "How are you, Dr. Ike? Having a good day today?"

"It keeps getting better." He closed the door, quickly, seeming to sense an urgency. "What can I do for you two?"

"I need a pregnancy test," Mags blurted before her aunt could say anything.

To Ike's credit, he didn't look shocked. "Okay," he said, as though he heard those exact words every day. "Do you have a reason to suspect you might be pregnant?"

No. She shouldn't have a reason. It would make no sense. "That illness Dahlia was bugging me about. It still hasn't gone away. It comes and goes. I'll feel fine one minute and then all of a sudden I'll feel like I'm going to throw up out of nowhere." But a lot of people had nervous stomachs. And she had been under a lot of stress.

"She's been tired," Sassy volunteered. "Very tired."

"Ah." The man nodded as though making a mental note. "Do you know when your last menstrual cycle was?"

"I can't remember exactly." After going off the treatments she'd stopped paying attention. "Things have been kind of messed up in that department. We were going through fertility treatments, but the last one failed." Her voice wavered. "And I've had three miscarriages."

Ike reached over to squeeze her hand. "That doesn't mean you'll have another one."

Mags nodded, letting a few more tears slip out. If Dahlia didn't go after this man, she was going to let her sister have it.

"All right." The man stood. "We're going to make this as quick and easy as possible. Why don't you go down to the bathroom and leave a urine sample? Then you can come back in here and we'll run the test. I'll come back the second I have results."

"That would be great. Thank you." She followed him out into the hall, her feet clunky, and found the restroom. Her hands shook as she went about the task, but, somehow, she left the sample and made it back to the exam room without crying again.

"I'm afraid to hear no and I'm afraid to hear yes." She sat down next to her aunt again, caught in the tug-of-war between hope and doubt.

"I can certainly understand that." Sassy turned to face her. "What scares you the most?"

She didn't even have to think about the answer. "That I might never be a mother." That was the missing piece of her. The broken piece she couldn't fix. It had become a hole in her heart she couldn't fill, and it was stealing everything from her—her joy, her marriage...

"Oh, but Mags...my dear..." Sassy pressed her cool palm

against her cheek. "You already are a mother. You might not have been able to hold your babies in your arms, but you've cradled them in your heart all this time. You know that love. You know how it changes you from the inside out. Maybe you know it better than most people because of all you've lost."

"Thank you." A sob rose up her throat. No one had ever acknowledged that before. No one had ever called her a mother. After she'd seen the blood in the toilet the first time she'd miscarried, she'd been whisked in to the doctor for a D&C and then sent home with post-procedure instructions. No one had said the word "baby." No one had said the word "mother."

A knock on the door set her heart ablaze. But with her aunt holding tightly to her hand, a strength rose up, trampling over her fears. "Come in."

Ike stepped fully inside the room and closed the door behind him. "We got the results and I'm thrilled to be the first one to congratulate you, Mags. You are definitely pregnant."

She let out the breath she'd been holding. A few tears escaped, too. "Wow. Wow." That was all she could seem to say.

"What wonderful news." Sassy wrapped her in a hug, both laughing and crying.

"Congratulations." Ike squeezed her shoulder. "I have a good friend who's an OB in Salida. They're supposed to be closed tomorrow since it's Christmas Eve and all. But I could call her and see if she'd be willing to take one patient."

"Yes." She held back another sob. "Please. Yes. Tell her I can be there whenever it works for her." That was what she needed most—to see the baby. To hear that little heartbeat.

"I'll call her right now," Ike promised, opening the door. "You can stay here as long as you like. Take as much time as you need."

"Thank you." Mags sprung up and hugged the doctor, feeling a sudden energy run through her. "I really appreciate this."

"It's nothing," he assured her. "Congratulations, Mama." He turned to walk out the door. "I'll let you know what my friend says as soon as I can."

Mags nodded, laughed, and cried, cradling her belly in her hands. She whirled to face her sweet aunt. "I'm having a baby." Saying it out loud made her heart bust at the seams. "Eric and I are a having a baby." It didn't matter if Eric had started to drift away, or if he was ready to give up. She wouldn't let him. She would fight for him. She would fight for this baby. She would fight for her family.

Chapter Twenty-Two

Dahlia

T hat's it. I'm not going on the date."

Dahlia threw the plaid shirt onto the mountain of clothes that had slowly piled up on her bed. She couldn't wear a plaid shirt on a date! When she'd packed for this trip, a date had been the last thing on her mind. She'd brought comfy clothes that you'd wear out on a cold walk or that you'd dress in to sit by a cozy fire. She hadn't even considered that she might have to impress a man.

"Who are talking to?" Rose walked in with Marigold trotting along behind her.

"Myself." Dahlia never thought she'd see the day when her sister had a furry sidekick. Rose's sudden bond with the dog only proved miracles happened. Maybe she should close her eyes and click her heels and her fairy godmother would appear.

"Whoa." Her sister stood back and evaluated Mount St. Clothing with a frown. "Is that the Goodwill pile or the trash pile?"

"Very funny." Dahlia slumped onto the edge of the bed, running her hand over Marigold's soft fur. "That, my dear sister, is the full extent of my wardrobe here. Apparently, I left all my dating clothes at home." Buried in the back of her closet where they'd probably been for the last fifteen years.

Rose started to pick up garments one by one, giving them a detailed appraisal. "Ew. Yes. Wow. You can't wear any of these tonight." She tossed a sweatshirt back onto the pile like it was contaminated.

"That's okay. I don't need to go on a date anyway." She couldn't date! She was out of practice. What would they talk about? Dancing with Ike in a crowd was one thing, but they'd be alone, sitting across the table from each other...

"Oh, you're going on that date." Rose pulled her up and prodded her across the hall to her bedroom. "We're pretty close to the same size, and you know I never travel without preparing for an impromptu special occasion."

That was a true statement. Her sister had been overpacking since the early nineties. "I don't need to borrow your clothes. It's fine. I don't even know how to act on a date anyway."

Rose took Dahlia's shoulders in her hands forcing her to look into Rose's eyes. "Act like you, Dahlia. The caring, nurturing, incredibly smart woman you are." She let her go. "And if Ike doesn't like that woman, then he's not worth a second date." Her sister's eyes gleamed. "But I highly doubt that's going to happen. I see the way he looks at you. Truthfully, I highly doubt that he'll care if you're wearing a sweatshirt or some chic blouse." Rose shook her head. "Scratch that. I care if you're wearing a sweatshirt or a chic blouse. Give me one minute." She hurried into the walk-in closet on the other side of the room.

Ah, so that's why her sister had insisted she had to stay in this guest room. It was likely the only closet in the house that would fit all of the clothes she must've brought.

"Okay." Her sister marched out of the closet with an armload of garments and proceeded to lay at least seven different outfits out on the bed.

Marigold walked around sniffing them as though trying to help them decide which one would work best.

"I'm feeling something blue for you tonight." Rose stepped back and seemed to evaluate two different blue sweaters.

Dahlia couldn't hold back a smile. "What have I done without you for the last thirteen years?" she teased. "It's a wonder I have ever been able to get dressed by myself."

"We'll talk about a shopping trip after this crisis is averted," her sister informed her. "Ah, yes." She snatched a beautiful, soft, baby-blue sweater off the bed. "This would go perfectly with these jeans." She lay the sweater across a pair of dark jeggings.

"Are you sure you want me to wear that?" Dahlia reached out to run her fingers over the soft sweater. It had to be the highest quality cashmere. It had probably cost five hundred dollars or something crazy. And she hadn't bought anything that wasn't on sale since before Maya and Ollie were born. As always when she thought of them, that pang of longing squeezed around her heart. She hadn't heard from them today, but they were also supposed to be traveling on to London. Hopefully she'd get an update tomorrow.

"Yes, you can wear it." Rose handed her the sweater and the jeggings. "Try them on. I think I have the perfect pashmina to go with them." She disappeared back into the closet.

"How many suitcases did you bring?" Dahlia slipped off her sweatshirt and jeans, neatly folding them on the bed. Next to all of Rose's elegant clothes they stuck out as frumpy mom attire.

"I only brought four suitcases," her sister called from the closet.

"Four?" Dahlia laughed. She'd managed to stuff everything she'd brought into one suitcase so she didn't have to pay for another one. Of course, she didn't have a whole closet full of designer clothes and fashionable boots, so there was that. Sucking in her waist an extra couple of inches, Dahlia pulled on the jeggings Rose had handed her, shimmying them up over her thighs and hips. "Wow." She smoothed her hands down her legs. The material had quite the slimming effect.

"Found it!" Rose rushed out of the closet as Dahlia pulled on the sweater.

"Oh my." She'd never felt cashmere so soft.

"This will be perfect." Rose wrapped the silk pashmina around Dahlia's shoulders, and then turned her around to face the mirror above the dresser.

"Well, well, well." Mags sauntered into the room and gave off a catcall. "Looking hot, Dally. Getting all gussied up for your date tonight?"

"Apparently." There was something to be said for expensive clothes. They were elegant but not overdone and most importantly they made her feel…pretty.

"You've still got it, sis." Mags sat on the bed and petted the dog.

"Definitely," Rose agreed, readjusting the pashmina and then standing back as though admiring her work. "Ike won't be able to resist you."

Well, she didn't know about that, but hopefully the outfit would show him just how interested she was in spending more time with him.

Mags stood and joined them in front of the mirror. "Speaking of Ike, he sure seems excited about tonight."

Dahlia eyed her. "What? How do you know?"

Her sister went back to the bed and sat down. "I just came from the clinic."

"Really?" Panic rushed in, prickling Dahlia's skin with sudden warmth. "Why didn't you tell me you were going? Did you feel sick again?"

"Not exactly."

Dahlia caught her sister's eyes in the mirror. Wait. Had she been crying? "What is it?" She spun, the pashmina unraveling from her shoulders. "What's wrong? Did Ike find something?"

"Yes." A slow smile reached her sister's eyes. "He found something all right. I'm pregnant."

"Pregnant!" Rose lurched for the bed, but Dahlia beat her there.

"Oh, Mags. Oh honey. That's amazing." She was so happy she couldn't seem to catch her breath. "Are you okay? Have you told Eric?"

"I tried to call him, but he didn't answer. We just got back. Sassy went with me." Her sister paused as though she was overwhelmed. "I'm not sure how to tell him. The last time we talked about the fertility treatments, he didn't want a baby. We've already lost a couple. There's a chance—"

"You won't lose this one." Dear God, surely they wouldn't. Not when they'd already endured so much heartache. Dahlia took off the pashmina and tossed it onto the bed. "I should stay home tonight. We should be together."

"No, no, no. You have to go." Mags wrapped the scarf back around Dahlia's neck. "Besides, I'm going to bed soon. I need some space to sit with the news. To think through some things." Mags had always been that way. More of an internal processor when it came to her emotions. It used to drive Dahlia crazy.

"But I could at least be here. In case you did want to talk or something. I could—"

"You're not finding a way out of this date my dear." Mags shut her down with an amused stare. "Frankly, Ike seems crazy about you and I'm crazy about him. So, I refuse to be the reason you stand him up."

"Agreed." Rose invited Marigold up onto the bed to lay across all three of their laps. "Mags and I will eat junk food and snuggle with Marigold in front of a Hallmark movie, and then when you get home, you can give us all the juicy details about your date."

"*If* she comes home." Mags elbowed Rose and they both laughed.

"Oh, come on you two." That wasn't happening. Was it? Nerves buzzed in her stomach, but quickly flared into something that felt more like a simmering anticipation. "It can't happen! It's been eons, given how sparse *that* was during the last few years of my marriage." She was out of practice when it came to sex. "And I can't remember the last time I had a bikini wax!"

"A man isn't going to care about a bikini wax if he gets to have sex," Mags insisted. "And don't worry...it's like riding a bike."

"Yeah," Rose added, laughing so hard she almost couldn't talk. "You gotta climb back on and ride the horse again someday."

Both of her sisters collapsed into giggles and threw themselves back onto the bed.

Maybe it was the nerves or maybe the relief at seeing Mags laugh, but Dahlia threw herself back and laughed, too. The whole thing was absolutely ludicrous. Her having sex after practically being a nun for the last three years? She laughed even harder, tears rolling down her cheeks.

Marigold inched up from their laps and started to lick their faces, which set off a whole other round of laughter.

When the giggles died down, Dahlia turned to Mags. "Everything's going to be okay," she told her. "I'm so happy for you."

"And I'm happy you get to go on a date with Ike." Her sister tweaked her nose.

"And I'm happy for both of you." Rose jumped up. "But we have work to do. Dally needs to be ready in T-minus fifteen minutes."

"What?" She bolted upright. How had it gotten that late?

"Not to worry." Mags pushed off the bed, too. "We've got this."

"Totally." Rose pulled her up and her sisters ushered her into the bathroom across the hall. Sitting her down on the toilet, they ambushed her with a blow-dryer and brush, makeup, and God only knew what else.

Fourteen minutes later, Dahlia stood in front of the mirror again, and it was almost like she was staring at a former version of herself. They'd taken ten years off her easy. "You two should start a makeover business together." They'd make millions.

Rose leaned in and fluffed Dahlia's hair. "It's not like we performed a miracle. You're already beautiful."

"Yeah." Mags handed her the lip gloss they'd used. "We only helped bring out your natural beauty a little more."

Dahlia peeked into the mirror again. "Whatever. You totally performed a miracle." She hadn't seen herself look like this since that night she'd tried to dress up for Jeff two years ago. It had occurred to her after he left for work one morning that it had been three months since they'd made love, so she'd arranged for the kids to go home with friends from school, and then she'd made dinner, put on her sexiest dress, and ended up getting a text that he was working late. Too bad he'd already been sleeping with someone else by then.

"Come on." Rose whisked her out of the bathroom. "Dr. Ike will be here any minute."

"You two aren't going to take pictures or anything. Are you?" Dahlia asked as they made their way down the steps.

Rose and Mags shared a bright-eyed look.

Fabulous. She shouldn't be giving them any ideas.

When they reached the bottom of the steps, the three of them stopped. She could hear Ike's engaging voice from the kitchen.

"I can't breathe." Dahlia clutched at the pashmina, loosening it, but that didn't make it any easier to inhale. It struck her that she wouldn't be this nervous if she didn't have already have some feelings for the man.

"You two are going to have the best time," Rose assured her, nudging her toward the kitchen. But Ike and Sassy came walking down the hall, and Dahlia didn't have time to argue.

Ike stopped abruptly when he saw her standing there. "Hey."

A distinct shifting in her heart gave her vertigo. "Hi." Even with her shyness trying to take over, she couldn't look away from him. He'd dressed in a deep green crewneck sweater with a worn brown leather coat. And those jeans...

"You two have a good time," Sassy sang, sweeping an arm around Mags and Rose. "We have a lot of work to do in the kitchen, right girls?"

"Right." Rose turned back to stare over her shoulder, but Sassy continued moving them down the hall.

"Goodnight!" Mags yelled.

"We won't wait up!" Rose added.

Wow, real subtle. The heat on Dahlia's face outmatched the warmth simmering low in her stomach, but Ike simply laughed.

"Must be fun to have sisters," he said, moving in a few steps closer. "I only have brothers myself. They hardly even keep in touch."

His easy way of conversation pulled her out of her earlier timidity. "It's hard to keep in touch when you live far away. I'm really grateful to have this time with them." Even if they were intent on embarrassing her in front of her date.

"Yeah. My youngest brother Mason is in Thailand. He's a wanderer." Ike casually slipped his arm around Dahlia and led her to the front door as if it was the most natural thing in the world. "And Brock, my older brother, lives in Alaska."

"So, you're really spread out." Dahlia pulled her winter coat off the rack, and Ike immediately helped her slip it on.

"We are. My mom's in California, so we all try to meet up there a couple times a year." He took a hat and gloves out of his coat pocket and pulled them on. "Ready?"

"Yes." After being unsure earlier, she was so ready to be alone with him, to get to know him. As they stepped outside, she put on her hat and the fuzzy mittens she'd picked up in town the other day. Snow fell softly, illuminating the night sky, making the evening sparkle.

Just outside the door, Ike paused. "I thought we'd do a choose-your-own-adventure date this evening."

She wasn't sure why she found it so easy to gaze into his eyes. She only knew she never wanted to look away. "What'd you mean?"

"I mean, I'm giving you options." His smile was all mystery. "We can either go out to dinner at a great restaurant about twenty minutes away, or I could make you dinner at my cabin." He took her arm and escorted her down the porch steps. "I would've said I could make you dinner here, but I don't want to kick out Sassy and your sisters for the evening."

"No. That wouldn't be good." But a quiet dinner just the two of them did sound amazing. And the fact that he'd given her a choice made it even better. "Let's do dinner at your place."

"Homemade pizza it is then." He led her toward his truck.

Dahlia stopped and gaped at him. *"Homemade?"* She'd never had a man make her homemade anything.

"It's my dad's secret dough recipe," Ike explained. "It was the only thing he ever made in the kitchen. I already put it together and had it rising just in case." He opened the passenger's door.

Dahlia was about to climb in, but her gaze stuck on the view of the barn farther down the hill. It was all lit up with colorful lights, which glowed festively beneath the thin layer of fresh snow. Beyond that, the decorated trees lit a path all the way down to the pond. "Actually, can we walk down to your cabin?" She took a step back. The air was freezing, but Ike made her warm. And what better way to start their date than with a romantic walk to his cabin?

"I'd like that." He shut the truck's door and they started off together, their boots crunching in the snow.

After a few steps, Ike grabbed her mitten-clad hand, holding it in his. "Colt and Rose went all out with the lights."

"They sure did." It seemed every tree sparkled with a different color. One had been draped with bright pink lights, another with blue. That one farther down had green, and then there was one with orange. "Oh, look at that one." She pointed to the juniper pine that had been decked out with silvery sparkle lights. A contented sigh filled up her chest. "It looks so much like it did when we would visit all those years ago." A magical Christmas wonderland.

They passed the barn, walking slowly, and for once, Dahlia felt no desire to rush, to be on a schedule. Instead she wanted to simply be. To breathe it all in.

"I bet you have some great memories of this place," Ike said softly.

"So many." She closed her eyes and could still see them, playing like a film reel through her mind. Opening her eyes again, she wrapped her arm through Ike's, moving closer to the man. "It's funny... I've been away for a long time but coming here has been like coming home."

"I feel that way about Juniper Springs, too." He paused, gazing up at the lighted statue of Santa's sleigh perched on the barn's roof. "It's the place I fit."

"I know what you mean." After floundering for the past year, it felt good for her to be in Sassy's house, to be with her sisters. In so many ways it had reminded her who she was before her marriage, before her marriage had fallen apart.

"Hey." Ike looked at something over her shoulder. "What's that?"

Dahlia turned. Beyond the barn, a glow of light and color lit up the aspen trees. "The camper!" Dahlia took off in a jog, her feet and heart light. Being the good sport he was, Ike followed behind.

"They decorated it!" The entire camper was outlined in twinkling pastel-colored lights. "It's beautiful." She and her sisters still hadn't managed to clean up the outside, but with the bright lights the camper had taken on a new life.

"Should we take a peek?" Ike tried the door, and it swung open.

"Yes!" She rushed up the steps and flipped on the lights. She hadn't seen the inside since Rose had put on the finishing touches. "Look at this," she breathed. Her sister had reupholstered everything with bright flowery fabric. She'd repainted all the old, ugly wood paneling white. "She made pillows." Cute fluffy pillows with ruffles. A few of their old stuffed animals and tea sets had been incorporated into the design scheme as accents.

"It's pretty cool," Ike agreed. "But I can't imagine camping in here."

Dahlia laughed. "It's a little fancy for camping. But it was always so special to us. It's where we used to play and daydream."

He approached her, sliding his arms around her waist, his hands meeting at the small of her back, and it was so good to be held that way—with gentleness and care but also with passion.

"What did you dream about back then?"

She slid her hands up his shoulders, wishing her coat wasn't so puffy so she could get even closer to him. "Growing up to be fancy and successful and beautiful."

"You are beautiful." His smile always had a way of bringing out hers. "Not just tonight, either. I think you're a beautiful person, and that's not based on what clothes you're wearing." He skimmed his thumb over her glossed lips. "Or the makeup you put on." His eyes held hers, seeming to see everything. "You're organized, ordered mind is beautiful. The way you care about other people is beautiful. The way you love your kids is beautiful. Your strength is beautiful."

"I haven't felt beautiful in a long time." Not until now. Not until him. "You make me feel a lot of things."

His gaze shifted to her lips. "Yeah?"

"Yeah." She moved to her tiptoes, bringing her face in line with his. "I want to feel more."

The whisper drew him closer, and his lips touched hers, drowning out everything except the beat of her heart, the ache in her lungs. This man was warmth and light—the sunrise after a long, dark, lonely night waking everything its rays touched.

Somehow the radiance spread all through her, reaching into the farthest corners, ending the lonely twilight that had descended over her heart.

Chapter Twenty-Three

Rose

Rose hung another bough of holly on the curtain rod she'd made for the camper, belting out a stanza of "Deck the Halls."

As had become her custom, Marigold whine-howled along, sounding even more off-key than Rose. "You know something, pooch? You're the only one in the whole world who can harmonize with me." To think she'd never had a dog before! In such a short time, Marigold had become her other half, her missing piece, the yin to her yang. She'd had no idea what she had been missing out on all those years, but apparently, she'd been living with a Marigold-shaped hole in her heart.

The dog jumped onto the dinette bench and put her paws on Rose's chest, her tail moving the curtain behind her.

"Deck the halls with boughs of holly," Rose sang loudly.

"Raw rooo raw," the dog took over, jumping up onto the table like she wanted a stage.

Laughing, she continued the song. "'Tis the season to be jolly—"

"I'll say."

Colt's voice startled her into silence. She'd been singing so loudly—and horribly—she hadn't heard him come in from behind her. "Hi!" She spun, a sudden happiness fluttering through her chest. But it was only because they'd become friends of sorts ever since that day on the ladder. At least she liked to think of him as a friend. He didn't seem to stew or glare anymore in her presence anyway.

He walked a couple of steps into the camper, stopping to pet Marigold's head. "I see you two are still getting along."

Rose's heart seemed to pause right in the middle of a beat. Had he found Marigold's owners? "She is everything I never knew I needed." She hadn't mean to sound so desperate, but she couldn't give up the dog now. They'd already bonded. They'd shared a bed!

"It's a good thing because I still haven't found her owners." Colt took a seat on the bench and continued to give the dog some love. "Even with the signs we posted around town. So, unless something crazy happens, my guess is you'll get to keep her."

"Forever?" She plopped down on the bench across from Colt, leaning to the left so she could see him past the dog.

"Yeah. If you want to, that is."

How could he even question her? "I want to. I really want to." But…she still hadn't figured out what her life would look like next week. How could she go back to Savannah and marry Gregory when every part of her wanted to be here. How could she walk into a marriage when she didn't feel the same kind of passion Sassy had felt for Larry and Robert? Worry started to crowd in, dampening her hall-decking capabilities.

Colt didn't seem to pick up on her emotional swing. He glanced around the trailer. "This place looks amazing. You're

really talented Rose. You're good at making things look nice."
She'd never seen his face look so boyish. Relaxed but also a little
unsure. "You could do a whole lot with the inn."

Oh, the inn. She'd love to get her hands on all of it—to work
on each cabin and Sassy's main house, to bring out the original
charm. There was a problem though. "I'm not sure Mags, Dally,
and I will be able to hold on to the inn." A crack split through
her heart when she said it, but there was the truth. Dally had
her kids back in Minneapolis. Mags was expecting a baby now,
and well, Rose had a lot of details to work out in her life. She
glanced up at Colt, doing her best not to sigh. "You should have
it. Or at least a part of it. I feel like it belongs to you, too." And
he lived right in town. He could likely do a lot more with it than
she ever could.

"I have good memories here." He peered out the camper
window, which was facing the pond. "I'm grateful to Sassy for
giving me a place. She didn't have to. A lot of people turned their
backs on my dad after he got arrested, but she never did."

"That doesn't surprise me at all." Sassy had never cared much
what people thought. Doing the right thing meant more to her
than appearances. Rose would like to think she could be that
way, too. "Were you upset with your father?" she asked, trying to
gauge the emotion in his eyes. This was the most Colt had ever
said about his past. He obviously didn't like talking about it.

"Yeah." He nodded slowly, as though taking his time to consider
the question. "I wasn't mad he'd robbed a bank though. I know
why he did it. Hell, I'd probably do the same thing for someone
I loved." His thoughtful stare grazed hers before lowering back
to the table. "I was mad he got caught though. As stupid as it
sounds. I blamed him for getting caught."

"That doesn't sound stupid." She reached over the dog and brushed her hand over his. "I think I would've felt the same way." Colt's whole world had likely changed when his father had been taken away. It was normal to direct that anger somewhere. "You wanted him with you, that's all."

"Yeah, I did." Colt cleared his throat as though he'd gotten uncomfortable. "Anyway. Let me know what you and your sisters decide about the inn. I'd be interested in buying it." Rose didn't have to remind him Sassy would likely give it to him. She could see the determination in his eyes. He wouldn't allow that.

"I have to talk to Dally and Mags." Neither of whom she'd seen yet this morning. She'd done her best to wait up for their older sister so they could debrief the big date, but by one o'clock in the morning, Rose had fallen into bed. After putting center-pieces on all the tables in the barn and setting out the poinsettias they'd purchased from the flower shop and giving Betty one final cleaning, she couldn't keep her eyes open. When she'd woken up and gone to Dally's room this morning, the bed was empty, but it looked like it had been slept in at some point. She planned to voice her staunch disapproval that Dally hadn't spent the night with Ike to her sister later.

"I don't see any of us being able to put in the time or effort to keep this place up." She hadn't meant to sound so sad when she said it. "It doesn't seem to fit in with any of our lives."

Colt shrugged. "Maybe take some more time to think on it. Seems to me you can fit whatever you want into your life."

"Sure," she said, even though it wasn't that simple. "We'll talk through things before we leave." They had another four days here after Christmas. Could that be right? Only five days left with her sisters?

Colt nodded and rose from the bench. "Everything ready for tonight?"

"I think so." This morning she'd panicked that Betty wouldn't look festive enough. Hence the boughs of holly. Though now she wasn't singing or humming anymore.

"I have to admit, I can't believe you pulled it off." She still hadn't gotten used to seeing his smile. He had a shallow dimple in his left cheek.

"*We* pulled it off," Rose reminded him. "We make kind of a great team." When they finally started working together everything fell into place.

"Yeah. I guess we do make a good team." There was that shy look again. "I guess I'll see you later. I've got to make sure the sleigh is all ready for flight tonight."

"I can't wait to—"

"Hello?" The door popped open, and Rose froze mid-sentence. That voice. It couldn't be...

Gregory stepped inside the camper.

Still sitting up on the table, Marigold barked.

Rose calmed the dog with a scratch behind the ears and blinked her eyes furiously, but each time she opened them, her fiancé still stood there. Her heart fell. This is not what she'd envisioned. Having him show up like this. How could she break up with him the day before Christmas? "What're you doing here?"

Gregory's million-dollar smile fell away. "Hello to you, too."

Colt stood between them looking silently back and forth.

"Sorry." Rose shook herself free from the shock. "I'm just...surprised." And sad. Seeing him standing there made her heart heavy.

"I couldn't do it, babe." Gregory inched forward but there

wasn't enough space for him to get around Colt. "I couldn't spend Christmas away from you. I thought I'd surprise you. So, I flew out on the jet, and your aunt told me I'd find you down here." He spread out his arms like he wanted to pull her into them. "Merry Christmas."

"Merry Christmas." Rose didn't move. She wasn't sure how. Colt still stood between them. But that wasn't all that stood between them.

"I should get going." Colt lurched toward Gregory, and they man-danced around each other so Colt could get past.

"I'm so sorry." Rose came to her senses and rushed to them. "Gregory...this is Colt. He's a friend of the family."

"Ah." Her fiancé gave Colt a quick appraisal. "Nice to meet you."

"Yeah. Same." Colt shot a quick glance at Rose. "Let me know if you need anything else before tonight." He headed for the door, and Gregory watched him go with an eyebrow cocked. "Aren't you taking your dog?"

Colt paused. "Uh..."

"Marigold isn't Colt's dog." She walked back to the table and hugged the dog to her. "She's mine."

"Yours?" Her fiancé laughed. "But you *hate* dogs."

"I've never hated dogs!" What kind of person would *hate* dogs? "I was afraid of them, but Marigold helped me see the error of my ways." Really, it had been Colt who'd helped her get over her fear, but she didn't say so. "We found her outside. She's a stray. And she's absolutely the sweetest dog in the whole world. You're going to love her." She wasn't sure why she said it. To keep up appearances, maybe? Because she couldn't face the thought of breaking Gregory's heart on Christmas Eve...

Gregory laughed again. "She's not coming home with you."

He glanced over his shoulder at Colt shaking his head as if to say *Rose is nuts.*

Heat rose from her neck to the tips of her ears. "Yes she is."

"I should go." Colt darted out the door. "See you tonight," he called behind him.

"Right! Yep!" She tried to keep her voice chipper, but the second Colt disappeared, her embarrassment boiled over. Rose marched to Gregory. "She's my dog. She loves me. She follows me around everywhere. I can't leave her here."

"Come on, babe." A sigh signaled his waning patience. "We don't have time for a pet. Especially a dog. We're way too busy. And she's too big for condo living."

"I don't like being busy." These last three weeks had been heaven. She'd hadn't spent all day every day running. She'd wandered. She'd watched movies. She'd actually had time to bond with her sisters. The rest of the words stalled in brain. *I'm sorry. I can't do this.* Why couldn't she say it? Because it would be best to wait. Until after the holidays. Until they were back in Savannah. Until she could warn her mother.

"Let's not fight about this right now." Gregory seemed to dismiss the whole discussion. "We can talk about it later. Why don't you go pack up your stuff and we'll go find a good hotel?"

"Hotel?" Now it was her turn to laugh. "I'm not leaving the inn."

A tic worked its way through Gregory's jaw. "We don't want to stay here. It's too crowded. And where am I going to work out?"

"In the woods?" she suggested. "There are no luxury hotels in town." She'd been looking forward to Christmas here. With her sisters. And now Gregory had walked in and was trying to change everything.

"I know there are no luxury hotels here." He eased his hands onto her shoulders, giving her a gentle massage. "I was thinking we could spend a few nights in Aspen. We would come here to spend Christmas Day with your sisters—"

"Aspen is two hours away." On a good weather day.

"So?" he argued. "We have a driver."

"I'm not leaving." Rose backed away from him. This was supposed to be her calm Christmas before the storm. "I like it here. I like the calm and the coziness. I like being with my sisters." Maybe that was selfish. But that's all she wanted for Christmas. To stay here.

"I came all the way out here to spend time with you…"

Her heart raced with panic. This was not supposed to happen. "I know. But we can spend time together *here*. Please. It's such a beautiful place. I know you'll fall in love with it the way I have."

"Fine. We'll stay here." He brushed a quick kiss across her lips. "I need to go check in with work. Where would be the best place to do that?"

"Aunt Sassy has an office in the main house. I'm sure she'd be fine if you used it." Rose prodded Marigold to hop off the table. "Come on." She led him out of the camper. Together, they tromped through the snow up the hill. "See." She smiled over at him. "You can get a great workout hiking through the snow." Keep things light. That was the only way she would get through this.

He smiled back, but it seemed tighter than normal. "I guess I'll have to give it a try."

The rest of the way back to the house, Gregory chatted about all of the events he'd been forced to attend over the last three weeks, and once they stepped inside, they shed their winter coats and hung them up on the coatrack.

Rose led him into the kitchen where Dahlia and Mags were seated at the table. "There you are." She studied her sister's face for any hints about how last night had gone with Ike. "I was hoping to see you this morning, but you were already gone."

Her sister smiled mysteriously. "Hello, Gregory," she said, instead of offering any information. "How are you?"

"I'm okay."

Rose noticed he didn't say *great*. They had that in common right now.

"How's Jeff?" he asked politely.

Rose gasped and elbowed him. "They've been divorced for a year! You knew that." Seriously? Didn't he listen to her?

"Oh right." Gregory shrugged. "Sorry about that." He turned his attention to Mags. "What about Eric? How are things at the fire department?"

"Things are great," Rose said before her sister broke down in tears. Poor Mags. One mention of Eric and her bottom lip started to tremble. "Didn't you say you have some work to do?"

"I do." Gregory pulled out his phone right on cue. "The service isn't great right here. Not sure I can use my hot spot. Where is that office you were telling me about?"

"Down the hall, off to the left of the living room." She all but pushed him in that direction. Once Gregory was gone, Rose dragged Dahlia back to the table. "I need details. How was the date? What happened? Why weren't you home when I went to bed?"

Mags laughed. "Geez. One thing at a time."

"The date was great." Dally couldn't seem to stop smiling. "Ike is…well, he's different than anyone I've ever met."

"Ohhhh." She couldn't remember the last time she'd seen her sister look so happy. "Did he kiss you?"

"Oh, he kissed her," Mags answered for her.

"There was a lot of kissing," Dally admitted. "Amazing wonderful kissing. We walked down to his cabin, and he made me dinner. Then he played the guitar for me, and we sat on his couch in front of the fire talking and kissing until he walked me home."

Rose let out a squeal. "I knew you'd have a great time." She reached over to squeeze both of her sister's hands. "You deserve it."

"She deserves it," Mags echoed, looking a little teary. Rose removed one of her hands from Dally's and put it over Mags's hand. "How're you feeling about everything today?"

"Still overwhelmed." One of those tears spilled over. "But also hopeful. Ike set up an appointment for me at a clinic today. You two are both coming, by the way. And I'm sure Eric will call me back anytime now."

"I'm sure he will—"

"I can't get service here and there's no Wi-Fi." Gregory stormed back into the kitchen. "Your aunt doesn't have Wi-Fi," he said in disbelief. "How is that possible?"

The back of Rose's neck tightened with tension. "This is a tiny inn located in a small mountain town." She did her best to rein in the impatience flashing through her tone.

"You can plug your computer into the router," Dahlia offered. "That worked for me. It wasn't the fastest, but it got the job done."

Gregory continued to stare at Rose. "I have files to send."

"Then go to the coffee shop in town." She forced a smile. "They have good Wi-Fi there." And it would be the best place for him. She had to focus on the extravaganza tonight. And then she'd figure out how to tell him it was over.

Gregory shook his head and walked back out, muttering to himself the whole way.

An awkward silence descended over Rose and her sisters for a few seconds before Mags asked, "Are things okay with you two?"

"No." There was no sense in lying, even to herself. "Things are not okay at all."

Chapter Twenty-Four

Magnolia

Magnolia leaned over the counter holding the pastry bag above the Santa cookie. *Steady, now.* Somehow, she had to stop the shaking in her hands so she could create Santa's eyeballs with a dab of frosting.

"Hey." Dahlia nearly floated into the room. Ever since her date with Ike she seemed to be walking with an extra bounce in her step. "Are you ready? Aren't we supposed to meet Ike's friend at the clinic in a half hour?"

Mags straightened, setting down the pastry bag. She'd been purposely avoiding looking at the clock, trying to ward off the anxiety by decorating the last few cookies they needed for tonight. But now she had to face it. Leaning against the counter, she pressed her hand against her stomach, willing that little baby in there to hold on, to grow, to feel the love she already had for him or her.

"Have you been able to get ahold of Eric?" Dally stole two cookies from the counter and held one out to Mags, but she couldn't stomach eating anything right now.

"No. He hasn't been answering his phone." He was likely still at work, but she'd hoped to catch him when he wasn't busy. "They must be out on a call or something." Never in her marriage had she felt so disconnected from her husband. They'd always been best friends. He'd always text her when he was on a big call, keeping her updated so she'd know he was okay.

"I'm sure he'll call you as soon as he can." Her sister slipped an arm around her.

"We have to go!" Rose rushed into the room, pulling on her coat. "Sassy is warming up the car."

"Right." Mags stepped away from the counter feeling a weakness in her legs. No more stalling. It was time to hear what the doctor had to say.

"I'm sure the baby is going to be completely healthy," Rose insisted.

"I really want to believe that." Mags made her way across the kitchen and down the hall to where her coat hung.

"But," Dally prompted, pulling on her hat and scarf.

"But there are so many ugly memories." Those horrible moments when the doctor confirmed there was no heartbeat, that she'd miscarried. When she'd fallen apart in Eric's arms. He'd held her. They'd gotten each other through it.

"I know, sweetie." Rose moved to her side. "No matter what happens we're here for you." She helped Mags into her coat. Even the soft down feathers didn't warm the cold hollowness spreading through her.

The three of them slipped out the door and hurried to Sassy's waiting car. Mags climbed into the front seat while Dahlia and Rose claimed the back.

"Look at you girls." Sassy beamed while she pulled the car out of the driveway. "This reminds me of when we always used to drive over to the ice-cream parlor. Do you remember?"

"We remember." The memory temporarily distracted Mags from her worries. "We used to get those amazing banana splits with that crunchy topping."

"Oh my God, the cereal topping." Rose sighed happily. "I loved that place." She leaned forward between the seats. "Is it still there?"

"I'm afraid not." Sassy turned the car onto the highway. "But I'm sure we could find another place to get ice cream after we get to see the baby."

The baby. Tears gathered in Mags's eyes, blurring the mountain scenery stretched out in front of her. After she'd lost her second baby, the doctor had told her it wasn't wise to let herself get too attached until after eight weeks, but that was impossible. The very same second Ike had delivered the news, something clicked into place inside of her. Her heart had already attached itself to the baby's heart. They were connected no matter what happened. She peered back at Dally. "I really appreciate Ike calling his friend to set this up for me." It would make such a difference being able to see the baby.

"He was happy to." Mags didn't miss the way her sister's eyes lit up.

"Are you going to go on another date—"

Her phone blared out Eric's ringtone. "It's him," Mags squealed fumbling in her purse to find it. "Hello?" She dropped the phone into her lap before bringing it back to her ear. "Eric? I've been trying to call you."

"I saw. I'm sorry." Static crackled across the line. "I need to know where you are, Mags. Right now."

The desperation in his voice lurched her heart. "Why? What is it? Is something wrong?" Had he been hurt at work?

"Nothing's wrong. I'm here. I'm in Juniper Springs. But I don't know where to go. I don't know where to find you."

"You're here?" A sob bubbled up and tears flooded her eyes. She hadn't realized how much she'd missed him, how much she'd missed them until right now. "You came all the way out to Colorado?" It would be a miracle if he could understand her with all the blubbering.

"We've never spent a Christmas apart, Mags." Emotion shook through the words. "Never. And I won't start now."

Mags continued to cry, not caring that she could hardly talk, hardly breathe. "I'm so glad you're here. So, so, glad." She wiped her eyes, trying to see where they were. "We're on our way to a clinic in Salida right now."

"A clinic?" Eric's voice raised the way it always did when he was on the verge of panic. "Why? What's wrong? Did something happen to you?"

"Everything'll be okay." It would've sounded more convincing if she could quit crying. But now that he was here—now that he'd come to be with her, she knew. Everything would be okay. No matter what they had to deal with. Even if they lost another baby, they would still have each other. And like Sassy had said, they were already parents. They knew love and they knew loss and that could be the thing that weaved their hearts together. "I'll explain everything when you get there." She had to see him. She had to tell him about the baby in person. "We just left about ten minutes ago." She rattled off the address. "Can you meet us there?"

"I'm on my way." The line clicked and Sassy and both of her sisters cheered.

"I knew Eric would come!" Rose leaned forward, looking at Mags. "He loves you too much to spend Christmas without you."

"And it couldn't be more perfect for him to show up now," Sassy added. "It's like it was meant to be."

Mags sniffled but laughed at the same time. She couldn't remember the last time she'd been hit with so many conflicting emotions, but the joy had a way of overpowering the fear. "I've obviously missed him more than I let myself think about." Now even twenty more minutes seemed too long to wait to see him again.

"Well, not to worry, my dear." Sassy stared out the windshield like she was on a mission. "We'll be there in no time."

Her aunt didn't lie. She shaved eight minutes off Google's estimated time of arrival. When they pulled up to the clinic, only one other car sat in the parking lot. Not all that surprising since it was Christmas Eve and Ike had called in a favor.

They all piled out of the car, and a woman met them at the doors. She had a round friendly face with warm brown eyes. "Hi there!" She beckoned them inside. "I'm Dr. Lamb."

"Dr. Lamb." Tears still ran down Mags's cheeks, but she found her brightest smile. "I'm Magnolia." She shook the woman's hand before introducing her to Rose, Dahlia, and Sassy.

"It's wonderful to have so much support," the woman said, leading them into a waiting room.

"My husband will be here too," Mags blubbered. "In about ten minutes."

"That's wonderful." Everything about the doctor seemed so calming and soothing. "Why don't we get you ready, and he can come back as soon as he arrives?"

"We'll wait out here and point him in the right direction," Sassy promised, ushering her on.

"Okay. Yes." She needed a few minutes alone with Eric to tell him she was pregnant.

"Ike explained everything to me," Dr. Lamb said as they wound their way through a maze of hallways. "We'll take a look at the baby, do some measurements, and I'm sure you'll be able to hear the heartbeat today as well." She paused outside of a door. "He said you believe you might be about nine weeks along?"

"I think so." She tried to go back and do the math again, but the days and facts jumbled in her head. Her heart was racing. "That's the last time my husband and I made love." It sounded so terrible. Nine weeks they'd been avoiding each other. It felt like a lifetime. A lifetime too long.

"Well, the measurements should be able to confirm that," the doctor told her. She opened the door and led Mags into an exam room with a portable ultrasound machine all set up. "Since it's so early we'll have to do the pelvic ultrasound, which isn't necessarily a picnic." She handed her a paper drape. "You'll have to undress from the waist down and then just get comfortable on the table. I'll give you a few minutes and hopefully your husband will be here by then."

Yes. Hopefully. The second Eric pulled her into his arms, everything inside of her would still. "Thank you." She waited until the doctor stepped out, and then undressed. Sitting up on that table, the fear assaulted her again. She'd sat in so many doctor offices in this exact position. Wondering, hoping, dreading. And for every appointment, Eric had been there. He'd always been there for her before she'd shut him out.

It seemed like years passed before the door opened, but it had probably only been minutes. Her husband was suddenly there by her side like he had been so many times before. "What's going on, Mags?" A weariness lurked in his eyes. "Why are you here?"

She reached for his hand and pulled him to her, a calm settling over her just as she knew it would. "I'm pregnant," she told him gently. "After I got here, I wasn't feeling well. I was tired and I had an upset stomach all the time."

"Why didn't you tell me?"

"I thought it was bug or something." She'd never dreamed this was possible. "But we're pregnant. It had to be that one night after the last treatment had failed. It's the only time we—"

"It was the only time we've made love in three years." Tears lit up Eric's dark eyes, sticking in those eyelashes she'd always been so jealous of.

She knew what he meant. All the other times they'd had sex it had been regimented—with an end goal, a purpose. That night had been about emotion, about need, about comfort. It had been about love.

"I'm sorry." She pushed her face into his chest and breathed him in, this man she had loved for so long. "I shouldn't have pushed you away. My heart was broken, and there wasn't room for anything else."

"I know." He held the back of her head, gently caressing. "My heart was broken, too. And I knew I was helpless. I knew I couldn't give you what you wanted most." He sat on the edge of the exam table next to her and gazed into her eyes. "What if—"

Mags closed a finger over his lips. "There are no what ifs. There is only what we know now. What we know now is there is a baby growing right here." She placed his hand over her belly and covered it with hers. "We're going to have to learn to live in the moment. I'm going to try to stop obsessing about the future." That had almost cost her her marriage. "We have to focus on what we have today." She leaned over to kiss her husband's lips. "Today we have each other. And today we have the baby"

"We have a baby," Eric repeated, leaning his forehead against hers. "We have our baby." He held her jaw in his palm and kissed her again, and the intensity of it, the desire it brought fortified her.

The door opened, and they separated, but Mags still held his hand tightly.

"Are you two ready to see the baby?" Dr. Lamb asked, peeking her head in.

"We're ready." Eric squeezed Mags's hand as he said it, and she couldn't imagine him not being here, not having his strong hand to hold on to.

"Yes. We're ready." Living in the moment wasn't something she'd ever been good at, but she wanted to make it a practice. Worry would only steal this time from her—the moments of her pregnancy, and she couldn't give into it.

"All right. Let's get started." Dr. Lamb walked fully into the room and repositioned the ultrasound machine. "Lay back and try to relax."

That would be a lot easier now that Eric was here. Mags eased down on the table and fit her feet into the stirrups.

The pelvic ultrasound was no picnic, but she didn't have time to be uncomfortable before a distinct drumming sound hummed from the speaker.

"That's the heartbeat." Eric leaned over her, tears running down his cheeks. "That's our baby's heartbeat!"

"It sure is." Dr. Lamb shifted the wand. "Sounds very strong."

Mags closed her eyes, listening. Just listening. Memorizing the way that tiny heart thrummed. It was the most beautiful sound in the world. She opened her eyes and found herself gazing directly into Eric's eyes, and she could see how deeply the sound touched him, too.

"Here's the baby." Dr. Lamb pointed to the screen. "That tiny little bean right there." She typed something on the keyboard and the picture zoomed in.

"And the baby looks okay?" Eric asked, his eyes fixed on the screen. "Is it normal for it to be that small?"

"Completely normal at this stage." Dr. Lamb moved something on the machine. "I'm doing some measurements, but I would say it appears you were right on with your estimation. It seems this little one was likely conceived roughly nine weeks ago."

"Nine weeks," Eric whispered in her ear. He'd been there when that doctor had told her about the eight-week point. "That's the most amazing thing I've ever seen."

"The most amazing," Mags agreed, sealing that image of the tiny little jellybean into her mind.

"So far, I would say everything looks completely normal." The doctor handed Eric a printout. "You'll want to follow up with your regular doctor when you get home, but I don't see anything to be concerned about now."

"Thank you." Mags rested her head back on the pillow but continued peering up at the grainy black-and-white image on the screen. This baby wouldn't fix everything that had gone wrong with her and Eric. But he or she had already brought them closer together.

Chapter Twenty-Five

Dahlia

Talk about Christmas miracles. Dahlia wandered into the barn and gasped at the transformation. While she and Rose had escorted Mags to the doctor's office, Ike and Colt had finished hanging the white lights from the rafters. And that wasn't all they'd done, either. They had set up well over one hundred folding chairs and had scattered propane heaters all throughout the room to warm the space into a cozy Christmas wonderland.

"What'd you think?" Ike sauntered over, looking especially handsome in a rust-colored sweater and dark jeans.

"It's just like I remember it from my childhood." She raised her eyes to the rafters, turning in a slow circle to take it all in. "So many lights. It's absolutely beautiful."

"Absolutely beautiful," Rose echoed, walking over to them. Marigold followed closely behind.

Ike leaned in and kissed Dahlia's cheek, causing a swell of desire. It had been so long since a physical touch had roused such a passionate response in her. She'd almost forgotten it was possible.

"How was the appointment?" he asked in his doctorly voice.

"It couldn't have been better." Rose was always the quickest to answer.

"Your doctor friend was amazing," her sister said. "The baby looks perfect so far, and Eric even showed up in time for the ultrasound!"

"He flew out to surprise her," Dahlia explained. "And yes, your friend was wonderful."

"I knew she'd be great." The man eased an arm around Dahlia's waist. "She's married to one of my good friends from medical school."

"She was very nice, and having a last-minute appointment was exactly what Mags needed. So, thank you." She'd have to thank him properly later when her younger sister wasn't standing five feet away.

"Happy to help." Ike's grin told her he knew exactly what she was thinking.

"Hey Rose…" Colt strode into the barn carrying another strand of lights. "We have one left. Where would you like it?"

"Hmmm." Her sister scanned the rafters. "I don't know. You guys did such a great job, maybe we don't need to use it."

"We could add some in that corner." Ike pointed near the window. "It looks a little bare compared to the rest." He started walking in that direction. "I'll help you get them up."

Dahlia watched him move across the room. What she would've liked to do is yank him out of this barn and head back to his place for the evening, but they had an extravaganza to get ready for.

"Oh, Dally. It's good to see you happy." Rose wrapped her in a hug. "I know Jeff put you through a lot, and now it's like you're finally getting the happiness you've always deserved."

"I am happy." She squeezed Rose back before pulling away

She'd been careful not to bring up Gregory in front of anyone else, but she couldn't help but wonder since she'd seen her sister's interaction with him in the kitchen earlier. "What about you? Are you happy?"

Rose's expression underwent an abrupt change. Instead of that shining smile, a sad frown pulled at her lips. "I was. Back in Savannah. Before I came here. Gregory and I were happy."

"But now?" Dahlia couldn't let this go. She'd been through a divorce, and she wouldn't wish it on her worst enemy.

"I guess having some space has made me realize I don't want that life. I don't love him like I should. Like I would do anything to be with him." Her sister sighed. "And I'm not sure what to do about it."

"Have you talked to Gregory?" She led Rose to a table and they both sat.

"Not yet." Her shoulders slumped. "It's terrible timing. I'm not sure I can do it here. Maybe it's best to wait."

"Don't wait too long." She couldn't let her little sister do what she'd done—put everything on hold for a man who would always love himself more than he could love anyone else. "Trust me on this, Rosie." She caught a glimpse of Ike again, standing on a ladder, hanging those lights. "You have to choose wisely. It's never a good idea to walk into a marriage with someone who won't be able to adopt your dreams."

Her sister nodded slowly. "Do you regret marrying Jeff?"

"No." Maya and Ollie were the best things that had ever happened to her, and every second with Jeff had been worth what they'd made together. "But I didn't marry him for the right reasons. I think I was more interested in security. In being able to plan out a future that would give me stability." She couldn't blame

Jeff for not loving her deeply and passionately when she hadn't loved him that way either. "We were both in it for the wrong reasons, and eventually that's going to cause problems."

"I don't know how to break up with him. Oh my God, we have to call off the whole wedding."

Dahlia could relate to the look of panic on her sister's face. The wedding had already been planned, the save the date notices sent. "It'll be better now than in ten years." That much she could promise. Even with the rumors, the gossip, the questions, Rose could get out before too much damage was done. "I'm still a mess," Dahlia confessed. "My heart is still a mess." She didn't know what the future held for her and Ike. Her family— her *children*—had a life in Minneapolis. And Ike's life was here in his beloved mountains. But he'd told her last night not to stress about it, not even to think about it. He'd said they'd simply take things one day at a time and see where it brought them. There was so much freedom in that.

"I don't know how to—"

The barn door swung open with a whoosh of wintry wind. Sassy appeared in haste. "Dahlia," she called. "You have visitors."

Before she could stand, her children ran into the barn.

"Mama!" Ollie hurled himself at her, landing himself in her lap, his arms around her neck.

Instant tears broke her vision. "What? Oh my babies." She shifted him and opened her other arm for Maya, who wasn't moving as fast, but was smiling from ear to ear.

"Surprise!" Her daughter hugged her too, though not with as much force as Ollie.

"What're you doing here?" She struggled to stand up, unwilling to let go of them.

"We came to spend Christmas with you!" Maya pushed back and clapped her hands. "It was Dad's idea! He has a special surprise for you."

The announcement made her blood run colder. Dahlia let go of her children and watched for Jeff. "Where's Jade?" Surely he wouldn't bring his girlfriend to Dahlia's family Christmas, would he?

"I don't know where Jade is." Jeff finally walked in, and she had to do a double take. Instead of his impish smile and polished appearance, the man looked weary and rumpled. "And I don't care. This whole trip has made me realize I've only ever loved one woman."

Dahlia stopped breathing. Everyone in the room had stopped moving. The awkward silence seemed to be sucking all of the oxygen out of the room.

He was not doing this. Not now. Not in front of Maya and Ollie. Not in front of Mags and Rose. And Ike. She snuck a look to the corner where he'd been standing only a few minutes ago, but he was gone. He must've walked out.

"Dahlia..." Jeff stepped forward. "I never stopped loving you. I was confused and selfish and stupid. I'm so sorry. I see everything clearly now." He dropped to one knee and pulled a box out of his pocket.

No. No, no, no. Her heart folded in on itself, withering and crumbling. How could he do this? How could he make the kids hope?

"It's a ring!" Maya squealed. "The prettiest ring you've ever seen in your entire life! We picked it out in France!"

"We're going to get married again!" Ollie added. "And we're moving to France for a year all together! Did you know there's a Disneyland in Paris?"

Dahlia tried to swallow, but the anger choked her. Both Maya and Ollie stared at her with such exuberance, such hopeful anticipation that she froze. "France?" she choked out. What in the world were they talking about?

"The company asked me to work out of the Paris office for a year." Jeff said it as though this should be the best surprise she'd ever gotten. "I didn't want to say anything until it was a done deal, but my boss confirmed it while we were there. How about it, Dally? I know I have a lot of work to do to make up for what happened," he said, still perched on that one damn knee. "But I'm committed to it. I'm committed to you. Let's get married again. Let's put our family back together."

"Put the ring on! Put the ring on!" Maya chanted.

Ollie stole the box from his father's hands and opened it so Dahlia could see. "We helped pick it out." He was so proud. "It was the prettiest one in the whole store."

She tried to smile at her son, but the sight of that diamond made her want to throw up. And France? Was he serious right now? She couldn't smile. She couldn't even breathe! How could Jeff do this?

"Wow!" Sassy floated over to them and pretended to admire the ring. "You kids did a great job. I'm your great-aunt Sassy, and I'm so happy you're here because I have a ton of Christmas presents up at that house for you! I was going to send them home with your mom, but now that you're here, you can come open them right now!" She put an arm around Maya and then an arm around Ollie. "Would you like that?"

"Yes!" They both yelled at the same time. "We love presents," Ollie informed Sassy. "We love opening presents before the real Christmas Day!"

"Well, then. Let's go up to the house and give your parents a moment."

Dahlia silently thanked Sassy with a tearful gaze.

"Can I help you two open presents?" Rose begged in her fun-aunt way. "I might even have a few more in my suitcases for you."

"Yay, Aunt Rose!" Maya attached herself to Rose's side and everyone tromped out of the barn.

"I know you must be shocked," Jeff said. He'd finally stood, thank God. "But I had this come-to-Jesus moment on the trip. Jade was yelling at Ollie. Can you believe that?"

She could, actually. "Jade is ten years younger than us! She doesn't have children, but you knew that when you started having an affair with her!" She didn't care that she was yelling. She'd earned the right to yell.

"I know, I know." Her ex-husband shook his head and paced. "I just…I felt like I was losing myself. Getting older, and she made me feel different. Like I said, I was stupid. It was just some midlife crisis." He spun back to Dahlia. "But that's over now. I know what I want. What I've always wanted. We can start over someplace different. You're going to love France. It'll be a whole new adventure for us." He took her hands in his and trapped her with a pleading look. "You're the only woman I've ever loved."

The desperation in his eyes refuted the declaration. What she saw wasn't love. It wasn't passion. It was panic.

Dahlia pulled her hands out of his and backed up to put some space between them. "It's too late." A month ago, she would've taken him back. She would've put aside all her doubts and put that ring on her finger so she could try to patch her family back together. But it wouldn't be enough. Not for her. Not for Jeff. Not for Maya and Ollie. They all deserved more than a façade. "I don't love you. And you don't love me. Not the way a husband and a wife should love each other."

"But we can." Jeff shifted into his negotiator mode. "We can figure it out. I'll do whatever you want. Counseling. A couple's therapy group."

"None of that will change the fact that you chose someone else." She wouldn't blame this whole thing on him. He had his reasons for betraying her, but she wanted to be chosen. She *needed* to be chosen. And not just when something else didn't work out, either. Jeff didn't want her as a wife, he only wanted her as a mother for his children. "I can't go back, Jeff." Resolve poured into her heart, making it stronger. "*We* can't go back. We have to figure out how to move forward. Especially with you taking a job in France. We both need to be there for our kids." She had no idea what that would look like, but she was not moving to a different country. Especially not now. Not after getting a glimpse of what she wanted. "Maybe I'll move here." She'd been too afraid to seriously consider it before but knowing Jeff's living situation would change made it a possibility.

How could she not consider it? Sassy wanted to give them the inn. This place was a part of her past, a part of her dearest memories, and it could be a part of her future, too.

"But I have to move to France for a year," Jeff said in disbelief. "I've already committed. And I can't take the kids without you. I can't."

That wasn't entirely accurate. He didn't *want* to take the kids. But that was more than fine with her. It would make things much simpler. "Then you'll go to France." It would be a difficult transition for the kids all the way around, but she could get them through it. They'd come through a lot of difficult transitions this year, and they were stronger. A calm came over her. This would work. They would do their best to give the kids a sense of family, even if it wasn't in the traditional sense of the word. "And the kids can FaceTime you every day. I can bring them to visit you there, and you can come visit them here. We'll figure out how to make it work for all of us." And she wouldn't be tied to Minnesota anymore. She would be free to move Maya and Ollie here—to raise them at the inn with its magical forests and quaint ice-skating pond.

Jeff must've seen the conviction in her eyes because he didn't argue. "I guess that's best. I'll be working sixty-hour weeks anyway. The kids need you. You're a good mom, Dally." He gave her a sad smile. "I'm sorry. I hope you know how sorry I am for hurting you."

"I do now." He was willing to marry her again just to make up for the terrible thing he'd done. But making another mistake wouldn't blot out the first one.

"Maybe we should wait to tell the kids." He obviously didn't want to face Ollie and Maya any more than she did right now. "At least until after Christmas."

It was tempting, but she couldn't wait. It wouldn't be fair to let them think there was a possibility they'd be a family again. "We have to tell them the truth. Now." They had to be honest and hope it didn't ruin Christmas.

"I guess you're right." He sighed. "You're always right."

"Well, I don't know about that." In this case, she hated being right. Dahlia led the way out the door, and they walked up the hill in a sullen silence.

"You should do the talking." Jeff gestured for her to go inside first. No surprise there. He'd never been great with having the hard conversations.

"Feel free to chime in," Dahlia whispered just before they walked into Sassy's living room. Rose and Sassy sat with the kids on the couch, looking through the new books they must've opened. It appeared Eric and Mags were still out grabbing an early dinner.

"Mama!" Ollie flew off the couch, holding out a stack of books. "Look! More *Magic Tree House* to add to my collection!"

"Wow." She glanced at the covers, not really seeing them.

"And I got this beautiful necklace." Maya tossed her hair over her shoulder so she could show off the pendant.

"Beautiful," Dahlia marveled.

"Oh my, would you look at the time." Sassy popped off the couch, too, gesturing for Rose to follow. "We'd better get down to the barn. In less than an hour, this place'll be packed." She winked at Ollie. "You two are going to love the Christmas extravaganza. I'll tell Colt to take you on a very special sleigh ride."

"Yes!" Ollie started to put his coat back on, but Dahlia took it from him. "We'll head down there in a few minutes. Dad and I need to talk to you two first."

"Don't worry," Rose assured the kids. "We'll save you the best seats in the house."

After Sassy and Rose walked out, Maya eyed Dahlia warily. "You're not wearing the ring. Why aren't you wearing the ring?"

"Well, honey…" Dahlia directed both of the kids to the couch and she knelt in front of them. There was no easy way to tell them after the spectacle Jeff had made in the barn. "Your father and I decide it would be best if we didn't get married again."

"But we'll still be a family," Jeff added quickly. "That won't change."

"No, we won't!" Maya leapt to her feet, her face reddening. "We can't be a family without Dad living at our house! He's moving to France! We'll never see him!" She seemed to direct the brunt of her anger at Dahlia. "This is your fault! We came up with the perfect plan and the perfect Christmas present, and you ruined it all!"

Jeff moved in, gently turning their daughter's face to his. "That's not true, honey. I made mistakes."

"But you always tell me to forgive people!" Maya started to sob. "You always tell me that being mad at someone will hurt me more than it hurts them!"

It wasn't the first time her daughter had thrown her own words back in her face, and it likely wouldn't be the last. Dahlia inhaled, feeling her daughter's heartbreak as acutely as she felt her own. "That's right. I do tell you to forgive people. And I've forgiven your dad. We both made mistakes and we've forgiven each other." She was surprised to realize the words were true. "I'm not mad at him, but we can't be married. We love you and Ollie very much. And both of us will always be there for your no matter what. We don't have to be married to be your family." She reached for Maya, but her daughter ripped away.

"I hate you! You're ruining everything! This is the worst Christmas ever!" She bolted out of the room and ran up the steps. Somewhere a door slammed.

Jeff rubbed at his forehead. "I'll go after her. Ollie and I will take her out for some hot chocolate to calm her down." He pushed off the couch and trudged in the direction of the stairs, but Ollie snuggled in against Dahlia's chest. That was the best feeling in the world, holding your baby against you. "You okay, buddy?" she asked, tousling his hair.

"I'm okay." He turned his head to look up at her. "As long as you're happy, I'm happy, Mama. You and Dad have done a pretty good job being parents. Even living at different houses." He leaned in closer, and whispered, "I hated France anyway. It smells like stinky cheese."

That made her smile. "What do you think about the inn?"

"It's so cool!" Her son bounced up to his knees on the couch. "I love the barn. It could hold horses, couldn't it? Maybe we could come for vacation and Aunt Sassy can get some horses!"

That answered her question. "Maybe vacation. Or maybe we could move here…" She said it like the idea had just occurred to her.

"Yes!" Ollie threw his arms around her neck. "That would be so much fun!"

"Well, you and Maya and I will all talk it through when she's feeling better." If her daughter ever forgave her. "Wherever your dad and I are, we're going to try to be the best parents we can be. We're not perfect, and we won't do everything right, but I promise you honey…your dad and I will both love you with everything we have always and forever."

Her son planted a kiss on her cheek. "I'll love you always and forever, too, Mommy."

"Thank you." She wrapped him up in her arms, still unable to believe he belonged to her.

Footsteps rattled on the wooden steps, but Maya didn't come into the living room to see her.

"Ollie," Jeff called from the foyer. "Let's go into town and get some hot chocolate before we come back for the big extravaganza."

"Yes! Hot chocolate!" He squeezed Dahlia one more time before worming his way out of her arms. "We'll be right back," he promised.

Dahlia sent him off with a kiss. Ollie would be fine. Maya, on the other hand? Well, it might take her a little longer, but Dahlia would give her all the support she needed to get through the transition.

She listened to the front door open and close, to her precious children walking across the porch, and even though everything was a disaster, she was glad they'd come. She was glad they wouldn't be thousands of miles away from her on Christmas.

Her eyes drifted to the clock on the stove. They had thirty minutes until everyone would start arriving for the extravaganza, which should give her plenty of time to take a detour to Ike's cabin before she met Sassy and Rose at the barn.

Dahlia quickly bundled up and slipped out into the cold night. She followed the same path she and Ike had walked together just last night. Her heart pounded harder when she saw his cabin all lit up. Without thinking about what she would tell him, she hurried up the steps and knocked.

Within a few seconds the door opened. "Hey." He stepped aside as though he'd been expecting her. "Do you want to come in?"

"Yes." She wanted to come in. She wanted to sit with him and make out on the couch again. But there would be more time for that later. "So, pretty crazy that Jeff showed up, huh?"

"Yeah." Ike seemed to study her face. "Sorry I left. I figured you all could use some time alone." He gestured for her to sit down on his comfy leather couch, and then he sat next to her, his body angled toward hers. "Everything turn out okay?"

"I think it will be. Eventually." Her daughter was so resilient. She would do whatever Maya needed to walk her through this. "Jeff asked me to marry him again."

Ike nodded. "I had a feeling that was going to happen when he showed up like that."

Dahlia inched closer to him. "I told him no."

The man's shoulders seemed to relax. He eased his hand into hers. "That must've been hard on the kids."

Dahlia closed her eyes. She would never forget the look of utter desolation on Maya's face when they told her. "It was awful. But I don't want to teach them to pretend." They had to learn to be honest with themselves, honest with others. "Jeff has to move to France for a year." In some ways she couldn't believe he'd accepted a position like that without consulting her first, but that was Jeff. He'd likely gotten caught up in the excitement of a new adventure.

That guarded expression took over Ike's eyes again. "What does that mean for you?"

Dahlia scooted closer to him. "That means I'm not tied to Minnesota. I told him I'm considering moving here. It'll take time. And I need to talk it through with Maya and Ollie, but I think they would love it here."

"I would love having you here." Ike gazed into her eyes. "And I can't wait to get to know Maya and Ollie."

"They'll love you." The kids would be drawn to that friendliness the same way she had been. "I think I could love you, too." The confession was shaky, but honest. "I'm not sure I've ever embraced my true feelings. Not until now. Not until you." It wasn't until her security had been taken away that her heart had been completely open and exposed. And maybe that wasn't a bad thing. With Ike there was no plan and no control and no guarantees for a white picket fence, but there was passion. And for the first time in her life, Dahlia decided she'd rather bank on the passion.

"I could love you too," Ike told her with a glimmer in his eyes. "Maybe when the dust settles, I can show you how much I feel for you." He reached for a Santa hat that sat on the coffee table and put it on.

Santa…"Oh no." She covered her face with her hands.

"What is it?" Ike's arm came around her. "You okay?"

"Santa." She popped off the couch. "I have to go shopping! I have all the kids' presents at home. I wasn't planning to celebrate with them until after the trip, and now they're going to think Santa forgot all about them." It would break their hearts!

Ike stood, too. "No, they won't. Santa never forgets."

It was amazing how the man could reach in and snatch her out of panic mode just like that. "What do you mean?"

"My brother and sister-in-law are vising with my niece and nephew next week." He pointed to a huge stack of wrapped presents under the small Christmas tree in the corner. "They're about Maya and Ollies ages. We can give them those and I'll go shopping again after Christmas."

"Really?" Tears heated her eyes.

"Really. Like I said, Santa never forgets anyone."

"I like Santa." Dahlia reached up to straighten the hat for him. "He made me believe in the magic again," she whispered. Then she leaned in for a long Christmas kiss.

Chapter Twenty-Six

Rose

Who wants more whipped cream?" Rose made her way past the dinette, squirting generous piles of whipped cream into the kids' mugs. If anyone was worried about the little ones getting a sugar rush the night before Christmas, they shouldn't have put her in charge of the sugar. "Oh, you need more sprinkles." She found the chocolate shavings and heaped a generous pile onto the whipped cream mountain she'd just sprayed on a little boy's hot chocolate.

"This is the best Christmas extravaganza ever!" he declared, taking a huge bite out of the whipped cream.

"I think so too," Rose agreed. Throughout the course of the evening, she'd managed to circulate through the different areas—the barn, down by the pond for ice-skating, but this camper warming hut had to be her favorite. It had been very popular with the kids. The copious amounts of whipped cream might have something to do with that.

"What do you think, Marigold?" She wandered to the back where the dog sat on the tiny built-in couch. "Would you like some whipped cream?"

The dog tilted her head up and opened her mouth.

"Just a little squirt." Rose gave her a taste.

"Ew!" The little boy sitting next to the dog made a grossed-out face. "You're not supposed to give dogs whipped cream!"

"You're not?" Rose watched Marigold happily lick remnants of whipped cream off her fur. "She sure seems to like it."

"But it's a dog." The boy gave her a dramatic roll of his eyes. "Dogs don't eat whipped cream."

"Well, this is my first dog, so I'm not very experienced." Rose gave Marigold a good scratch behind the ears. "I'm just trying to make her happy. It's her fav—"

"Rose?" Gregory poked his head in.

With all the excitement she hadn't seen him since before Mags's appointment. Not that she had been in a huge hurry to break up with him. The truth was weighing on her, though. "Where have you been?" she walked over to greet him, but Gregory didn't step foot in the camper. He simply stood outside in the snow.

"I had a ton of work to finish up this afternoon." The tight scowl on his face put a damper on her Christmas spirit.

"The coffee shop owner finally kicked me out," Gregory went on. "He's not the politest person I ever met."

"Oh, that's Grumpy." She carefully maneuvered down the steps and stood across from him. "There's a reason he earned his nickname." But she loved the old man and couldn't imagine Juniper Springs without him.

Gregory didn't seem to see the charm in the name. "Anyway, I think I'm going to head back up to the house and settle in for the night."

Rose glanced at her watch. It was all of eight o'clock.

"I'm not in the mood for some big festival tonight," he went on. "You should see the text my mom sent me about missing tomorrow's family Christmas dinner."

It always came back to Evaline. She not only influenced Gregory's life and schedule. She also influenced his moods.

Dahlia's earlier words blared back at her. *You have to choose wisely.* Rose hadn't. The whole time she'd been engaged to Gregory, she'd been more concerned about what he wanted. Or, more accurately, what his family wanted. But this was her moment. She had to make the right choice now, before she lost what she wanted most. "Sassy offered us the inn, and I want to keep it."

Gregory sighed heavily and leaned his shoulder against the camper. "It's not practical. Talk about a money drain. This place is too run-down. We'd never make a profit on it."

"I don't care about a profit." He should know her better than that by now. "The Juniper Inn means something to me. It means something to my family." In a way, it had become the place where she could be the truest version of herself. She could be creative and wandering and casual and contemplative. "I'm happy here."

"I don't understand." Gregory threw up his hands and paced a few steps away from her. "What happened to you when you left?" He didn't wait for an answer. "Whatever it is, you need to snap out of it. You've changed. You're different. I feel like I don't even know you."

"I *am* different here." This was who she got to be when all the labels were stripped away. This is who she got to be when she wasn't Gregory Cunningham's fiancée. "I like who I am here." She was a better person here than she'd been in Savannah. "And I can't do it. I'm sorry. I can't be who your family wants me to be. I can't be who *you* want me to be." Dally was right. She had to follow her heart, no matter how much it cost her.

"All I want is for you to be the same woman I fell in love with."
Anger put a brittle edge into the words. "I don't think that's too
much to ask."

Tears heated her eyes. "But I'll always be changing. Growing.
Trying to be better." At least she hoped she would. "I'll always
be trying to live deeper." That wasn't what he wanted though.
He wanted predictable and controllable. He wanted to work out
every morning and then go to work and get home in time for a
late dinner and then he wanted to wake up and do the same thing
the next day so he could fulfill every expectation he'd been living
under since he was a child. And that wasn't love. That wasn't
passion. "I can't marry you." The tears fell. "We have to call off
the wedding."

"Are you crazy?" Even in the dim light outside the camper,
she could see his face turning the same shade of red it did when
she was running late somewhere. "We can't call off the wedding
now. After we've already made such a big deal about it. What will
everyone think?"

"It doesn't matter what anyone else thinks." That question only
confirmed this was the right decision. He wasn't at all upset about
losing her. Calling off the wedding wouldn't break his heart. It
would damage his image, his family's image.

"I can't live my life trying to meet everyone else's standards."
Not after seeing this glimpse of what her life could be. "I especially can't meet your mom's standards." And she wasn't willing
to spend her whole life trying.

"You're walking away from me?" He marched to her and got
in her face. "You've lost your mind. I think the altitude has made
you crazy."

"And I think it's helped me see things clearly for the first time in a long time." The mountains, her sisters, her aunt. This charming little town. "I care for you very much. But we want different things out of life." Admitting it finally freed her. One month ago, she wouldn't have been strong enough to walk away. She would've marched down that aisle with a push from her mother, but her sisters inspired her. Sassy inspired her. She needed to live the life that made her happy.

"Obviously you're not who I thought you were," Gregory sneered.

"I'm not," she agreed. "I guess I didn't know who I was." She'd been too busy trying to make everyone else happy. "I'm sorry." But she had no doubt he would find a woman who was willing to fill her place.

"Sorry?" He turned and stomped away from her. "A lot of good sorry is going to do me." He continued talking as he walked away from her, but the light wind stole his words.

Children still chattered inside the camper, as though too engrossed in their treats to pay any attention to what the adults were saying. "Hey guys, I'll be back in a few minutes." She handed the little dog expert the can of whipped cream. "You're in charge."

"Yes!" He went about refilling everyone's mug.

"Come on, Marigold," she called, wrapping her scarf around her neck. Together, she and her dog stepped outside and tromped over through the aspens en route to the barn. She'd best tell Aunt Sassy and her sisters Gregory wouldn't be joining them for their Christmas breakfast in the morning. "I'm not getting married," she informed sweet Marigold. "Wait until my mom hears. She's going to lose her mind." But she didn't have to think about that right now. She wouldn't think about that right now.

A swooshing came through the trees—the gentle sound of runners on the snow. Rose stopped and stepped aside as Colt steered the sleigh through the narrow path in the trees. He looked like a cowboy sitting on that bench seat all bundled up.

"Whoa." Pulling on the reins, he slowed the horses to a stop next to Rose. "Need a lift?"

"A lift would be great." She'd decided to wear her cute boots instead of the clompy snow boots, and now her toes were numb.

"Here we go." Colt reached out his hand to help her into the sleigh, and Marigold jumped in behind her. They all settled in, and he handed her a warm wool blanket. "It's pretty chilly when you get going."

"I remember." But it was also beautiful—the lights in the trees, the white fluffy snow. With views like this, she would take the cold any day.

"Where to?" Colt prodded the horses to get moving, and the sleigh glided effortlessly over the ground.

"I need to head to the barn," she told him, her gaze entranced by the colorful lights.

"That's where I'm headed anyway." He steered the horses with an expert hand. "Sassy wanted the sleigh rides to start at eight thirty on the nose. I figured I'd better get down there early."

"Everyone is going to love this." Rose closed her eyes, letting the cold wind bite at her cheeks.

"Should I ask why you were walking alone when your fiancé showed up for a surprise visit?" Colt finally broke the silence between them.

"I wasn't alone." She guided Marigold's head to lay in her lap. She wouldn't be alone with Marigold around.

The man next to her shot her a knowing look, but simply asked, "You okay?"

"Not really." Gregory might not've been the one for her, but they'd shared a lot. At one point she'd imagined a future with him. And watching him walk away had hurt. "I broke up with my fiancé." Colt wasn't your typical heart-to-heart talker, but he'd likely hear eventually anyway.

"I'm not sure what to say," he admitted, keeping his eyes on the tracks in front of him. "Breakup advice isn't my specialty."

"Are you sure?" she teased. But then she let him off the hook. "You don't have to say anything. It was a long time coming." For her, the breakup had been a process of evaluating her doubts and then finally finding the strength to give in to them. "It's for the best." In this case, those words weren't trite. "He's a good person, but we want different things."

"So, what're you going to do?" Colt asked, pulling the sleigh to a stop near the barn.

"I'm going to stay here. In Juniper Springs." The answer came easily. Think of everything she could do with this place! She could pour all of her creativity into these old cabins. Maybe she would make each one a different theme. She slid a smile in Colt's direction. "But I promise not to redecorate anything in this town without getting permission first."

"Ha." He climbed out of the sleigh and then walked over to help her down. "You don't need permission. This town could use some flair."

"I'll remember that." She walked by his side to the barn doors, smiling at the music and laughter echoing inside. "I can't believe I'm starting over. I hardly know anyone here. And my mother…" Her emotions seesawed back and forth between elation and terror. But she had to do this. She couldn't live for Lillian anymore.

"Well, Sassy loves you, so you won't be totally alone." Colt nudged her shoulder with his. "And Grumpy seems to think you're okay."

"That's true. I guess I'll have two friends here." She stared him down, lifting her eyebrows in wait.

"Two's not too bad," Colt said with a straight face.

Oh, come on. Was he going to make her beg? "But maybe I could make it three?" she prompted.

He opened the door for her, smiling as they went in. "We'll see."

Chapter Twenty-Seven

Magnolia

"Here, let me take that." Eric swooped in and took the box of cookies out of Mags's hands, bringing it to the large table where her confections were rapidly disappearing.

"I can carry a box of cookies," she informed him with a playful smile. "Just this morning, I carried my laundry basket downstairs all by myself."

"That's because I wasn't here." Her husband set the box of cookies on the table and crept up behind her, weaving his arms around her waist. "Now you don't have to carry your own laundry, or your own box of cookies."

Shaking her head at him, Mags turned into his embrace. "You're not going to be around twenty-four/seven, you know. What about when we're back home and you're at work?"

He settled his hands on her hips. "Maybe I should take the next thirty-eight weeks off so I can do all the lifting and cleaning and laundry."

That made her laugh out loud. "Last time you did the laundry you turned all of my underwear red."

Eric laughed, too. "Those buttons on the washing machine are confusing."

"Leave the laundry to me." Mags rested her palms on his chest, and that was enough to bring a swell of desire. Whoa Nelly, it had been way too long since she'd touched this man. "We're not going to worry, remember? I can lift things. I can clean, and I can still do laundry." As unfortunate as that was. "It's good for me to exercise, to be active. You don't want me to gain a hundred pounds, do you?"

"I'd still love you." His hands met at the small of her back, pressing her in a little bit more. "God, I was so afraid I was going to lose you, Mags. I was so afraid we weren't going to find each other again. I can't imagine my life without you."

For at least the tenth time that day, tears crowded her eyes. You'd think she'd run out of them eventually. "I can't imagine my life without you either." She'd been so closed off to him, closed off to everything because of the pain. But now her heart was opening again, and she would let everything back in. The love and the grief. Both were part of life and healing.

"Let's dance, *mi bella amor*." Eric moved her body with his to the dance floor where other couples were swaying to "I'll Be Home for Christmas." But Mags was oblivious to everyone else. She stared into Eric's eyes, seeing the love that had brought them back together.

Mags settled her ear against his chest, dancing with him, savoring the feel of his arms around her. "You know what else I can still do besides laundry and cleaning?" she murmured, peering up at him.

Eric stopped, his gaze turning hungry. "Is it too early for bed?"

Laughing softly, Mags started to sway again, pulling him back into their dance. "We should probably stay for a little while longer." From a distance, she'd been trying to keep tabs on Dahlia and Ollie and Maya. From what she could tell, her niece still wasn't talking to Dahlia, but the girl seemed to be having fun. Right now, she was over in the craft corner making an ornament. Jeff was nowhere to be seen. Smart man. "I want to make sure Dally is okay. And Rose, too." Her younger sister had walked in a few minutes ago and was chatting with Sassy near the makeshift bar they'd set up.

"Where's the hotshot fiancé? Eric scanned the room.

"I'm not sure he'll be her fiancé much longer." Mags had sensed a change in Rose. Sort of a stepping into her own skin the last few weeks, and she couldn't imagine the Cunninghams would put up with a woman who spoke her mind and did her own thing.

"That's good," her husband grumbled. "I've never really liked that guy. But, I liked Jeff even less." That protective fierceness she loved lit his eyes. "Wish I would've been here when he'd paraded in and proposed to Dally again. I would've told him where he could stick that ring."

"She likely told him that herself." Dally had changed, too. She'd finally stood up to Jeff. She'd stepped way outside of her comfort zone and had gone on a date with Ike.

"I think they'll be okay. And I think we'll be okay, too." Mags held on tighter to Eric, grateful for what they had. It wasn't perfect. It wasn't even easy. But she knew he had grit. She had grit. And that gave them staying power. Even if they drifted apart, even if they fought, even if they made mistakes, these last few weeks had given her hope that they would always find their way back to each other.

Across the room, Dally and Rose retreated to a corner with their heads together. Uh-oh. This looked like something she needed to be part of.

Before she could even ask, Eric let her go. "It's fine. You can head over there and see what's going on."

"Thank you." She moved to her tiptoes to kiss his cheek, then whispered, "Twenty minutes tops. Then you and I will make it an early night."

"Hell, yes we will."

She could feel Eric watching her all the way across the room, and the anticipation of spending the night with him nearly sent her running back to his arms. But Dally and Rose were still huddled in the corner, and things looked serious.

"Everything okay?" she asked, hoping they'd simply say yes and she could drag Eric out of here.

"Rose broke things off with Gregory," Dally announced.

Now that she was closer, Mags could see Rose had been crying.

"I don't know what these tears are about," her younger sister whimpered. "I think deep down I've known this was coming since I got here. But it's just so final."

"I know." Mags hugged her. "It's always hard to walk away, even if you knew it was coming."

"We can all tell Mom together," Dally offered.

Mags nodded her support. That would be the worst part of the whole breakup. Their mother was going to be sorely disappointed that she wouldn't be part of the Cunningham family after all. "You're doing the right thing, Rosie. The hard thing is usually the right thing."

"And we're here for you," Dally added. "Whatever you need. We're here to support you."

"I'm so glad." Rose raised her head and pulled Mags and Dally in closer. "I have no idea what my life is going to look like in a month, but I know I want you both to be a bigger part of it."

"I want that, too." Damn those silly tears. Mags was powerless against them. "Eric and I both want that. I want you to know the baby. I want him or her to grow up knowing his or her aunties."

"Oh, don't you worry about that." Dally squeezed her hand. "I can't wait to get my baby fix. You're probably going to get sick of me visiting you all the time."

"Impossible." Mags looked around for Ollie and Maya again. They'd both moved on to the cookie table where Eric was entertaining them by balancing a stack of sugar cookies on his nose. "The kids seem to be taking everything okay."

Dally blew out a lengthy sigh. "I know Ollie will be okay. He's so much better about talking through his feelings." Her sad gaze seemed to follow Maya. "But my baby girl...she takes too much on herself. I know she's angry and disappointed with me right now."

"It won't be the last time," Mags reminded her.

"That's part of doing what's best for them," Rose added. "Can you imagine if you would've said yes to Jeff? After everything he put you through?"

"No." Their sister blanched. "I just have to show the kids that even though our family will look a little different, we can still find joy."

"We can," Mags agreed. "All of us together."

"Look at Eric." Dally laughed. "He's going to make such a great dad."

Mags turned to watch her husband laugh with Ollie while

Maya was talking with another girl about her age. "I know." She couldn't wait to see him holding the baby, dancing with the baby, feeding him or her bottles, doing all the things they'd dreamed about doing for so long. "I think Eric and I are going to go to bed early." She couldn't wait to have him all to herself anymore, to rediscover that connection their bodies had always had.

Rose smiled. "We'll make sure not to disturb you."

"Don't stay up too late," Dally teased. "The kids are probably going to be up at sunrise ready to open presents."

"That's what we used to do." Those were some of her favorite memories, getting up before sunrise to drink hot chocolate. Their parents always made them wait until the sun was "all the way up" before waking them, so the three of them would make a nest of blankets in front of the bay window in the living room and they would watch the sun inch its way over the horizon.

"I'm so grateful I get to spend Christmas with my sisters this year." Rose gave them each a hug, and then sent Mags off with a pat. "You go with Eric now. You two deserve some good quality time alone."

Mags had already walked away with a wave before Rose even finished the sentence. Her husband must've seen her coming. Right as she walked up, Ollie said, "Aw, Uncle Eric. Do you hafta go to bed already?"

"I'm afraid so, buddy." He winked at Mags. "Gotta gear up for the big day tomorrow, know what I mean?"

"Yes!" Ollie bounced around. Judging from the frosting smudges on his chin, he'd had more than one cookie.

"We'll see you in the morning, though," Mags told him. "We have some special surprises for you."

"Oh boy, oh boy!" Her nephew hugged her. "I can't wait to see what it is! I love surprises! I love Christmas!"

"Me, too." Eric took ahold of Mags's hand. "Don't stay up too late now," he told Ollie.

"I won't," the boy promised. "Maybe I'll just have one more cookie." He took off for the cookie table at Mach speed.

"You ready?" Eric pulled Mags's coat off the back of a chair and helped her slip into it before putting on his own.

"I'm so ready." Her whole body seemed to be humming with a warm, simmering anticipation.

Her husband tucked her under his arm, and they walked out into the snow moving as quickly as they could without slipping.

"You sure you're all right?" he asked, tightening his hold on her as they made their way up the hill.

"I'm better than all right." Christmas would come tomorrow. She had the love of her life by her side. And they were preparing to cherish this new life they'd made together.

"Careful on the stairs. They're icy." Eric led her to go in front of him, and they tromped up the porch steps. By the time they slipped in through the door, both of their coats were already off.

"Come on, come on." Mags tried to kick off her boots impatiently, but they wouldn't budge.

Eric knelt down and untied them for her, gently pulling off the right and then the left. When he stood back up, he pulled her into a kiss, a foreshadow of everything to come. Mags clung to him, and they continued to kiss their way down the hall, through the living room.

"Stairs," Eric murmured breathless against her lips.

"Right." Mags held on to him and tried to focus on staying upright even with her knees weak. At the top of the stairs, Eric danced her into the guest bedroom that had become hers, and somehow shut the door without breaking their kiss.

Mags started to unbutton his shirt.

"Hold on." He stumbled back a step and seemed to collect himself with a breath. "There's something I want to give you first." Eric went to his suitcase and rummaged around until he pulled out a small gift bag.

His expression had gotten so serious that Mags eased herself down to sit on the edge of the bed.

"Open it." He handed it to her and then knelt so that his face was level with hers.

Carefully, Mags pulled apart the tape that held the top of the bag together. She fished her hand inside and pulled out the tiny little Christmas stocking that was folded up inside. The one she'd bought for the baby they didn't have.

Still on his knees, Eric looked at her, tears overflowing from his eyes. "After you left, I bought paint and trash bags, and I went into that room to clean it all out. To erase every reminder of what we'd lost. I thought that would fix things. I thought it would help us move on."

Swallowing against her own tears, Mags clutched the stocking to her chest.

"And then I found that in the drawer," Eric went on. "I sat down in the rocking chair and held on to that stocking, and I finally understood. I realized you weren't giving up hope. I realized if you weren't giving up hope, then I couldn't either." He eased closer to her, his hands on her thighs. "I couldn't stand being helpless, so I wanted it all to go away. But sitting in that room, holding on to that stocking, I could feel all the love you have for our children. All the love you have for me.

And I knew I had to come to you. I never should've said I didn't want a baby, Mags. I didn't mean to hurt you. The truth is, I was afraid."

"I understand." She pushed off the bed onto the floor with him, both of them on their knees, clinging to each other. "But we won't be afraid anymore." They would find the strength they needed in each other.

Chapter Twenty-Eight

Dahlia

Mommy?"

Dahlia's eyes fluttered open. Maya's face materialized in front of hers, and she bolted upright in the bed, her heart galloping straight into panic. "What is it, baby? What's wrong?"

"I'm sorry for what I said last night." Her daughter started to cry. "I don't hate you. You're not ruining everything."

"Oh, sweetie." She pulled back the covers so Maya could crawl into bed with her. It was still dark outside, but the clock read five thirty. "It's okay. I know you didn't mean it. You had every right to be upset."

Her daughter climbed in next to her, snuggling up against Dahlia's body. "I miss it. I miss our family the way it was." She yawned. "I hate leaving you to go to Dad's house all the time. And I hate leaving him, too. I wish we could all be together."

"It's hard. I know." Dahlia stroked her daughter's hair. "But think of it as having two homes. Two homes where you're loved no matter what. Two homes where you get to make beautiful memories." She peeked down at Maya's face, and saw her little girl. Even though she acted so much older, in many ways she was still her baby. She would give anything to protect her from sadness and hurt, but that would never be possible. The best she could do was help her learn how to process her feelings, how to still look for the bright moments, the positives, even when things were hard.

"I guess at least you and Daddy don't fight," her daughter said sleepily. "My friend Gigi's parents are divorced, and they're mean to each other."

"Your father and I will always be friends." That was one thing she would promise. She would never put them in the middle of any ugliness or anger. "We'll always have a bond because we have two of the most amazing kids in the world together." She kissed Maya's forehead. "I'm proud of you, sweetie. You're very mature and thoughtful. But I also don't want you to take so much on all by yourself. I want you to know you can talk to me about any—"

A soft snore cut her off.

Dahlia gently brushed her daughter's hair away from her face, watching her sleep in the dim light filtering in from the moon outside. There was nothing like watching her children sleep. The utter peace on their faces, the cute noises they made. She was tempted to try to reach for her phone so she could take a quick video, but Maya would kill her. Besides that, something told her she wasn't the only one awake in this house.

It had been a late one last night. After they'd finished cleaning up from the extravaganza, she and the children had come back to the house with Sassy and Rose. They'd made more hot chocolate and had watched *Home Alone*—one of the kids' favorites before Dahlia had tucked Maya and Ollie to bed in Sassy's study. But even with the late hour she'd be willing to bet Rose hadn't slept much. When they'd gotten home, Gregory and all of his things had been gone. Her sister had put on a brave face, but it wouldn't hurt to go check on her.

She peeked at her soundly sleeping daughter once more and then inched her way out of the bed, doing her best not to wake Maya. Jamming her feet into her slippers, she slipped into the fuzzy bathrobe Sassy had lent her for freezing mornings like this one. Quietly, she padded down the hall. Rose's door was already open, and, not surprisingly, her sister wasn't in her room. Dahlia made her way down the steps, wincing at the creaks and crept past the study where Ollie was still sawing logs.

When she walked into the kitchen, she laughed. "What're you two doing up?" Both Mags and Rose sat at the kitchen table. A mug sat in front of each of them, and a bottle of whipped cream sat in the center of the table. Marigold, of course, had sprawled herself out on Rose's slippers.

"I couldn't sleep," Rose grumbled. "Every time I closed my eyes, all I could think about is everything we have to do to cancel the wedding." She put her head down on the table. "It's going to be a nightmare."

"Then let's not think about it," Dahlia suggested, joining them. "It's Christmas. We can start helping you make a spreadsheet of wedding cancelation tasks tomorrow." She turned to Mags. "What're you doing up so early?"

"I'm too excited to sleep." Mags sighed happily. "Eric and I spent half the night talking about what we need to do to plan for the baby and the other half...well..." She paused, a pinkish hue on her cheeks. "Never mind. I'm just happy. Really happy."

Rose raised her head back up. "Then I can be happy, too." She angled her head toward Dahlia. "What about you? Were you having some insomnia thinking about Ike?"

"Nooo." Though she was pretty sure she'd had a dream about him. "Maya crawled into bed with me and apologized for telling me she hated me."

"Sweet girl." Mags added another squirt of whipped cream to her hot chocolate.

"She's so much like you," Rose said.

"I know. That's what I'm worried about." But she would also do her best to bring out her daughter's strengths since they so closely mimicked her own. "Hey…" She popped up and grabbed a mug to make herself a hot chocolate. "What'd you say we watch the sunrise together?"

"Yes!" Mags stood, too. "Oh my God, it's been years."

Rose seemed a little less enthusiastic. "But isn't Ollie sleeping in the den? We don't want to wake him up."

This was true. Her son was a complete angel…unless he didn't get his required nine hours of sleep. "We can sit on the porch!"

That got Rose out of her seat. "Yes! It'll be beautiful with all that snow outside."

Now it was Mags's turn to frown. "Outside? Seriously? It's probably ten below out there."

"We'll have hot chocolate." Dahlia put the kettle back on the stove.

"And we can bundle up in coats and blankets." Rose scurried out of the kitchen and came back in with an armload of blankets. "Come on, Mags. When are we going to have another opportunity to watch the Christmas sunrise?"

"Fine." Their sister pouted a bit, but she helped Dahlia make more hot chocolate, and didn't complain as they bundled up in their coats and hats and scarves and boots.

"I can hardly move," Rose said, tromping to the porch steps.

"At least we'll stay warm." Dahlia plopped down on the first step, not even feeling the hard wood beneath her thanks to all the padding. Once they sat down, Rose unfolded a warm fuzzy blanket and they squeezed in together, wrapping it around their shoulders.

Whining, Marigold climbed in between Dahlia and Rose.

"I couldn't think of a more perfect way to spend Christmas morning." Dahlia gazed out on the inn's frozen landscape, the sky a light shade of gray. Farther down the hill, smoke rose from the chimney of Ike's cabin, and she wondered if he was up yet.

"It's beautiful," Rose murmured, holding her mug in her mitten-clad hands. "We need to talk about the inn. About Sassy's offer."

"Yes, we do." Dahlia had been turning the offer around and around in her head. She already knew what she wanted—what she hoped for. But she didn't want to make this all about her either. "What do you want to do?" she asked Rose.

Her sister took in a deep breath. "I'd like to take it over. To stay in Juniper Springs and reopen the inn as a vacation resort." Her face seemed to brighten at the possibility. "And I know you both have lives far away from here, but I'd love for all of us to have a part in it."

"I'm so in." She laughed. They were doing this. They were going to stay in Colorado! "With Jeff taking a job in France, I won't have to stay in Minnesota. The kids would be so happy here." She could see them taking long walks in the woods and fishing in the pond in the summer. It would be like a constant vacation.

"Well if you two are keeping it, then I will, too." Mags pulled the blanket tighter around her shoulders. "I'm just not sure how much time we'll be able to spend here after the baby's born."

The baby! Dahlia couldn't resist hugging Mags.

"You could be a silent partner," Rose suggested. "And maybe we could have one or two weeks a year when we all gather here together. The whole family."

"That would be perfect." It would be like it was when they were kids.

"So…um…" Rose played with a loose thread on the hem of the blanket. "I'd like to offer Colt a twenty-five percent share, too."

Well, that was interesting. Dahlia studied her younger sister. "You want to offer him a share of only the inn or of something else?" She couldn't help but tease her. Colt and Rose were the epitome of opposites attract. She could see potential there.

Rose ignored the insinuation. "He spent a lot of his childhood here. I feel like it belongs to him, too."

Dahlia shrugged. "I'm fine with that." They would need all the help they could get to bring this place back.

"Me, too." Mags grinned. "I like Colt."

"Good, then. That's settled." Rose seemed to bail on the Colt line of conversation. "There's something else I've been thinking about, too." She waited until they both looked at her. "I don't want us to drift apart again. I've lost my fiancé, and I'm pretty sure Mom is going to disown me once she finds out I broke up with Gregory. I need my sisters."

Amen. "We need each other." Dahlia thought back to that awkward bathroom conversation right after they'd arrived in town. They'd come a long way in a few short weeks. "Hey, do you think maybe, someday, we could help Mom and Aunt Sassy reconnect?"

"We could *try*." Rose didn't appear to have high hopes.

Sure, Dahlia would be the first to admit it might take a miracle of epic proportions, but crazier things had happened. "Maybe we could plan something next summer. Isn't Aunt Sassy turning seventy in August?"

"Yes, but she'll never admit it." Mags laughed. "She keeps trying to tell me she's only forty-five."

Dahlia had heard the same thing from her aunt on more than one occasion. "That's what surprise parties are for." They didn't have to tell her they were going to celebrate her seventieth birthday. And they didn't have to tell their mother she was coming to the party.

"Can you even imagine the fun we're going to have here?" Mags asked wistfully. "Someday—when Rose is ready—all of our kids will be playing right out there together."

Dahlia gazed down to the pond, picturing Ollie and Maya and their future cousins. "It'll be the perfect place to gather."

"Oh!" Rose jumped up suddenly, taking the warm blanket with her. "I have a gift for both of you that I want you to open before everyone else wakes up." She ran into the house with Marigold hot on her heels and then quickly shuffled in her slippers back to them. She handed Dahlia and Mags each a wrapped package.

Dahlia carefully unwrapped the beautiful paper. It was picture frame with two photographs side by side. The first one had been taken when they were eight, six, and four. They were all dressed up in Sassy's finest posing in front of the camper. And the second photograph had been taken only a few weeks ago, when they'd found those silly hats in one of the boxes. She traced the inscription with her finger: "Sisters are different flowers from the same garden."

"It's beautiful." They were beautiful. She'd forgotten how much her sisters were part of her. "Every time I look at it, I'm going to remember this Christmas." The one she was sure would be lonely and devastating without her children.

"It's been pretty eventful so far," Mags said with a laugh.

"And there was quite the eclectic mix of people and surprises," Rose added.

Dahlia hugged her sisters in against her side. "This wasn't exactly the family Christmas season we were envisioning." Not with ex-spouses and an ex-fiancé and a mysterious sickness that turned out to be a surprise baby on the way. "But somehow it's still perfect."

READING GROUP GUIDE

YOUR BOOK CLUB RESOURCE

Home for the
Holidays

A LETTER FROM
THE AUTHOR

Dear friends,

I hope you enjoyed spending some time at the Juniper Inn. There really is no place like the beautiful Rocky Mountains during the holidays. I grew up traveling over the river and through the woods to my aunt and uncle's house in the mountains for Christmas, and those family gatherings are some of my most treasured memories.

When I envisioned the Juniper Inn, I found myself drawing on the inspiration from those times with my family. We would bundle up and sled down the huge snowdrifts and build snowmen and have snowball fights. Then we would go inside and enjoy a festive meal together—complete with turkey and sweet potatoes and some Scandinavian delicacies like lutefisk and lefse. There were always more desserts than I could count—cookies we'd decorated with my aunts, and homemade pies, and usually a chocolate yule log cake. My favorite part of our celebration, though, was when we would all gather around the towering Christmas tree to exchange gifts. It wasn't the gifts themselves, however. It was all of us being together in one room, seeing the joy on everyone's faces as each of us experienced the gift of giving.

One of the things I love the most about my extended family is that we have always welcomed anyone and everyone to join us for holiday celebrations. Over the years, we've expanded our family by inviting neighbors and friends who didn't have their own family nearby, and most of them became part of our family, too. We take the term "the more the merrier" to heart. Maybe that's why I found it so easy to write Sassy's character. Like my own wonderful aunts, Sassy brings people together. Her openness and welcoming spirit are really what the holidays are all about.

Christmas these days doesn't look exactly the same as it did when I was young. We've lost some of our beloved family members. And with our numbers growing by the year, it's a bit more chaotic than it used to be. (As an adult I now fully appreciate how much work goes into the preparations.) But even as I drive with my little family over the river and through the woods into the mountains, I still feel the magic. It's in the peacefulness of the snow-laden evergreen branches. It's in the joy of coming together. It's in the spirit of gathering around the tree to give.

I hope reading *Home for the Holidays* helped you feel the magic, too. My desire was to write a story about reconnecting with loved ones who offer the strength and support and closeness we all need more of in our lives. Throughout the story, Dahlia, Magnolia, and Rose rediscovered the gift of simply being together, of being there for each other, and that made Christmas even more meaningful. Whether you're gathering with family or friends or neighbors, I hope you find those heart connections this upcoming holiday season, too.

All the best,
Sara

QUESTIONS FOR READERS

1. Dahlia, Magnolia, and Rose each have a very different personality. Which sister did you find yourself relating to the most throughout the story? Why?

2. In *Home for the Holidays*, each sister takes a reprieve from their current life situation. What would an ideal reprieve look like for you? Where would you want to go? Who would you want to connect with?

3. A major theme in the book is learning that courage comes from vulnerability. At the beginning of the story, the sisters found it difficult to share their disappointments and struggles with each other. Why do you think that was? Who do you draw courage from?

4. Why do you think Lillian was so centered on appearances? How did that influence her daughters and their interactions?

5. Motherhood is another major theme in the book: Sassy never had children of her own but was a mother figure for the sisters; Dahlia is navigating life as a single mom; and Magnolia hopes to become a mom. How do you define the role of a mom? Is there anyone who played that role for you outside of your immediate family? Have you ever played that role for someone?

6. What was your initial impression of Dr. Ike? Was he right for Dahlia? Why or why not?

7. Why do you think Magnolia and Eric were able to find their way back to each other while Dahlia and Jeff could not? Discuss the differences in their relationships.

8. Aunt Sassy was an important figure in the sisters' early lives, but they eventually lost touch with her. Have you lost touch with someone who once played a significant role in your life? Is there anyone from your past you would like to reconnect with?

9. Part of Rose's journey is recognizing she has been living her life for others rather than pursuing her own passions. What about Juniper Springs and the inn helped her come to the conclusion she wants more?

10. In some ways, Aunt Sassy is at a crossroads in her life, too. Starting over can happen at any age. Do you have

big life transitions coming up? How will they impact your life moving forward?

11. The sisters didn't exactly have the Christmas they'd envisioned, thanks to some last-minute surprises. Talk about a time the holidays didn't turn out exactly the way you planned.

12. What do you think the future holds for each of the sisters?

About the Author

National bestselling author Sara Richardson composes uplifting stories that illustrate the rocky roads of love, friendship, and family relationships. Her characters are strong women journeying to define their lives and pursue their dreams. Her books have received numerous award nominations and critical acclaim, with *Publishers Weekly* recognizing her stories as "emotionally rich, charmingly funny, and sensitive."

After graduating with a master's degree in journalism, Sarah realized she was too empathetic to be a reporter and started writing her first novel. When not writing, Sara can be found promoting women's health and empowerment by teaching Pilates or hiking the trails near her house. A lifelong Colorado girl, Sara lives and plays near the mountains with her husband, two sons, two fur babies, and a tortoise named Leo.